HUMMUS AND HOMICIDE

HUMMUS AND HOMICIDE

Tina Kashian

KENSINGTON BOOKS

http://www.kensingtonbooks.com

KENSINGTON BOOKS are published by

Kensington Publishing Corp.
119 West 40th Street
New York, NY 10018

Copyright © 2018 by Tina Sickler

All rights reserved. No part of this book may be repro-
duced in any form or by any means without the prior
written consent of the Publisher, excepting brief quotes
used in reviews.

If you purchased this book without a cover, you should be
aware that this book is stolen property. It was reported as
"unsold and destroyed" to the Publisher and neither the
Author nor the Publisher has received any payment for
this "stripped book."

All Kensington titles, imprints and distributed lines are
available at special quantity discounts for bulk purchases
for sales promotion, premiums, fund-raising, educational
or institutional use. Special book excerpts or customized
printings can also be created to fit specific needs. For
details, write or phone the office of the Kensington
Special Sales Manager: Kensington Publishing Corp.,
119 West 40th Street, New York, NY, 10018. Attn. Special
Sales Department. Phone: 1-800-221-2647.

Kensington and the K logo Reg. U.S. Pat. & TM Off.

ISBN-13: 978-1-4967-1347-6
ISBN-10: 1-4967-1347-8
First Kensington Mass Market Edition: March 2018

eISBN-13: 978-1-4967-1348-3
eISBN-10: 1-4967-1348-6
First Kensington Electronic Edition: March 2018

10 9 8 7 6 5 4 3 2 1

Printed in the United States of America

For Mom and Dad.
Growing up in the restaurant was the best!
I miss you both every day.

CHAPTER 1

Ocean Crest, New Jersey

"Lucy Berberian! Is that you?"

Lucy's car was stopped at a red light when the excited shout caught her attention. Her gaze turned to the crosswalk, and she lowered her sunglasses an inch to peer above the rim. A tiny old lady with an abundance of gray curls was pushing a rolling cart filled with groceries. She waved. One of the plastic bags stuck out from the cart and flapped in the breeze.

Lucy glimpsed the name *Holloway's* printed on the bag—the sole grocery store in the small New Jersey beach town. "Hello, Mrs. Kiminski," she called out her open window.

The old lady smiled, revealing pearly white dentures. "You're visiting? Your mama will be so happy."

No doubt her mother and father would be thrilled when they learned Lucy was back, not only for a visit, but longer. Lucy swallowed hard. She'd hit the first stop light out of three in town and already her nerves were getting to her. It felt like a corkscrew was slowly winding in her stomach the closer she came to her destination. And to *him*.

Don't think about it.

The light changed, and Lucy waved as she continued down Ocean Avenue. Parking spots in the town's main street were vacant in late April, and only a few people strolled about. The tourist season wouldn't begin until Memorial Day. A month later and the town would be crammed with seasonal tourists, and a parking spot would be hard to find.

Lucy drove past a ramp leading to the town's mile-long boardwalk, and she spied the Atlantic Ocean between two buildings—a blue line to the horizon. The Jersey shore was in Lucy's blood. She'd been born and raised in Ocean Crest, a tiny town located on a barrier island about six miles north of Cape May. Even off-season the scent of funnel cake drifted from one of the boardwalk shops and through her window. The bright morning sunlight warmed her cheeks, and she spotted the single pier with a Ferris wheel and an old-fashioned wooden roller coaster. Soon the Ferris wheel would light up the night sky and the piercing screams from the coaster would be heard from a block away.

The small ocean town was so different from the rapid pace of the Center-City Philadelphia law firm and apartment she had grown accustomed to over the last eight years. But now that part of her life was done, and she needed to figure out what she was going to do next. When her work had thrown her a curveball, returning home had come to mind. Other than hasty holiday visits, she hadn't stayed for longer than a weekend.

A few blocks later Lucy parked before a quaint brick building with a flower bed bursting with yellow daffodils and red tulips. A lit sign read KEBAB KITCHEN FINE MEDITERRANEAN CUISINE.

A flash of motion by the front door caught her eye as soon as she killed the engine. Gadoo, the calico cat with yellow eyes her mother had adopted when he kept coming around the restaurant, cocked his head to the side as if to say, *What took you so long to come home?* and then swished his tail and sauntered down the alley.

Taking a deep breath, she got out of the car, then pushed open the door to the restaurant.

The dining room was empty and the lights were dimmed. Sunlight through the front windows shone on pristine white tablecloths covering a dozen tables and a handful of maple booths. Small vases with fresh flowers and unlit tea light candles in glass votive holders rested upon the pressed linen. Cherry wainscoting gave the place a warm, family feel. The ocean shimmered from large bay windows and seagulls soared above the water. The delicious aroma of fresh herbs, fragrant spices, and grilled lamb wafted to her. It was only ten o'clock in the morning, well before the restaurant opened for lunch, and that meant her mother was preparing her savory specials.

Lucy walked forward and stopped by the hostess stand. The place hadn't changed since she was a kid. As a young child, her mom carried her around to greet customers and kiss the staff. When she was eight, she started rolling silverware in cloth napkins and refilling salt and pepper shakers. Lucy eyed the cash register behind the counter with its laminated dollar bill showcasing the first cash the restaurant took in as well as the required heath department notices that hung on the wall. A low wall separated a waitress station from the dining area, and a pair of swinging doors led to the kitchen. She recalled her days as a hostess and cashier, seating customers and handing them menus, then ringing them up to pay on their way out. A waitress pad sat on a nearby table, and she remembered how excited she'd been as a teenager the day her father promoted her from hostess to waitress. The cash tips had helped pay for her prom gown.

Footsteps sounded on the terra cotta tiles. Lucy turned to see her older sister carrying a tray of sparkling glasses.

"Lucy! What are you doing here?" Her sister set down the tray on a nearby table.

Lucy smiled and embraced her warmly. "Hi, Emma. I've come for a visit."

At thirty-seven Emma was five years older than Lucy. Lucy had always been a bit envious of her sister who was slim and attractive with long, curly brown hair. She weighed the same as she had since college, and she'd never had to worry about how many carbs or pieces of pita bread she consumed. "How's Max?" Lucy asked.

Emma wrinkled her nose. "He's the same. The king of real estate in town. He works a lot and is never around."

Emma tended to frequently complain about her husband, but they had a ten-year-old daughter they adored. "And my little niece Niari?"

"Most of the time Niari's great," Emma said. "She's good in school and likes soccer. But she's also a tween who can drive us crazy. I dread the puberty years to come."

Lucy chuckled. "I imagine we drove Mom and Dad nuts as teenagers."

Emma perched on the edge of a table and crossed her arms. "How's work? I'm surprised you could get away."

Lucy cleared her throat. "Well, that's just it. I have some time to—"

"Lucy Anahid Berberian!"

Lucy whirled to see her mother and father emerge from the swinging kitchen doors. Her Lebanese, Greek, and Armenian mother, Angela, had olive skin and dark hair that she'd styled in a beehive since the sixties. Her Armenian father, Raffi, was a portly man of average height with a balding pate of curly black hair. Both had arrived in America on their twenty-first birthdays, met months later at a church festival, and married soon after. They'd meshed cultures and languages, and Emma and Lucy were first-generation Americans with ethnic roots as strong as her parents' prized grapevine clinging to its trellis.

Lucy found herself engulfed in her mother's arms, flowery perfume tickling her nose. The large gold cross—the one piece of jewelry her mother never left the house without—was cool as it pressed against Lucy's neck. Her mother was a tiny woman, only five feet tall even with her beehive hairdo, but she was a talented chef and a smart businesswoman.

Angela passed Lucy to her father, and Lucy smiled at his bear hug and the light scrape of his whiskers as he brushed her cheek with a kiss. He released her to study her face and grinned. "My little girl, the big city lawyer."

Her mother touched Lucy's arm. "It's Tuesday. Shouldn't you be at work?"

Lucy's insides froze for a heart-stopping moment. "I'm taking a vacation," she blurted out.

Why did she have to sound so nervous? She'd rehearsed the perfect excuse over and over in her car on the way here.

"A vacation?" Angela folded her arms across her chest. Her gaze filled with suspicion as it traveled over Lucy from head to toe, taking in the worn jeans, Philadelphia Eagles T-shirt, and Nike sneakers.

Lucy's attire was far from her normal business wear, but it was surprising how quick a week of unemployment could affect one's desire to dress in anything but yoga pants or jeans.

"It's true," Lucy said. A small streak of panic ran through her at her mother's continuing inquisitive gaze.

"Well, it's about time." Her mother nodded curtly and unfolded her arms from across her chest. "That law firm works you too hard. You only visit for Thanksgiving, Christmas, and Easter. You stay two, maybe three days, and then you're off again. Plus"—she eyed Lucy with an admonishing glare—"you didn't visit last Mother's Day."

Lucy's pulse quickened. Here it was. Her family's ability to layer on guilt. She'd always made an effort to visit for the holidays, but the truth was she didn't always want to come home. The smothering could be as thick as the sugar syrup on her mother's baklava—sticky, sweet, and as effective as super-glue.

"You know I had a big case and couldn't take time off. You could have visited me," Lucy said.

"Bah!" Raffi said with a disgusted wave of his hand. "What company makes its employees work so many weekends? And you know we don't like to drive into the city."

Lucy knew crossing the Delaware River via the Ben Franklin Bridge into Philadelphia was like traveling to another country for her parents.

"How long is your vacation?" Emma asked.

"A month." At their stunned looks, Lucy quickly added, "It's really what we call a sabbatical." She wasn't ready to admit she was no longer employed.

Knowing her parents, they'd think she was home for good. Why give them false hope?

"You'll stay with us. I'll tidy your room," her mom said.

Heck no. Seeing her parents was good, but living with them was something else entirely. "I'm staying with Katie and Bill, Mom."

Her mom hesitated and glared at her as if she'd been denied access to Lucy's firstborn. Katie Watson was Lucy's long-time friend. When Lucy had called her to tell her that she was coming home and staying for a while, Katie had offered for Lucy to stay with her and her husband, Bill, an Ocean Crest police officer.

"Fine," Angela finally said. "I've always liked Katie, and she comes from a good family."

Raffi cracked a wide grin. "You came at a good time, Lucy. With Memorial Day in less than a month, the tourist season will begin. Millie left to have a baby. We need your help."

Lucy's smile faded. Millie had worked for her parents as a waitress for years. From what Lucy recalled, Millie had married right out of high school and started having kids. Was she on baby number four by now?

"It's her sixth boy," her dad answered as if reading her mind. "We need a waitress. We're already short for today's lunch shift."

Lucy felt as if she were being sucked back into the fold like quicksand; no amount of professional accomplishments mattered. Family helped family, and their expectations could be stifling and overwhelming. It was partly why she'd fled years ago.

But she was older and more experienced now. "Dad, I don't think—"

"You can borrow Millie's apron and Emma's clothes," Angela said.

Good grief. Millie's apron was one thing. But how would she fit into her skinny sister's black pants and white shirt? Lucy was bigger than Emma in every way. From her breasts, to her hips, and definitely her derriere.

Angela pulled out a chair. "Sit. You're too thin." She glanced at Lucy's father behind her shoulder. "Raffi, please bring Lucy something special to eat. We can catch up while we wait."

Her dad disappeared through the swinging kitchen doors.

Lucy rolled her eyes as she sat. Their mother never seemed to notice any physical differences between her two daughters. To her, everyone appeared in need of food.

Emma smiled mischievously as she set a glass of water in front of Lucy. "Good luck," she whispered, then followed their father into the kitchen.

Lucy inwardly groaned as her mother pulled up a chair beside her. She didn't need her sister's warning. She knew what was coming as soon as she spotted the gleam in her mother's eyes. The maternal message was clear. *Let's talk about how old you are and remind you that your biological clock is ticking louder*

*than a pounding drum and that you should be married
and birthing my grandchildren by now.*

Her mother patted her hand. "You know I think
you work too hard."

Once again, a nagging guilt pierced Lucy's chest
for not revealing the truth. "It's okay. I'm home for
a while now, remember?"

Angela's face lit up. "Good. We need to focus on
finding you a husband."

"Mom," Lucy whined. "I'm not opposed to mar-
riage, but only if the right man proposes. Meanwhile, my career is important to—"

"Posh," her mom said, waving a hand. "A career
doesn't keep you warm at night when you get old.
Granted, men are far from perfect. Your father is a
good example," she said, motioning toward the
kitchen, "but he's *there.*"

Lucy wrinkled her nose. She didn't consider herself a romantic, but she'd hoped for more than just
there when it came to a man.

"I saw Gadoo," Lucy said, hoping to change the
topic.

Angela always loved to talk about the cat. "He
waits for me every morning by the back door. Actu-
ally, he's waiting for his breakfast. As long as I feed
him, Gadoo keeps coming."

Gadoo was Armenian for cat. Not very original,
but it fit the patchy orange and black calico cat with
yellow eyes.

Before long the kitchen doors opened again and
her father emerged with a large shish kebab platter

and set it before her. Two skewers of succulent lamb and a skewer of roasted peppers, tomatoes, and onions were accompanied by rice pilaf and home-made pita bread. The aroma made her stomach grumble and her mouth water.

Lucy may not have missed her mother's lectures about husband hunting, but damned if she hadn't missed the food. She picked up a warm piece of pita bread, then stopped. "Is there hummus?"

Her gaze followed Emma's pointing finger. "You have to see our newest addition."

Lucy stood and looked toward the corner of the restaurant where a long sidebar stood. She hadn't noticed it earlier. At first glance, it looked like a salad bar, but instead of lettuce, tomatoes, and salad, bins of hummus were displayed, each tray a different variety.

"Specialties of the house, and all my own flavors. Roasted red pepper, extra garlic, Mediterranean herb, lemon pucker, artichoke, black bean, sweet apricot, and of course, my own recipe of traditional hummus," Angela boasted with pride.

"Customers love it," Raffi said.

Lucy carried her plate to the bins full of the creamy dips and added a large spoonful of tradi-tional hummus next to the pita bread, then returned to her seat. "Wow! Business must be good, Dad." She dipped a piece of pita into the hummus and shoved it into her mouth.

Heaven. The lemon blended with the garlic,

chick peas and sesame seed puree perfectly, and the texture was super-creamy.

Silence greeted her. Lucy looked up from her plate to see all three members of her family staring at her. "What's wrong?" she mumbled.

Emma broke the awkward silence. "Dad wants to sell."

Lucy nearly choked on a mouthful before managing to swallow it down. "Sell?"

"Not right away, but I've been thinking about it," Raffi said.

An uncomfortable thought crossed Lucy's mind. Her gaze swept him from his balding head of curly black hair to his sizeable belly back to his face. "Are you sick?"

His brows furrowed. "No. I'm old."

The irony was not lost on her. Less than an hour ago she was hesitant to set foot in the place. But selling the restaurant? For thirty years, ever since her parents had opened it, Kebab Kitchen had been the center of their lives, socially and economically. What would they do without it?

"But I don't understand why—"

"I have no sons or sons-in-law who want it. Emma doesn't have a head for business, and Max is into real estate." Her father eyed Lucy hard, his glare cutting through her like one of his prized butcher knives. "If you'd married Azad Zakarian this wouldn't be a problem."

Lucy's stomach bottomed out at the mention of the man her parents had so desperately wanted her to marry. He was one of the main reasons she'd left to take the job in the Philadelphia law firm. It had taken months, years, to dull the heartache. Her throat seemed to close up as she felt the all-too-familiar pressure from her parents' unreasonable expectations—that the ultimate fate of the restaurant rested upon her shoulders and that *she* had to be the one to keep everything together. Lucy reached for the water glass and took a big swallow.

"Dad, stop," Emma said. "No sense nagging Lucy. Max has a buyer."

"Who?"

"Anthony Citteroni."

Lucy sat upright at the name. "The bike man next door to the restaurant?"

Every summer, Mr. Citteroni's bike shop rented a variety of bicycles to tourists. Ever since she was a kid, she'd heard stories that he had mob connections in Atlantic City, and his many businesses were how he laundered money.

"He wants the property," Raffi explained.

"Why?" Lucy couldn't fathom what Mr. Citteroni would do with it.

"He wants to open a high class Italian restaurant, but he's not the only interested buyer," Raffi said.

"A local woman wants to convert Kebab Kitchen into a diner," Emma said.

"Another Jersey diner? The state is loaded with them. And Ocean Crest already has the Pancake Palace," Lucy said.

"Don't forget that Azad's interested," Angela announced.

There it was again. *His* name.

"Why would he want it?" Lucy asked.

"Azad graduated from culinary school and is working as a sous chef for a fancy Atlantic City restaurant. He wants to buy Kebab Kitchen and keep it the way it is."

Of course, he did. He was perfect. Hand-picked by her parents. He'd started working as a dishwasher for the restaurant when he was in high school. He'd soon worked his way up to busboy, then line cook, and had earned her parents' respect. Not to mention their hopes of a union with their younger daughter. The pressure tightened in Lucy's chest.

She glared at her parents. "What will you do if you retire? Where will you go?"

"We'll stay in Ocean Crest. It's a peaceful place," Angela said.

Raffi waved his hand toward the window and a view of the calm ocean and blue sky. "After all, what bad things happen here?"

CHAPTER 2

Lucy lowered the visor to shield her eyes from the late morning sun as she drove down Ocean Avenue. Scanning the sidewalks, she drove past Magic's Family Apothecary, Holloway's Grocery, and Cutie's Cupcake Bakery. The memory of Susan Cutie's lemon meringue pie made Lucy's mouth water. It had been too long since she'd savored one of her homemade, calorie-packed desserts, and Lucy made a mental note to stop by soon.

She drove two more blocks before reaching her destination. A neon lit sign blinked MAC'S IRISH PUB.

As soon as she parked, a woman rushed toward the driver side door. "I can't believe it! My best friend's staying with us."

Lucy laughed and stepped out of the car to hug Katie Watson, her best friend since grade school. Tall and thin with straight blond hair and blue eyes, she was Lucy's total opposite. The pair also came from different worlds. Lucy was a first generation

American, and Katie often joked that her ancestors sailed on the Mayflower. She was raised on meat, potatoes, and apple pie while Lucy grew up eating stuffed grape leaves and hummus.

"I got your text to meet at Mac's. Are you sure you can take the entire morning off from work?" Lucy asked.

Katie worked at the Ocean Crest town hall as a clerk handling everything from real estate taxes to zoning to renewing dog and cat licenses. "You bet. I know it's still before noon, but we should celebrate properly." She opened the pub door and motioned for Lucy to step inside.

Lucy blinked as her eyes adjusted from the bright sunlight to the dim pub lighting. The smell of beer and fried bar food wafted to her. A long mahogany bar, its surface polished but nicked from years of use, ran the length of one wall. Mac's was a hometown favorite and boasted a large selection of microbrews and classic beers on tap. Several tables were occupied by locals drinking beer and watching a large television mounted above the bar.

As Lucy and Katie slid onto a pair of bar stools, a bubble gum chomping barmaid slid cardboard coasters advertising domestic beers before them. "Lucy! What are you doing back home?"

"Hi Sue. I'm here for a bit. A long vacation of sorts."

"What would you two like?"

They ordered beers, and Sue filled frosted mugs and placed them on the coasters.

Katie tucked a stray lock of straight blond hair behind her ear, swiveled on her stool to eye Lucy, and raised her mug. "To the return of my BFF. Since when are you an Eagles fan?" She pointed to the football logo on Lucy's T-shirt.

Lucy tapped her glass to Katie's and they sipped their drinks.

"Since living in Philly. The cheesesteaks and soft pretzels are also favorites."

Katie chuckled. "I'm thrilled you're home, but I want details. What happened at the firm?"

Lucy's thoughts turned back to recent events and she frowned. "I was passed over for partner in favor of a male associate."

"That's the second time in two years, isn't it?"

Lucy tried not to flinch. "It's true. Apparently eight years of working crazy billable hours and toiling over legal briefs isn't enough to break through the proverbial glass ceiling."

"Who'd they pick?"

"An associate named Stanley Upton."

Katie's brows drew together. "That name sounds familiar."

Lucy fidgeted in her seat. "That's because I mentioned Stanley over the phone once. I was never interested in him, but he kept asking me out for a drink. After the fifth time, I said yes. Little did I know he wasn't interested in me, but in a potential client I had met at a city fundraiser. Once Stanley learned her name, he wined and dined her. When the firm's partners learned about Stanley's new client, they chose to make him partner. If I complained, I'd look like a whiner. So, I quit."

"What a jerk!"

Lucy's throat tightened as she recalled how betrayed and upset she'd been when the managing partner of Parker and Weinstein had knocked on her office door to tell her that Stanley Upton was being promoted to partner.

Katie took a sip of her beer. "How are your parents handling your long visit?"

Lucy ran her fingers down the frosted glass. "They're happy. But they're still as stubborn as ever and immediately brought up Azad. They'd be more than thrilled to see him back in my life."

Even after all this time her parents still had hopes. She felt like she was a daughter during medieval times when handfasting and arranged marriages were the norm. It was ridiculous, really. When would they leave it be?

Katie chuckled and the corners of her lips tilted in a smile.

"My parents want to sell the restaurant," Lucy said.

"It's true, then?"

She looked at Katie in surprise. "You knew?"

"I've heard rumors at the town hall, but I never gave them much credit. Your restaurant has been around since I was a kid." She gently squeezed Lucy's arm. "Coming home was a good decision. You can clear your head and think about what you want for the future."

"I didn't have much choice. I quit, remember?"

Kate waved a dismissive hand. "It was the right move. After we finish our drinks, we'll head to my house, and I'll help you unpack."

Lucy cocked her head to the side and studied Katie. "Are you sure Bill is okay with me staying with you?"

Bill and Katie had married three years after high school just as Bill had become a beat cop in Ocean Crest. He was perfect for Katie since she'd always been obsessed with detective and crime TV shows.

Katie took a sip of her beer. "Of course. Bill's happy if I'm happy."

Lucy couldn't help but feel a stab of envy. She hadn't had much luck in the boyfriend department. The earlier break up with Azad had blindsided her. Her more recent dating life was dry as burnt toast.

Before Lucy could express her gratitude for Katie's hospitality, the front door opened and a couple strolled inside. The man was unremarkable—ordinary-looking with brown hair and eyes, slim build, and average height. His plain attire, khakis, and a white collared shirt, would not have attracted Lucy's notice except for the woman by his side. Four-inch black stilettos clicked on the hardwood floor as the woman sauntered past in a skintight yellow and black pantsuit with a low neckline, which revealed a good amount of cleavage. Her long, bottle-dyed red hair was brushed back in loose curls that could only be accomplished with lots of Aqua Net and a screaming-hot curling iron. Her fingers clung to the man's arm like a lifeline, and sunlight from the window glinted off her red painted nails. They took stools at the opposite end of the bar.

Something about her was familiar.

Lucy realized she was staring at the red-haired woman when she looked up and caught Lucy's gaze. She smirked, her lips like a thread of scarlet, and raised a well-plucked eyebrow.

Lucy's face grew warm, and she quickly averted her gaze.

"Well, well, if it isn't Lucy Berberian." The woman's voice carried from across the bar.

Lucy's head snapped up. The nasally voice was eerily familiar, and she struggled to place it. The woman eased off her stool, whispered something into the man's ear, and they walked over to where Katie and Lucy sat.

She flipped a long lock of hair across her shoulder and looked at Lucy. "You don't remember me, do you?"

"Hello, Heather," Katie said.

Lucy's memory sparked like the Fourth of July, and she blinked. "Heather Banks?"

"You do remember," Heather said.

Lucy forced a smile as she stood. Heather Banks had been an egotistical cheerleader in high school. She'd also been one of the most popular girls who wouldn't give Lucy the time of day. Lucy had attempted to try out for the cheerleading squad, but it soon became clear that she wasn't welcome by the team's captain, aka Heather. Lucy had lasted a week. It had been a humiliating experience.

Looking at Heather, Lucy realized why she hadn't recognized her. Heather's hair had been bleached blond in high school, and her currently dyed red hair and expertly applied makeup made her look like an entirely different person. That, and it had been fourteen years ago.

"What are you doing back in town?" Heather asked. "Last I heard you were a city lawyer. Something to do with inventions and such."

"I'm a patent attorney, and I'm visiting for a while. I'm taking a sabbatical," Lucy said.

Heather's gaze swept over Lucy with a smirk, taking in the Eagles shirt, worn jeans, and sneakers. Lucy straightened her shoulders.

"A sabbatical? How nice for you," Heather said in a tone that suggested it was anything but. She turned to the man standing beside her and reached for his arm. "This is Paul Evans. He's a writer. I'm sure you've heard of him."

The Paul Evans? Lucy stared dumbfounded at him. "Are you the suspense writer?"

"Yes," Heather answered. "Paul's latest book, *Killer Status,* just hit number one on the *New York Times* best seller list."

Paul shifted on his feet and his complexion turned a shade red. He was clearly uncomfortable with Heather's comments. He extended his hand. "It's nice to meet you."

Lucy couldn't help but stare as she shook his hand. This unassuming man was the famous best-selling suspense writer? Reading his books had often kept her up late. They'd also scared her into checking her doors and windows to make sure they were closed and locked each night. Paul Evans wrote about serial killers that made your blood run cold—highly intelligent and downright evil. Villains that made Lucy glance behind her when she walked the streets of Philadelphia after a long day at the firm.

"I'm a fan of your books. You are very good at scaring a lady at night," Lucy said.

Paul smiled. "Thank you. I'll take that as a compliment."

"Do you live in Ocean Crest?" she asked.

"I was born here, but I moved away with my mother to Chicago when I was very young. I've been back for about six months," he said.

"We met at one of his book signings." Heather patted his arm, her long red nails catching a glimmer of neon from a flashing beer sign hanging above the bar.

Paul looked from Lucy to Katie, then back to Heather. "How do all of you know each other?"

"We graduated from high school together," Heather said.

"You were friends, then?" Paul asked.

Heather wrinkled her nose as if she smelled a bad odor. "We didn't hang out together. Lucy's parents are foreigners who own that Mediterranean restaurant."

Katie laughed outright at Heather's blatant insult. Paul had the good grace to look uncomfortable.

Lucy gritted her teeth. "My parents aren't *foreigners,* Heather. They've been US citizens since before I was born."

"Well, they still own that restaurant and speak different languages."

Lucy's voice rose an octave. "You mean Kebab Kitchen? Yes, they still own it and continue to employ town residents and pay taxes." Lucy folded her arms across her chest, braced her feet apart, and faced the other woman.

The tension between them grew. She was aware of several of the locals sitting at tables nearby looking up from their beers to stare at the two of them. Gossip spread like wildfire in town, and they were giving everyone present plenty to talk about.

Damn.

She hadn't even been back more than a few hours.

Lucy wasn't the only one to notice.

Paul tugged on Heather's arm. "Our food has arrived. Perhaps we should go back to our seats," he suggested.

Heather shot Lucy a scathing look. "I expect I'll see you and your parents soon." She turned and allowed Paul to steer her back to their barstools.

Katie slapped money on the bar and ushered Lucy outside.

As soon as the door shut behind them, Lucy whirled to face her. "I don't believe it. It's like I never left high school. I couldn't stand Heather Banks then and it doesn't look like time has given me any reason to improve my opinion."

"She's always been obnoxious," Katie said. "She's also a fixture in town. I just laugh at her antics and then ignore her. Besides you can't blow your nose without someone announcing it in the paper. You don't want to give people something to talk about, do you?"

Lucy halted and clenched her fists at her side. She had worried about the same thing, but her temper had been quick to flare after Heather's comments about her family. A shiny, candy apple red Lexus with a license plate that read BANKS1 caught her eye.

Ugh. Even Heather's car was flashy.

"I wish I could ignore her," Lucy muttered. "What did she mean when she said she'd see me and my parents soon?"

Katie kept walking. "Your brother-in-law has to apply for a health inspection for the restaurant before he can list it on the real estate market."

Lucy frowned, not sure what that information had to do with Heather. "I remember her father was the town health inspector."

"Mr. Banks recently retired. Heather took over the position."

Lucy's breath caught in her lungs. "You're kidding? Me and my big mouth. I didn't mean to pick a fight with her. Doesn't anyone aspire to leave this small town?"

"Hey, watch it!"

Lucy raised a hand. "No offense. I shouldn't talk. I'm already scheduled to waitress for today's lunch shift."

Katie laughed. "That didn't take long, did it? Tell me if you want a job at the town hall. We could use a good file clerk in the tax office."

Lucy rolled her eyes. "I just may take you up on that offer."

Later that afternoon, Lucy arrived at the restaurant a half hour before her scheduled lunch shift to find her mother busy in the kitchen. A container of chick peas soaking in water sat beside a food processor on a wood worktable.

"You're just in time," Angela said. "I'm preparing traditional hummus. You can help."

Lucy eyed the worktable with unease. Cooking had never been one of her talents. She'd disliked spending time in the kitchen, and her past attempts to create meals had never resulted in success. She'd once invited two fellow female associates to her apartment and tried to cook an "easy" lasagna dish using no-boil lasagna noodles. It ended up dry and nonedible, and they'd quickly ordered Chinese takeout.

Her mother must have read the anxiety on her face. "Don't worry. You won't even have to preheat the oven."

Lucy let out a held-in breath. "Okay. Tell me what to do."

Her mother handed her a glass jar of tahini. "Stir this well, then give me a cup."

Lucy knew tahini was a paste made from ground sesame seeds and a key ingredient in hummus and many Mediterranean dishes. The oil tended to separate on top and had to be thoroughly mixed with the ground sesame seeds.

She could handle this task. She reached for a long spoon and began mixing. "A whole cup?" Lucy asked.

Angela waved a dismissive hand. "About. I never measure."

Lucy frowned. Some things never changed. Her mother rarely measured ingredients when she cooked. How on earth could Lucy hope to learn without a recipe?

Angela strained the softened chick peas and poured them into the food processor. Fresh garlic, lemon, salt, and extra virgin olive oil followed, none of them precisely measured. Lucy, on the other hand, measured a full cup of tahini and added it into the machine.

"Now go ahead and blend everything," her mom instructed.

Lucy snapped the lip on the food processor, then hit the button.

Nothing.

"Did you plug it in?" Angela reached around the machine for the cord.

Lucy felt her face grow warm, and she batted her mother's hand away. "I got this, Mom," She plugged the cord into the socket and tried again. The machine whirred to life. After a few minutes of blending, Lucy removed the lid. "It looks right."

"Go ahead and taste it," Angela said.

Lucy dipped a clean spoon inside the food processor and tasted the hummus.

Amazing. The blend of ingredients was smooth, flavorful, and just right. Her mother's cooking always tasted the same, no matter the accuracy of her measurements. Lucy's logical mind couldn't comprehend it.

"Now that you know how to make traditional hummus, next time you can prepare it," Angela said.

A streak of panic hit Lucy in the chest. "I don't think that's a good idea."

Her mother untied her apron. "Why not?"

First, Lucy couldn't cook. It was one thing to have her mother stand beside her and instruct her step-by-step. It was another thing entirely to prepare it on her own. Second, she wasn't planning on staying in town for long. She knew family and food went hand in hand for her mother, and that making hummus would give her the wrong idea.

Angela poured the fresh hummus into a container and handed it to Lucy. "Put this in the walk-in refrigerator, swap it with the cold bin I made earlier, then refill the hummus bar in the dining room. Lunch service starts soon, and it will get busy."

Lucy took the container and headed for the refrigerator.

"Oh, and Lucy?"

Lucy halted and glanced back. "Yes?"

Satisfaction pursed her mother's mouth. "I'm glad you're finally home."

Waiting tables was like riding a bike. You may have to brush up on your skills, but you never forgot how to do it.

The lunch shift had a steady stream of customers, but Lucy knew better than to think it was busy. In less than a month, business would triple as the ocean town officially opened for the summer. Sweat beaded on her brow as she retrieved platters of shish kebab, pilaf, and cucumber salad from the warm kitchen and hurried to serve customers in the dining room. Working at a law firm might tax her mind, but it was nothing compared to rushing around to serve dozens of hungry locals.

Emma and Sally waitressed, too. Sally, who had

been with her parents for years, reminded her of Olive Oyl from the Popeye cartoon. Tall and willowy with short dark hair, she was friendly and chatty and always remembered personal facts about the regular customers—the progress of a knee replacement, the birth of a grandchild, and who were selling their homes. She was like a walking encyclopedia of local folk, and customers loved her. Together, the three of them managed to cover the dining room, but barely had time to say a word to each other as they worked. Lucy's dad manned the register and seated customers as they arrived.

The restaurant's head line cook, Butch, was an African-American man who'd been working for her parents since Lucy was in kindergarten. He was large and tall, with a chest the size of a small armoire, and he always wore a checkered bandana on his bald head.

"Good to see you back, Lucy Lou," Butch said as he slid a plate of stuffed grape leaves across the stainless steel pickup counter for her to deliver. He smiled, revealing a gold front tooth.

Lucy smiled back as she took the plate. He'd always called her nicknames and *Lucy Lou* was his favorite.

The new hummus bar was busy. Lucy's mom kept running back and forth with clean plates and refilling the bins with fresh creamy hummus and raw carrots and celery sticks for dipping. Homemade white or whole wheat pita bread was served warm and soft from the oven and had to be ordered. The chick pea and tahini based dip was clearly popular.

Angela's authentic recipes and unique variations with fresh ingredients drew the customers and satisfied finicky taste buds. Lucy had tried them all, but her favorite was what she'd helped prepare earlier in the kitchen—her mother's traditional hummus.

Lucy's feet were throbbing by the time lunch service died down.

"Sit," Emma said. "I'll wipe down the booths and change the used table linens." She wrung out a clean rag from a small bucket of warm, sudsy water.

Lucy didn't have to be told twice. She pulled out a chair, stretched her legs, and sighed in relief. "How do you do it all these years, Em?"

Emma moved sugar, salt, and pepper shakers aside to wipe a table. "You mean why did I stay here with Mom and Dad at the restaurant?

"Yes. You have a degree in fashion design."

Emma leaned across the table as she tackled her task. "All the fashion design jobs are in the city and I prefer it here. Plus, Max handles most of the home sales and a large portion of the summer rentals in Ocean Crest. Waitressing gives me something to do when Max is busy."

"It helps that you stayed around, married a local guy, and added a twig to the family tree," Lucy said.

Emma grinned. "Mom and Dad don't pressure me the way they do you. Have you seen Azad yet?"

Lucy stiffened. "No, and I'd rather not."

Emma halted to look her square in the eye. "He's changed, Lucy. It was a long time ago."

"Not long enough. And you're starting to sound like our parents."

"Sorry, but you have to face him sometime."

Lucky picked a piece of lint off her apron. "Only if I'm unlucky enough to run into him."

"He's working at a five star restaurant in Atlantic City, but he still visits Mom and Dad. You already know that he wants to buy Kebab Kitchen," Emma said.

Lucy blinked. She was still processing the news that Azad had become a successful sous chef and that he wanted to buy the restaurant. Did it make a difference to her personally?

Nope. She didn't want to see Azad. No matter how much her parents wanted them to get back together. Or how much Emma insisted he'd changed. She refused to go down the path to heartache.

Again.

Emma untied her apron and folded it into a neat square. "I'm off to run errands, but I'll be back at five. You okay to stay?"

Lucy nodded. "I'll manage."

Emma waved on her way out. "I'm confident you can hold down the fort."

Lucy stood with a sigh when she noticed that Emma had missed wiping down one of the booths. She picked up the discarded rag and started on the dirty table when the little bell on the front door sounded. Lucy's first thought was that Emma had forgotten her purse. She turned around.

And stopped short as Heather Banks walked inside.

Lucy dropped the rag and headed to the hostess stand. "May I help you?"

Heather had exchanged the tight yellow pantsuit she'd worn at Mac's Pub earlier today for a tight pink one, but she still wore the stilettos that gave her a four-inch height advantage over Lucy. The only other difference was that now she carried a clipboard. "I'm here on official business." She began to tap her pen on the clipboard. "I'm the town's new heath inspector."

As if I could forget. Lucy couldn't help but wonder if Heather had purposely shown up on the same day they'd exchanged words at the bar. Heather had said she'd see Lucy and her parents soon, but this seemed ridiculous and contrived.

Lucy eyed Heather warily. "I'll get my parents." She hurried into the kitchen to find her father chopping onions on a large wooden cutting board. "The health inspector is here."

His knife halted in midair as he looked up. "Mr. Banks?"

"No. Ms. Banks. His daughter."

He rubbed his brow. "Ah, I forgot she'd taken over."

Lucy waited as he removed his apron and washed

his hands. Together they met Heather in the dining room.

"I've always dealt with your father," Raffi said.

"He's retired." Heather tapped her clipboard with her pen in an increasing staccato. "I've taken over his position."

The full impact of Heather's power struck Lucy. If her father wanted to put the restaurant on the market, it had to pass inspection. Then again, in the thirty years her parents had owned the business, they had never once failed a health inspection.

Her father waved Heather forward with a cheery smile. "Please do your job, Ms. Banks. If you need anything, Lucy will help you. I have paperwork I need to see to in the office." He headed to the storage room where his office was located, leaving Lucy alone with Heather.

Just great. Her dad had no idea of the animosity between them, and he clearly wasn't concerned about passing inspection. Why should he be? If his past record was any indication, he had nothing to worry about.

Lucy turned to Heather. "Will it take long?"

Heather arched an eyebrow. "It depends on what I find."

Lucy watched as Heather walked through the restaurant, taking notes on her clipboard. She inspected the sinks in the kitchen to ensure proper hand washing stations were in place for employees and that surfaces used for raw meat were not also used to prepare ready-to-eat foods like fruits and salads. Lucy wasn't worried. Her parents were stringent when it came to cleanliness.

Her confidence didn't last long.

"Why only three sinks?" Heather asked.

Lucy's brow furrowed. "Pardon?"

"There should be more. At least four total," Heather said as she scribbled on an official looking carbon copy paper pinned to the clipboard.

"The kitchen has always had three, and it's been more than sufficient in the past," Lucy argued. "Plus, your father never said otherwise." She added the last statement to back up her reasoning.

Heather's head snapped up. "Times have changed, and I'm *not* my father. The restaurant should add another sink." She pointed to a corner with a long, red fingernail. "Over there would be best."

"You're kidding, right?" Lucy planted her hands on her hips. "It doesn't make sense to install a sink there. All the food is prepared near the prep table where a sink already exists. Also, there's insufficient space and no plumbing where you're pointing. You know how much that would cost?"

Heather tossed a lock of red hair behind her shoulder. "Cost is irrelevant to me. I'm the health inspector, not the owner of the establishment, remember?"

Lucy wanted to throttle her. Heather pivoted on her stilettos, and headed toward the kitchen's overhead exhaust. She studied it from below. "This looks ancient. Is this up to code?"

"Yes," Lucy snapped, pointing to an inspection sticker displayed prominently in the corner. "The fire chief has never had a problem with the exhaust system."

Heather grunted. Lucy had the distinct impression she would have marked that down on her clipboard if it was within her job scope.

But the worst was yet to come. As she went along, Heather scrawled notes for additional violations in the walk-in-refrigerator, freezer, and the commercial dishwasher. Finished with the kitchen, Heather wandered into the back storage room. The shelves were loaded with cans and dry goods—flour, salt, bags of rice, lentils, bulgur, and exotic spices— the essentials of Mediterranean cuisine. Heather checked each shelf to ensure no pests were present. By the time she made a few more notes, Lucy was fuming.

Heather left the kitchen and returned to the dining room where she spotted the new hummus bar in the corner. She studied it for a long moment and walked its perimeter. "What type of salad bar is this?"

"It's not. It's a hummus bar," Lucy said. "All different varieties. Customers love it."

Heather pulled out a measuring tape from her purse. She scribbled dimensions down on her note pad. When she was finished, she looked at Lucy. "The sneeze guard is too low."

"Too low? I thought the only concern was if it

was too high and people could accidentally sneeze into the food."

Heather shot her a haughty look. "We've revised the regulations. And I personally dislike salad bars."

"Like I said, it's not a salad bar."

She snorted as she tore off a carbon copy from her clipboard and handed it to Lucy. "See that all these violations are immediately remedied."

Anxiety spurted through Lucy as she studied the paper. "These are all absurd!"

Heather's eyes narrowed. "Excuse me?"

"These are bogus violations and you know it."

"I know no such thing."

"Is this because of our little tiff today at the bar or does it go way back to our high school years?"

Heather's eyes narrowed to slits. "I don't know what you're suggesting."

"Kebab Kitchen hasn't been cited for a single health violation in *thirty* years," Lucy snapped.

Heather's lips curved into a malicious smirk. "There's always a first. See that the violations are remedied or I'll have the place closed down. You have seven days." She turned on her heel and stalked out of the restaurant.

Lucy's heart hammered as she stood clutching the carbon copy in her fist. She barely heard Butch approach.

"What's wrong, Lucy Lou? Is it the inspection?"

She shook her head. "I've dealt with a lot of difficult clients over the years, but I can't remember the last time I've wanted to strangle someone."

"That bad?"

"What's so bad?" another voice chimed in.

Lucy and Butch turned at the sound of her father's voice.

She dreaded telling him the news. "We didn't do so well with the new health inspector."

Raffi held out his hand for the inspection report. "Let me see." His olive eyes widened and his face turned a mottled scarlet as he read. Lucy met Butch's eyes, and they both held their breath for her father's expected burst of anger.

"*Hent!* She's crazy! In all my years here, I've never seen a report like this."

Lucy couldn't have agreed more. "You're right, Dad. But there's not much we can do but comply. She has the power to shut the doors when she comes back."

Raffi's brows drew together. "She has to be the one to come back?"

For the first time she noticed how her father was aging. He looked . . . well . . . older and almost fragile. The wrinkles around his eyes and the downward slope of his shoulders didn't sit well with her. He was still a large, robust man, but she could see how the daily stress of running the restaurant was taking its toll.

She also sympathized with her father's dread regarding the new health inspector. Lucy hoped she wasn't there when Heather came back. Something about Heather Banks . . . and something about this place . . . made Lucy act irrationally.

She'd always prided herself on her control. She'd never lost her temper in her legal practice no matter how difficult a client or adversary.

She glanced at her watch. Twenty minutes.

Heather had been in the restaurant for only twenty minutes, and Lucy felt as overheated as a radiator about to explode. Was she becoming hotheaded after just two days back? What would happen after a week? A month? Was anger management in her future?

CHAPTER 3

The following afternoon, when Lucy showed up for her shift, the aroma made her mouth water as soon as she opened the door. Butch announced the day's specials—grilled halibut kebabs, and stuffed peppers and tomatoes with meat and rice, a traditional Armenian dish called dolma. Lucy's mother encouraged her to taste each dish in case their customers had any questions. Lucy had been more than eager to comply. The halibut was fresh, flaky, and divine in a lemon, cumin, and garlic sauce, and the dolma was hearty and full of spices and flavor. She'd wanted to consume both plates.

Lunch service started soon and quickly grew busy. Butch put out dish after dish. Her mother was busy seating customers and covering the cash register and her dad was in the back office working on payroll.

Close to three, came the usual lull before the dinner hour. Only a few straggling customers remained, sipping coffee while talking and enjoying an extra piece of baklava. Emma and Sally left, and, with no place else to be, Lucy agreed to stay. She began to refill the salt and pepper shakers.

"Thank you for staying," her mother said, kissing her cheek. "Payroll is due on Friday, and I need to help your father in the office."

"No problem, Mom." Lucy could easily handle a stray customer or two.

The pepper made Lucy's nose itch, but she found the simple task relaxing. She hadn't thought of the law firm much in the two days she'd been home. She knew she needed to update her resume soon. What would the law partners and her colleagues think if they saw her in her bright red apron surrounded by dozens of salt and pepper shakers? They probably wouldn't even recognize her and would just hand her a tip on their way out the door. The thought made her laugh out loud.

Lucy's back was to the door when she heard it open. She reached for a menu to welcome a late lunch customer when she froze at the sound of a long-ago, but not-so-forgotten masculine voice.

"Hello, Lucy."

Lucy turned, and her stomach flip-flopped at the sight of Azad Zakarian in the entrance.

Oh, no.

He was even better looking than she remembered. With his dark hair, coffee brown eyes, and bronzed complexion, his features no longer held a soft, youthful appearance, but were chiseled into a man's. A very handsome man. He'd always been athletic, but his shoulders were broader and his chest more muscular beneath his button-down shirt. Well-worn jeans encased his lean legs. The familiar scent of his cologne wafted to her, unleashing unwanted memories.

The last time she'd seen him was two years after college graduation. It had been at the boardwalk, at the town's family-friendly amusement pier. Their eyes had briefly met through a throng of tourists waiting to ride the Ferris wheel. For an instant, an electric current had passed between them and burned as hot as the billion watt bulbs lighting the Ferris wheel, but they'd both looked away. Their past break-up was too fresh.

That had been a long time ago, and she was different now. She was a successful attorney, no longer a lovesick college student with stars in her eyes.

Lucy's chin shot up a notch. "Hello, Azad. My parents are in the office."

He tilted his head to the side and studied her with those dark eyes. "I'm not here to see your parents. I heard you're back for good."

Her heart thumped uncomfortably. "No. Not for good. I took a sabbatical." The lie came easier this time.

He looked at her as if there was no difference between the two. "Either way, I'm glad you're back, Lucy. We should talk."

Alarm bells went off in her head. No way. That was so not going to happen. She had no desire to be alone with Azad. She was past this. *Way* past this. "I don't see why."

At his confused look, a sudden thought crossed Lucy's mind, and she felt her cheeks grow warm. "Wait a second. I've heard you want to buy the restaurant. Is that why you want to talk?"

He studied her with a curious intensity. "Not entirely. I was thinking we could get together and talk . . . you know . . . about us."

Lucy held up a hand. "No. I—"

"We were young." He raked his fingers through his hair, drawing the dark strands away from his forehead, before shoving both hands into the pocket of his jeans. "Right out of college and just twenty-one."

"There's nothing to discuss." This was not a topic she wanted to delve into. "It no longer matters."

"I wasn't ready to commit. I panicked and handled us badly."

Lucy wanted to cover her ears, but that would be childish and stupid and would show she still cared— which she didn't. What was it about this place that made her feel like she'd been stuffed into a time machine and spit out ten years in the past? She was glad her parents were squirreled away in the office with sheets of payroll. They'd be all too happy to learn that Azad had come to see her. She could just imagine her mother's enthusiasm.

"How about we get together for coffee? Don't you want to talk?" he asked.

"No. We are not going there. End of discussion. Period," she added for extra emphasis. "If we're to talk about anything it should be about business. Like why do you want to buy this place?"

He met her gaze and appeared to stand an inch taller. "I've been to culinary school."

"I've heard. But why this?" Lucy said, sweeping her hand across the dining room.

He shrugged broad shoulders. "It's a good investment. I practically grew up here. Your father gave me my first job, and I know this place inside and out. I have what it takes to make it more successful."

"Maybe, but—"

"It was your father's plan years ago," he said as a slow grin formed on his lips. "Remember what he said?"

A heavy feeling settled in Lucy's stomach. She remembered, all right. She'd been dating Azad their senior year in college when they were both home for spring break. As soon as her father had sat them down at the kitchen table, she'd known it was serious. The kitchen of her family home was where all important matters were discussed.

"You two have been together for a year now," Raffi had started. "I can't take the restaurant with me when I die. Emma may be older than you, Lucy, but she doesn't have a head for business. You and Azad are perfect."

She should have been outraged at her father's plotting. But the truth was she had fallen for Azad. Hard.

Apparently he hadn't felt the same. If only he'd had the guts to tell her . . .

Azad took a step toward her, and a traitorous

tingling began in the pit of Lucy's stomach. "I was young and stupid. If only I could go back and—"

Lucy whirled at the sound of shattering glass and loud voices coming from the kitchen.

Azad frowned. "What the hell was that?"

"Wait here." She rushed to the kitchen to find a large jar of grape leaves scattered across the floor and Butch laughing with a strange man. The man was short and stocky, with legs that looked like mini tree trunks and, as he turned, she saw a familiar face.

"Big Al!" she cried out.

"Look who's returned to the nest." The man enveloped Lucy in a big hug.

Lucy's arms didn't reach halfway around his large girth. Ali Basher, otherwise known as Big Al, was one of her father's food suppliers who specialized in ethnic food items and made small weekly deliveries. He looked just as she remembered—a head of curly salt and pepper hair and warm brown eyes in a large fleshy face. He waddled when he walked, and, when she was young, Lucy had thought he looked like a penguin.

She eyed the dark grape leaves, liquid brine, and shattered glass on the floor. Her mother would have used the jar's contents to prepare savory wrapped grape leaves with meat and rice. "What happened?"

A toothy grin spread across his face. "Just a small accident. Don't worry. I brought an extra jar, and I'll help Butch clean it up."

"What else have you brought today?" Lucy peeked

inside a box on the counter to see fresh apricots, phyllo dough that would be used to make baklava—her favorite flaky pastry dessert with walnuts and cinnamon—crushed mint to prepare tabbouleh salad, and jars of aromatic spices like sumac and paprika.

"A little of this and that," Big Al said.

Lucy smiled at his description. "My parents are in the office working on payroll."

"Don't disturb them. I don't need them for this delivery. By the way, is that Azad's truck I saw outside?"

She kept forgetting how everyone knew everyone in the restaurant business, especially in the small town. "He's in the dining room."

Big Al began unpacking his box and placing items on a wooden prep table. The sight of the fresh apricots caught Lucy's eye, the fruits' pale skins shining beneath the kitchen's florescent lights. How long had it been since she'd eaten one?

"As soon as I'm done here, I'll say hello to him," Big Al said as she worked.

"I don't know if he's still here," Lucy said on her way out of the kitchen. If she were lucky, Azad would be long gone.

No such luck. As soon as she walked into the dining room, she spotted Azad sitting at one of the tables checking his e-mail on his cell phone. Thankfully, the last of the customers were waiting to pay, and Lucy could avoid him and busy herself making change at the register until the place was empty.

She eyed the back of his dark head and broad shoulders. Straightening her shoulders, she headed for where he sat, fully intending to have an impersonal, business-like conversation with him. She opened her mouth to call his name when the front door opened.

Lucy turned with a smile to greet a customer only to see Heather Banks walk inside. Dressed in another tight business suit—a lime green one this time—and holding the dreaded clipboard, she halted by the hostess stand. Lucy couldn't help but wonder how many restaurants she'd failed today.

Putting Azad out of her mind, she took three deep breaths, slowly exhaled, then walked over. "You gave us seven days. It's only been one."

Heather arched a perfectly drawn-on brow. Her gaze raked Lucy's length, taking in her simple white collared shirt, black slacks, red apron, and sneakers. Heather's red-glossed lips twisted with distaste. "I know. I can read a calendar. I'm here to eat."

Lucy's jaw dropped as she gawked at her. "Eat?"

"Yes. Eat. That's what people do here, isn't it?"

Lucy stiffened. She wouldn't have been more surprised if Heather had said there was a pack of wild dogs running through the restaurant. "Of course. You can sit anywhere."

Heather chose the best table in the restaurant, one with a nice view of the ocean and cloudless sky.

"I'll get you a menu." Lucy headed for the hostess stand where the menus were stored.

"I don't need one," Heather called out.

"Pardon?" Lucy halted mid-step.

Heather plopped her lime green Gucci purse—a perfect match to her outfit—on the table. "I know what I want. Are you just going to stand there or are you going to take my order?"

Lucy was determined not to lose her temper. Pasting a smile on her face, she pulled out a pad and pen from her apron pocket. "What can I get you?"

"Pita bread. Wheat only."

This was just getting weirder and weirder. Lucy looked at her questioningly. "That's it?"

"A glass of fresh-brewed, unsweetened iced tea."

"Got it." Lucy made a pretense of scribbling on her pad. It was preferable to looking at her infuriating customer.

Heather drummed red nails on the table. "I also want the all you can eat hummus bar."

After citing the restaurant for the hummus bar? Lucy felt a simmering anger. She clenched and unclenched the pen. "I'll bring the pita and you can help yourself to the hummus."

Heading to the kitchen, she ripped off the slip from her pad and tucked it in the ticket spindle and gave it a good spin. Butch appeared in the kitchen, glanced at the order, and blinked. "Pita only? That's it?'

"Guess who?" Lucy said.

Butch arched a bushy brow.

"The lovely Ms. Banks."

He scratched his red bandana. "The new health inspector? The one that gave us a hard time?"

Lucy held up her hands. "Go figure. But she's here as a customer, not on official business."

Butch handed her a basket of warm pita bread. "You better be quick for her highness."

Lucy hurried into the kitchen to fetch the iced tea when she spotted Azad and Big Al talking at the entrance to the storage room. Azad must have left the dining room and wandered into the kitchen when she was busy taking Heather's order.

"What are you two doing back here?" she asked.

Big Al shot her a smile. "Just catching up. Azad's agreed to help me unload the rest of the boxes from my truck."

"Happy to help." Azad grinned as he folded his arms across his chest and leaned against a tall shelf.

Lucy quickly averted her gaze from his tautly stretched shirt. *Damn.* She mentally shook herself. He'd be gone soon. She just had to get through waiting on Heather and Azad unloading Big Al's truck, then she'd finish her shift and sprint out of the place.

"Only one lone customer out there?" Azad asked.

Lucy nodded, anxious to get away. "Excuse me while I see what else she needs." She left the two men in the kitchen and delivered the basket of pita bread.

Heather's blindingly white teeth flashed as she tore into the bread. They must have been recently bleached. Lowering the half-eaten piece of bread, she glowered at Lucy and snapped, "Where's my iced tea?"

Lucy had forgotten all about the tea. The sight of Azad talking with Big Al had unsettled her more than it should have. Mind whirling, she came up with a quick excuse. "You said fresh. It's brewing and will be right up."

Lucy went back to the kitchen to see Big Al packing up empty boxes. There was no sign of Azad.

"Azad had to leave," Big Al said, anticipating her question.

A heaviness centered in her chest. He hadn't even said good-bye. She couldn't possibly be disappointed, could she?

"Please give this to your father." Big Al handed her a slip of paper—an itemized bill for the goods he'd delivered.

Seeing Azad had been trying and Lucy longed to go back to Katie's place, change, and take a boardwalk jog.

Unfortunately, before she could do that she had to check on Heather.

Lucy passed the hummus bar on her way to Heather's table. For someone who had recently written a report about its noncompliance, Heather had a healthy appetite. There wasn't a single type of hummus she hadn't tried and it looked like her mother's traditional hummus was her favorite. Large scoops had been carved out from the containers.

"Do you need anything else?" Lucy hoped the answer would be no.

"More pita."

Heather's complexion was flushed and she fanned herself with papers she'd removed from her clipboard. She was breathing rapidly. It was hot outside, but the restaurant was air-conditioned. Maybe she had hot flashes? They were the same age—early thirties—but Lucy liked to think she was still years off from that change of life.

Heather's plate was covered with clumps of hummus. Each variety had its own space around the perimeter of her plate, reminding Lucy of an artist's palette. *How strange.*

Lucy hurried to fetch another basket of pita. She wanted Heather gone and hoped she ate quickly.

At last, Heather waved a hand and called out loudly, "Check."

Lucy was tallying the bill by the register when Heather's cell phone trilled. "I said don't call me on this number," Heather hissed into the phone.

Lucy's ears perked up at Heather's harsh tone, and she strained to hear. Even from where she stood, Lucy could see the sheen of perspiration glistening on Heather's brow as she shifted restlessly in her seat and resumed vigorously fanning herself with her papers.

"It doesn't matter," Heather said through gritted teeth. "No exceptions. Have I ever let you down before?"

Whoever she was talking to must have been determined, because Heather's caustic tone softened a bit. "I see. Yeah. I'll have it by the end of the week."

Heather pressed the END CALL button on her cell, then spotted Lucy by the cash register. She extended her hand and snapped her fingers.

Lucy jumped, fearful that she'd been caught eavesdropping, until she realized that Heather just wanted her check. Really? Snapping fingers was beyond rude.

She delivered the check, then breathed a sigh of relief when Heather finally paid and left.

"Good riddance," Butch said when Lucy went back into the kitchen. "Big Al left, and your parents will be in their office for a while. Let's hope the rest of the evening is calm."

She couldn't agree more. "Emma's coming back soon for the dinner shift. I'll clean up a bit before I leave."

Keeping herself busy, she wiped down booths, filled the small flower vases with additional water, cleaned the juice and soda machines, and swept the tiles behind the waitress station. An hour and a half later, after everything was to her satisfaction, she found Butch stirring a large pot of lentil soup for the dinner service. Lucy smiled wearily and pointed to a bag by the back door of the storage room. "How about I take this trash out to the Dumpster on my way?"

He smiled, revealing his gold tooth. "Thanks, Lucy Lou."

Lucy removed her apron and hung it on a hook in the storage room. Grabbing her purse with one hand and the trash bag with the other, she exited through the back door. It was cool outside and early evenings at the Jersey shore were always her favorite time of day to jog. Nothing calmed the tension of a hard workday like a run on the boardwalk, the sound of the ocean waves, and the smell of salty air.

She hefted the trash bag toward the Dumpster in the back of the parking lot, spotted Gadoo walking past a red Lexus with its distinctive BANKS1 license plate, and frowned. Did Heather have car trouble and have someone pick her up? Lucy adjusted the trash bag over her shoulder and continued her trek to the Dumpster, eyes still on the shiny, red Lexus. Halfway to her destination she tripped, dropped the trash bag and her purse, just catching herself from sprawling flat on her face. She looked down to see what she'd stumbled over.

On the blacktop lay Heather Banks, faceup, mouth agape, eyes wide open and unfocused, a pool of vomit nearby.

CHAPTER 4

Lucy sucked in air and choked back a scream. Her hand flew up to cover her mouth. Heather's head was turned to the side, the skin of her neck unnaturally pale, and her dyed red hair was spread out on the blacktop. A few strands lay in the puddle of vomit.

Years ago, Lucy had taken a CPR course and her training told her what to do, but her body wouldn't cooperate. *Get a hold of yourself! Stay calm and help her.* Lucy reached down for Heather's wrist to take her pulse. Her flesh was cold. Lucy felt nothing.

Oh my God.

Heather was dead.

Lucy sprinted back through the storage room and into the kitchen where Butch was still stirring the large pot of lentil soup over the stove. "Heather's dead!"

The spoon clattered against the side of the pot, and Butch looked at her like she'd grown two heads. "What are you talking about?"

Thank goodness she had the presence of mind to pick up her purse from where she'd dropped it along with the trash bag. She had no intention of going back outside to retrieve anything or running to reach the nearest landline in the dining room. "I'm calling 911."

Lucy punched in the numbers on her cell with shaky fingers and explained to the dispatcher what she'd found. As soon as she hung up with the police, she called Katie.

"Hello," Katie answered, slightly out of breath. Loud music played in the background and Lucy remembered that Katie exercised to kickboxing DVDs after work.

"Katie! You have to come to the restaurant. Heather Banks is dead!"

"What?" There was a pause until the music stopped and Katie switched from speaker phone to the receiver.

Lucy's pulse battered erratically through her veins. "She came here to eat and then left . . . and I went out the back. I tripped over her body and she's dead." Lucy knew she was not being totally coherent.

"Did you call the police?" Katie asked.

"Yes. They're on their way."

"Are you alone?"

"No. Butch is here." Lucy suddenly remembered her parents were in their office. "My mom and dad are here, too."

"Good. Stay together. It may not be safe." Katie's voice was low and troubled.

Lucy immediately halted her pacing, and her fingers tightened on the phone. She hadn't thought of that. Was it safe? Did someone attack Heather? She hadn't seen any injuries or blood. But that didn't necessarily mean . . .

My God. Was there a killer outside?

"Stay there with Butch and your parents. I'll be right over." Katie hung up.

Stomach clenched tight, Lucy ran to the tiny office in the corner of the storage room and threw open the door. Her parents sat behind the desk and looked up from their work. Papers and time slips cluttered the surface of the desk.

Angela removed her reading glasses and they dangled from a chain around her neck. "What's wrong?"

"Heather Banks is dead in the back parking lot," Lucy blurted out. "The police are on their way."

Raffi pushed back his chair and stood. *"Asvadzt!* My God! What has that crazy lady gotten herself into?"

In all the crime fighting TV shows Lucy had watched, the police arrive in minutes. It took the Ocean Crest police close to seventeen minutes to show up. Officer Bill Watson was the first to come inside. Tall and fit with blue eyes and close-cropped light brown hair, he had the look of a seasoned officer. In contrast, he was followed by a younger officer with a freckled face and a crew cut who looked fresh out of the police academy.

A look of concern crossed Bill's face as soon as he spotted her. "Are you all right, Lucy?"

Lucy worried her bottom lip. "I've been better."

"Your call said there was a body," the young officer said. "Where is it?"

"Out back."

The officers followed Lucy into the kitchen, through the storage room, and out the back door. Her stomach turned at the sight of Heather splayed out, eyes unseeing. The faint stench of vomit permeated the air.

Bill squatted down to press two fingers against Heather's carotid artery. Lucy could have told him not to bother. He muttered a curse under his breath, reached for his walkie-talkie, and called for backup.

She wondered why they didn't show up with the entire police force in the first place. How common were dead bodies in the small shore town anyway?

Bill stepped away from the body and approached her. "We needed to be sure," he said as if reading her mind. "It's not very often someone dies of unknown causes here." Taking her arm, he led her back into the dining room.

Her knees were wobbling, and she feared she would trip.

The front door burst open and Katie flew inside.

Still wearing her workout gear, her blond hair was pulled back into a messy ponytail and her face was flushed. "Lucy!" Katie ran over and hugged her.

Bill turned to his wife in astonishment. "What are you doing here?"

Katie's lips parted. "Lucy called me."

He stared at his wife. "You shouldn't be here. There's a body out back. We need to secure the scene."

"I'm not leaving her." Katie put her hands on her hips and faced her husband.

Bill took one look at his wife's determined expression, sighed, and shook his head. "Fine. Then sit." He pointed to the closest table. "And please don't interfere."

The door burst open again and two more officers in uniform and the paramedics arrived. The group charged through the dining room and out the back. Lucy trailed behind and peeked out the door. The paramedics were quick to confirm that Heather was dead, and the officers began taking pictures. She blinked at the blinding flash of numerous cameras.

The restaurant was secured. No one was permitted in or out.

The county medical examiner was called in, and he went right to the body with his own camera. Soon after, another police officer arrived—a tall man in his late-thirties with a full head of straw-colored hair and a bushy mustache, dressed in a gray-checked suit. His sharp nose looked like a wedge of cheese. He seemed familiar, and Lucy struggled to place him. A name kept slipping through her thoughts.

"I'm Detective Clemmons." His expression was grave as he pulled out a small notebook from his shirt pocket and flipped it open.

Her face burned as she remembered. Calvin Clemmons. Her sister's former high school boyfriend. Emma had broken up with Clingy Calvin, as she'd called him, to date and eventually marry Max. From what Lucy recalled, it hadn't ended friendly. Emma hadn't been known for her faithfulness.

"You found the body, correct?" Detective Clemmons asked

"Yes."

"Your name?"

"Lucy Berberian."

He lowered his notebook. "Well, well. If it isn't Emma's little sister. Is your sister here?"

"No. Emma left hours ago." Hopefully Calvin Clemmons wouldn't hold a grudge against her family because of something that happened years ago in high school. Would he?

He cleared his throat and looked her in the eye. "Okay, Lucy. I need to ask you a few questions about what you know."

Lucy pointed to the body with a shaky finger. "That is . . . was . . . Heather Banks."

"When did you first see Ms. Banks today?"

"She came into the restaurant to eat. I waited on

her, she paid, then she left. I never saw her again until the end of my shift when I went to take the trash to the Dumpster. That's when I stumbled over her body."

"What did she order?"

"Hummus and pita bread."

His stare drilled into her. "That's it? Kind of odd, isn't it?"

Lucy's fingers tensed at her sides. "I guess that's all she wanted." The way he watched her made her anxious.

"Did you know Ms. Banks?"

Her unease increased. Detective Calvin Clemmons was older and had graduated before Lucy and Heather had started high school as freshmen. But Lucy wasn't fooled. She may not want to delve into her past with Heather, but she knew the detective would quickly learn that she'd known Heather. "We went to high school together."

The Detective raised an eyebrow and wrote a note in his pad. "Do you know of anyone who had a conflict with Ms. Banks?"

Lucy's nervousness escalated. "A conflict? Are you saying there was foul play?"

His straight glance seemed to be accusing her. "I'm not saying anything. I'm just asking a question."

"Didn't she have a heart attack or something?"

"Answer the question, please."

Her mind spun as she recalled her argument

with Heather at Mac's Pub. Their raised voices had been overheard by several locals. She knew that it would eventually come out. It was best if she told him before he found out from another source and it looked like she was withholding information.

"Like I said, we went to high school together. We weren't the best pals. We had a run-in at Mac's Pub yesterday," Lucy said.

One brow shot up. "What do you mean by a run-in?"

She shrugged, hoping to make it look like no big deal. "We argued."

"About what?"

"She thought my parents weren't citizens, and I corrected her. That's all. No biggie."

He glared at her, frowning, then scribbled in his pad. "Anything else I should know?"

Lucy recalled Heather gripping her cell phone, her scowling expression. "I overheard her arguing with someone on her cell phone when I handed her the check. She yelled at someone for calling her."

"That's it?"

"That's all I heard." Lucy's nerves were frayed as the medical examiner began covering Heather's body in a black body bag. The sound of the zipper made her cringe.

"This is your parents' restaurant, correct?"

"Yes."

"I understand you're staying with Officer Bill Watson and his wife," Detective Clemmons said.

She looked away from Heather's body back to the

Detective. "Yes. Bill's wife, Katie, and I are longtime friends."

"All right. If there's anything else, I'll be in touch."

Butch was interviewed next, then Lucy's parents. Unlike when he questioned Lucy, Calvin Clemmons was quick with them. The county medical examiner and the other officers continued to process the scene. Everything Heather had touched and had eaten and drunk from, her plate, glass and utensils, the bins in the hummus bar, the pita bread and the iced tea, was collected in evidence bags and taken away. Even the trash in the restaurant was collected, and the Dumpster was emptied for processing. Last to be carried out was Heather's body.

Sitting in the dining room with her parents, Katie, and Butch, huddled around a table with glasses of ice water, Lucy said, "I can't believe she's dead." *Had she died of natural causes or was there foul play?*

Heather had been Lucy's age, thirty-two. Lucy considered herself young, but it wasn't unheard of for thirty-somethings to have heart attacks and strokes. She hadn't seen anything to show Heather had been attacked, but Lucy wasn't a detective. Unlike Katie, she didn't even like crime shows.

Angela wrung her hands on the table. "Why here? Why couldn't she have died at any of the other restaurants she cited? It's a bad omen. Someone put the *achk* on us." She crossed herself.

"Nonsense. I don't believe in the evil eye or bad omens," Raffi muttered.

"How do you explain it, then?" Angela said.

"She was bad news. She got herself into trouble," Raffi said.

"Either way. I'm worried about the business. What will people think of not only a customer dying here, but the health inspector. Good God! Could it be any worse?" Her mother sniffled, then began to cry.

Her father's brows drew downward. He could never stand to see tears, from his wife or either of his daughters. He pulled a handkerchief from his pocket and handed it to her, then wrapped an arm around her shoulders. "No . . . no. All will be well. You'll see. The business will be fine. People in town know us. They trust us."

Angela blew her nose and shook her head.

Katie spoke up. "Mr. and Mrs. Berberian, please don't worry. There must be an explanation. Maybe she had a heart attack or some other medical condition."

Lucy set her water glass down. "Katie's right. What else could the police think it could be?"

Silence. All eyes turned to look at her, and she inwardly flinched. She didn't have to be a mind reader to know what everyone else was thinking.

Lucy sat up straight. "Well, it wasn't the food. She ordered hummus and pita. That's all."

"No one has ever gotten sick from eating here in

thirty years. Thirty!" Raffi slammed his fist on the table, causing water to slosh onto the tablecloth.

Butch removed his checkered bandana and rubbed his bald pate. "No one's saying that, Mr. B."

"There's no sense in arguing," Katie said. "The medical examiner will find out what happened. Then it will be business as usual for all of you."

Angela rubbed her forehead and sobbed even louder. "Business? How could I forget? It's almost tourist season. It's even worse than I thought."

Lucy bit her lip over her mother's distress. "They'll know the truth before then, Mom." They had to know by then. The consequences of Heather's demise struck Lucy like a falling brick. She may not have been involved in the day-to-day running of the restaurant for years, but she knew how important the tourist season was to their economic survival.

The kitchen door swung open and Bill stepped into the dining room.

Her parents jumped to their feet. "What's going on?" they asked in unison.

Bill removed his hat and ran his fingers through his fair hair. Two deep lines of worry appeared between his eyes. He looked wearier than when he'd first arrived after Lucy had called the police. Wearier and older. She didn't envy him his job.

"The scene is still being processed, Mrs. Berberian. We won't know anything until the medical examiner has a good look at the body," Bill said.

Raffi frowned. "That's it?"

"I'm afraid I'm not able to work the case. There's a conflict of interest. Lucy's good friends with my wife and is staying with us. It looks bad for everyone if I'm involved," Bill said.

Angela's gaze was clouded with tears as she waved a hand in exasperation. "Of all the places to die, why did that woman have to pick here?"

Lucy was thinking the same thing.

CHAPTER 5

The following morning, Lucy woke to sunshine streaming through the slats of the guest room's blinds. The window was cracked and a pleasant breeze stirred sheer curtains as the faint scent of ocean wafted into the room. Somewhere in the distance seagulls squawked. Memories of lazy summer mornings lingered around the edges of her half-sleepy, half-awake mind. No city traffic, no obnoxious car honking, and no squealing of trucks' brakes as they made early morning deliveries to bustling city businesses.

She yawned, rubbed her eyes, then glanced at the clock on the bedside table. Seven o'clock.

She was surprised it was so late. Years of working at the law firm had programmed her to wake up at five. She rarely overslept.

As soon as she sat up, last night's nightmare came back in a rush. It had taken four hours before the last of the police officers, crime scene technicians, and Detective Clemmons had left the restaurant.

Lucy had been exhausted by the time Katie had taken her home.

Katie and Bill lived in a charming, cozy rancher with a white picket fence two blocks from the beach. The guest room was airy with plenty of natural light. Sheer curtains embroidered with starfish and shells matched the daybed's thick, matching coverlet and throw pillows. Cheerful watercolors, featuring a variety of Jersey beach scenes, added bursts of color to the pale blue walls. The furniture was white, and a wicker chair with a pad covered in a horseshoe crab pattern completed the beach theme.

The smell of freshly brewed coffee made Lucy's mouth water. She threw on a robe, thrust her feet into slippers, and padded into the kitchen. Katie and Bill were standing at the kitchen island, sipping coffee from steaming mugs and speaking softly. Bill was dressed in his uniform. They froze when they saw her, their mugs poised in midair.

Lucy instantly became alert. "What's up?"

"We know more about last night," Katie said.

Bill's brows drew together. "I'm not supposed to talk about it, remember?"

Katie touched his sleeve. "I understand, but she has a right to know." She walked to the cupboard for a mug and poured Lucy a cup of coffee.

Bill let out a slow breath and set his mug down on the Formica counter. "The medical examiner hasn't yet conducted the autopsy, and it will take weeks to get the tox results back, but after his preliminary examination it looks like Heather Banks did not die of a heart attack or a stroke."

Oh no. This couldn't be good. Lucy's mind scrambled for some kind of explanation for why Heather had dropped dead in the restaurant's parking lot. "What about her health history? There must be some explanation."

"We looked into her medical history. She recently had a physical and was given a good report."

"Then what?"

Bill's shoulders hunched forward, and he hesitated before speaking. "Like I said we won't know until the toxicology results are final, but the medical examiner thinks she died from something she ingested."

Food poisoning? Lucy bit her lip until it throbbed like her pulse. "How can he tell so soon?"

"There were signs. After her clothing was removed, her skin was pinker than usual and he detected a distinctive odor. And she'd vomited."

Lucy sagged against the counter. "The police can't think that the food Heather ate at Kebab Kitchen killed her, can they? It's not possible."

"If it was something she consumed, they have to look into everything."

"Wait a minute. Doesn't food poisoning take time? I've never heard of a person dropping dead of salmonella or botulism after thirty minutes," Lucy insisted.

Bill shifted uneasily. "You're right."

"The medical examiner would know that. So

what else could the police think?" Lucy's mind spun and a frightening thought struck her like a bolt of lightning. "That Heather was murdered? By poison?"

The slightest flinch of Bill's features told her more than any words could convey.

Holy crap. It was one thing to accidently die of food poisoning, but another entirely for the police to believe Heather was intentionally poisoned and murdered.

"Don't panic. Like I said, it's too soon to tell, and the autopsy is scheduled for this morning. The ME may find something else."

The medical examiner *had* to find something else to explain Heather's death. Lucy opened her mouth, then shut it. Arguing with Bill wouldn't help. He was already taking a professional risk by revealing more than he should. "Thank you for sharing this. I don't want to get you in trouble."

Bill's gaze traveled from Katie to Lucy, then back to Katie. "Then please stay out of it and let us do our jobs, okay?" He placed his mug in the kitchen sink, grabbed his hat from the counter, and walked to the door. Katie trailed behind to say good-bye before he left for his shift.

Lucy remained in the kitchen as she struggled to make sense of what she'd learned. It was her nature to question things. Who, then, had disliked Heather enough to murder her? Lucy's thoughts churned. If curiosity killed the cat, what would it do to an out-of-work lawyer sticking her nose where it didn't belong?

Don't meddle with police business, Lucy. Still, it couldn't hurt to ask a few questions, could it?

Lucy parked her car in front of the restaurant and sat with the engine running. She dreaded walking into the place, but it was because of an entirely different type of family drama. For a heart-stopping moment, she contemplated backing out of her parking spot and speeding all the way back to Philadelphia. She could get another job, start over, and ignore the entire mess.

Then she envisioned her parents' expressions and she couldn't do it. She'd fled once before, years ago. But she was a "big girl" now, and she wouldn't do it again.

Lucy killed the engine and entered the restaurant. Her parents were waiting for her. So were Emma and her husband Max.

Emma rushed to her side. "Lucy! Thank goodness you're all right. I can't believe Heather Banks died here."

Max gave her a hug. "You okay?"

Lucy nodded and kissed her brother-in-law's cheek. Max was handsome, with blue eyes and sandy hair that brushed his collar and gave him a roguish look. His quick smile and charming personality were assets in his thriving real estate business. He worked long hours, and his schedule was a point of strife between him and Emma. Lucy's sister had been the first to marry outside of their culture, and the church wedding was as humorous and stress-ridden as the movie *My Big Fat Greek Wedding*.

"You should have called us last night," Max said. "We could have been here in five minutes flat."

Lucy shook her head. "There was no need. The police had to secure the scene and do their jobs. No one was allowed in or out."

Angela flipped through a stack of menus, righting each one to face the same direction, then banged the stack hard on a table. Her cheeks were flushed with anger, and a loose pin flew from her beehive to the floor. "I still can't believe it. The woman complained about our hummus bar and then came back to eat. How dare she touch my hummus!"

Lucy was relieved her mother's tears were gone. She didn't blame her for her show of temper. Lucy had displayed more of it in the past two days she'd been home than in the past six months.

"What does Bill say?" Emma said.

A tight knot formed inside Lucy as she recalled what Bill had told her. Did she want to tell them or wait until more information was available, at least until the autopsy was completed? "Bill isn't at liberty to tell me all the details."

"It was a heart attack, wasn't it?" Emma pressed.

Lucy decided being truthful was best. They

needed to know . . . to prepare themselves. "That was their first thought."

"What do you mean their *first* thought?" Emma said.

Lucy took a deep breath before answering. "After an initial examination of the body, it appears that Heather died from something she ate."

"You mean food poisoning?" Emma said.

A collective gasp followed from her parents.

Emma whirled to face their mother. "How fresh was your hummus, Mom?"

"Nonsense," Angela snapped. "I make my hummus every morning and place it immediately in the refrigerator until it's ready to be served. We bring it out in small batches and replenish it as needed. My hummus did not kill that woman."

"We've never been accused of such a foul offense," Raffi grumbled.

Max spoke up. "It doesn't make sense. A person doesn't eat and then croak of food poisoning as they're walking out."

"Maybe she was unhealthy and took a wrong dose of medication by accident," Emma suggested.

Lucy swallowed and shook her head. "Not according to the initial examination by the medical examiner."

Emma's eyes widened. "Then if Heather died of something she ate and she wasn't unhealthy and didn't accidently mix up her medication, they must think she was *murdered*."

Angela dropped the stack of menus with a thud. Everyone turned to look at Lucy in astonishment.

Lucy ran a hand through her hair in exasperation. "They won't know for sure until the toxicology results are final. It could take weeks."

"Weeks?" Angela asked incredulously. "This is a small town. News travels fast. Tourist season will begin in less than a month. What will happen to us? To the restaurant?"

"They wouldn't even have to shut us down. Who would come eat at Kebab Kitchen?" Raffi asked.

"What about Ocean Crest? Who will want to spend their vacation in our small town if they believe a murderer lives here?" Emma said.

"It will affect the sale of the restaurant for certain," Max said. "How do you expect me to sell the place if the authorities suspect that the health inspector was poisoned after eating here? Even *I* can't fix that."

Lucy's breath solidified in her throat. They were all looking to her for answers. "I don't know."

Her father pointed a finger at her chest. "You have to find out who did this, Lucy. You need to learn what happened to that woman."

"Me?"

His eyes held a sheen of purpose. "Yes. You're the attorney in the family."

Even though she'd considered doing a bit of snooping on her own, the family pressure was entirely different. It was much, much worse. "I'm a *patent attorney*, Dad." Her voice was shakier than she would have liked. "I have no law enforcement experience, and I'm not an investigator."

"So? Family helps family. Find out who did this."

Lucy sat on the sofa in Katie's family room and rested her head in her hands. Thank goodness her friend was home on her lunch break. "My dad expects me to turn into Sherlock Holmes."

Katie made a sound that was part snort, part chuckle. "He wants you to find Heather's killer?"

Lucy felt a headache beginning and rubbed her temples. "If the autopsy confirms the medical examiner's initial guess of murder by poison, then yes."

Katie handed her a mug of coffee and sat in an armchair cradling her own cup. "It's not a bad idea for us, Lucy."

Lucy took a sip of her coffee and nearly burned her tongue. "What do you mean by *us?*"

"Don't get your panties in a twist. Of course, I want to help. I'll do as much as I can during lunch breaks and after work hours. You'll be Sherlock and I'll be your Watson. It will be just like old times. We were inseparable, remember?"

Lucy set the mug down on the end table. "In high school gym class. We were good badminton partners and one of us could hold the bottom of a rope while the other climbed up. This is entirely different."

Katie leaned forward and met Lucy's gaze.

"Tell me you haven't thought about the possibility already?"

Lucy swallowed. "I won't lie. I was planning to ask around to see who else disliked Heather."

Katie tapped her chin with a forefinger. "It's a good start, and I have ideas too. After all, I've been married to a cop for fourteen years."

"Bill would be furious if he found out we were poking around. He already warned us to stay out of it, remember?" Lucy pointed out.

Katie waved a hand. "I'm not worried. We'll be careful, and Bill will never find out. Besides he has to stay out of the investigation to avoid a conflict of interest. It's Calvin Clemmons who concerns me. He's a small-minded detective in a small town. He's under pressure to close the case before tourist season starts. He won't dig deep. He'll look for the easiest way to solve the crime, even if it's not the right one."

Lucy's brow crimped. "You think so? I'm worried he still holds a grudge against Emma and possibly our family for their high school breakup. My parents never liked him and he knew it."

"Like I said, he's small-minded."

"Maybe he's not the one in charge."

Katie's eyebrow shot up. "This is Ocean Crest. He's the town's sole detective and is in charge of investigating all crime, not that we've had any. If Calvin suspects foul play, he'll report it to the county prosecutor so fast our heads will spin."

A wave of apprehension swept through Lucy. "You think so?"

"I do." Katie opened a slim drawer of an end table and withdrew a pad and pencil. "Think back. Who else was in the restaurant when Heather was there?"

"Butch was in the kitchen and I was in the dining room. My parents were in their office working on payroll."

Katie scribbled on the pad. "That's it?"

"That's who was working." Lucy's mind went back to that afternoon. "Azad stopped by."

Katie looked up, an eager expression on her face. "He did? What happened?"

Her coffee hadn't quite kicked in yet, but Lucy knew to be cautious. "Nothing. I thought he was there to see my dad, but he'd heard I was home and wanted to see me."

A mischievous gleam lit Katie's eyes. "Interesting. He's looking good, isn't he? I always thought Azad was cute, but now he's handsome with those dark eyes, broad shoulders, and—"

"It's not like that," Lucy snapped. "I'm over him."

"I believe you, but we still need to add him to the list of people present that afternoon." Katie wrote Azad's name on the pad.

Katie was right. Maybe Azad saw something. Or maybe he knew Heather. But that meant Lucy would have to speak with him to find out. Her fingers tensed in her lap.

"Anyone else?" Katie asked.

Lucy recalled the crash in the kitchen and the appearance of Big Al. "One of my father's food suppliers made a delivery. Big Al is friendly with Azad." She remembered how that had irked her. Everyone in the town seemed to know everyone else's business.

"Did either of them have a reason to want Heather dead?" Katie asked.

"If they did, I can't think of one."

"Clemmons already questioned Butch and your parents. He will question Big Al, too." Katie rubbed her chin. "From what you told me last night, Heather drank unsweetened ice tea, ordered pita bread, and ate from the hummus bar."

Lucy reached for her coffee again. This time it wasn't as hot. "That's right. The police took Heather's leftovers and the trash, even the garbage from the Dumpster."

"If something in the hummus killed Heather, they'll know when the state lab results come back," Katie said.

"What could possibly be deadly in the hummus? An overdose of garlic?" Lucy said sarcastically.

"You're right. Bad breath never killed anyone," Katie said.

"My mom swears her hummus is made fresh each morning and promptly refrigerated. I believe her. Plus, I helped her make a fresh batch the other day. There's no meat or dairy that could spoil quickly in the hummus. It's a mystery to me."

Katie tucked the pencil behind her ear. "Maybe Heather had a food allergy."

Lucy shook her head. "I don't think so. She was very particular about what she ordered and drank. She wouldn't have eaten anything that would make her sick."

Katie shimmied forward on the couch and looked Lucy in the eye. "What else can you remember?"

Lucy rubbed her forehead. "Heather was sweating. I thought it was odd since the restaurant's air conditioning system works well."

"Maybe she was physically reacting to the garlic in the hummus or, heaven forbid, poison. Anything else?"

Lucy let out a long exhale. "I overheard Heather arguing with someone on her cell phone. She told the person never to call her on that line. I told all of this to the police. But I've been thinking about it since. What if she was arguing with her boyfriend, Paul Evans?"

"I think we should talk to him," Katie said. "Bill always says victims are often murdered by someone close to them. Husbands and boyfriends are usually prime suspects."

A flash of blue outside the living room window caught Lucy's eye. Katie saw it too. They stood and parted the curtains to see a blue Ford F150 truck park in Katie's driveway.

"Who's that?" Lucy asked.

The door of the truck opened, and Azad climbed out. He wore a T-shirt and jeans that clung to his long legs and made him look lean and sinewy. His features were chiseled and a lock of dark hair brushed his forehead.

Watch it, Lucy!

"Well, well," Katie drawled, a note of appreciation in her voice. "Look who's decided to pay a visit." She grinned and shot Lucy a sidelong glance. "And you said nothing happened between you two yesterday."

Lucy's heart skipped a beat as Azad walked up the driveway. She trailed behind Katie and paused for a quick glimpse in the hallway mirror before they reached the front door. In her haste this morning, she hadn't used her trusty spray gel and her long dark curls were already a halo of frizz from the ever present Jersey shore humidity. She attempted to smooth the wayward strands just as Katie yanked open the front door.

"Hello Katie," Azad said.

"Good to see you, Azad. You're here to speak with Lucy, right?"

"If you don't mind." He grinned, a charming smile that said he knew the effect he had on women and he was taking full advantage.

Lucy stepped onto the porch. She decided it was best if she talked to him outside. That way, she could make a fast escape back inside if necessary.

"I'll be in the house if you need me," Katie said, then left the two of them alone.

Lucy faked an ease she didn't feel. She awkwardly cleared her throat and attempted to look anywhere but in Azad's dark eyes. Katie's stone driveway was lined with pinkish and pearly shells that shimmered in the sunlight. Spring blooms of crocus, hyacinth, and tulips added splashes of color to her porch.

It was some consolation that Azad didn't look all that comfortable either. He stuffed his hands into his jeans pockets and shifted his feet. "I heard what happened at the restaurant last night."

Lucy didn't bother to ask how he had heard. News traveled as fast as electricity in the town.

"It makes for an interesting first week back home."

"Do the police have any information?" Azad asked.

"You mean about what could have caused a customer to die out back?" she asked.

"Heather looked fine when I saw her in the restaurant that day."

Lucy looked at him in surprise. She wondered what else he'd noticed. Had he spoken to Heather? Did he know her well? If so, when and where did the two meet? Here was her chance to investigate and start asking questions. "Did you know Heather Banks?"

He stopped short and shot her a strange look. "Not personally, but I'd met her before. I was working at Kebab Kitchen when her old man came in to inspect the place years ago. She sometimes tagged along."

It made sense that Azad would have seen the health inspector and his daughter after working in the business for years. "Did you talk to her the other day?"

"No. I went into the kitchen and chatted with Big Al. You saw us."

Lucy's tension eased a bit. She had seen the two men talking when she went to fetch Heather's iced tea. "Well, I feel horrible about what happened. I just wish she hadn't died after eating at Kebab Kitchen. We won't know anything until the autopsy and toxicology results are complete. It could take weeks." Lucy withheld the most damaging news—that the police thought Heather was poisoned.

"That long?"

Another thought crossed her mind. "I know you want to buy the restaurant, but have you ever helped my parents in the kitchen since you graduated from culinary school?"

"Sure. I go back sometimes. Your dad gave me my first job, remember? I even helped your mom plan the menu for the hummus bar. We came up with a few of the new varieties."

Truly? Did he know Heather had ordered from the hummus bar that day? Funny how her mother had never mentioned Azad's help when she'd raved about her hummus.

"What varieties did you help my mom come up with?"

"The bruschetta, black bean, roasted pepper, and sweet apricot. Why?" he asked.

"No reason," she said offhandedly

He watched her intently. "I'd still like to have that talk, Lucy. You know . . . about us?"

She cocked her head to the side and studied

him. He'd been a large part of her college years and she used to know him as well as any family member. His mannerisms and quirks had been as familiar as her own.

"I should go. Katie's waiting," she said.

"Not yet." He reached out to grasp her hand.

Her skin prickled with awareness, and her heart fluttered in her chest. He stood close enough for her to feel the heat from his body. The simple touch relit some tangible bond between them, and she found herself strangely flattered by his interest. For a brief moment, she felt like a breathless girl of eighteen again.

"Don't run away. Lola's Coffee Shop still has the best coffee at the Jersey shore. How about I buy you a cup? We can just talk business if you want. You can grill me about why I want to buy your parents' place."

Her parents would be relieved he was still interested. She wouldn't want to jeopardize that, would she? "Business? That's it?"

He gave her a smile that sent her pulses racing. "Great. How about Saturday morning at ten? I'll pick you up here."

Despite her sworn vow not to get involved with him, she found herself nodding her head. "All right. Saturday at ten." He squeezed her hand, just enough pressure to send a small tingle down her spine.

Business. It's fine if you keep it to business, her inner voice warned.

The front door opened, and Katie stepped onto the porch.

Lucy pulled her hand out of his grasp. Thank goodness for the interruption. Azad looked good. Too good. After he touched her, she realized she may not be as strong as she'd thought.

Lucy looked at Katie's face and froze. Her complexion was ghostly pale as she held a phone to her ear. Her left hand covered the receiver.

"What is it?" Lucy asked.

Katie stepped down from the porch. "It's Detective Clemmons. The autopsy was completed, and he wants you at the station for questioning."

CHAPTER 6

"Thank you for coming, Lucy." Detective Calvin Clemmons smiled from behind the desk in his office and extended his hand, which she briefly shook.

He motioned to the chair in front of his desk. He was dressed as he had been last night—navy suit, white shirt, and striped tie. His manner was slightly more polite today, but his arrogant sallow features and cold brown eyes were still unfriendly. He removed his reading glasses, leaving a ridge at the bridge of his nose where his glasses had trenched, and Lucy couldn't help but think he looked like a constipated accountant during tax season. Katie's warning that he was under pressure to solve the crime before Memorial Day heightened her uneasiness.

Lucy sat down in a faux leather chair. His office was spacious—twice as big as her parents' cramped space in the corner of the restaurant storeroom. One end of the detective's desk held a pile of papers beneath a polished stone paperweight. A computer sat in the center, and a battered metal filing cabinet stood close by. A picture of Clemmons on a boat holding a large tuna hung behind him on the wall. Various stuffed fish were mounted around the room. A bluefish. A salmon. An openmouthed trout. She wondered which he spent more money on—fishing or taxidermy?

Clemmons opened a drawer, pulled out a manila file folder, and placed it on the desk. The tab read HEATHER BANKS typed in bold font. "I want to ask you a few more questions about last night."

Lucy dragged her gaze from the folder. "I told you everything I know."

He nudged the folder with a forefinger. "This is the medical examiner's autopsy report. He completed it this morning."

Eagerness buzzed through Lucy's veins. "What does it say?"

He drummed his fingers on the desk. "I'm not at liberty to discuss the information."

Her voice was hoarse with frustration. "Then why display the folder in front of me like dangling fruit?"

His smile didn't reach his eyes. "You're an attorney, correct?"

"I'm a patent attorney. What does that have to do with anything?"

"Still. You must know the way this works."

Why on earth did everyone assume she was an

expert in solving crime or criminal procedure? "I've only handled patent applications . . . you know"—her hands fluttered before her—"for inventions."

"I see," he said in a tone that suggested he didn't think there was a difference between the two.

"There must be *something* you can tell me," she said, clenching her fingers in her lap.

"We don't have a complete picture yet. The toxicology results won't be available for several weeks."

Lucy knew all this after talking to Bill, but Calvin Clemmons made her uneasy. "It's just all so upsetting."

"Of course. A woman is dead."

She could feel his sharp eyes boring into her. "Why am I here, Detective?"

Springs squeaked as he leaned back in his chair. "I need clarification. Walk me through the restaurant's process from start to finish when a customer walks in."

At least this was comfortable ground. "A customer is seated and orders from the menu. As a waitress, I write their order on a check pad, tear off the check, and clip it onto the cook's wheel. I would then get the customer's drinks, and when the food is ready, the cook calls out my number."

"Your number?"

"I'm number six. It's pretty basic. Each waitress is assigned a number. She writes that number on every check. When an order of food is ready, the line cook calls out the specific number on the check so that the waitress knows her order is ready and to fetch it for delivery. A waitress always delivers the food, unless customers order from the hummus bar. Then customers get a clean plate by the hummus bar and help themselves."

"Are the orders and checks generated by a computer?" Clemmons asked.

Lucy made a face. "My parents are old school. It's all done on paper. Emma has been nagging them for years to have a computer system. But they're comfortable with the way things are."

"What about a carbon copy?"

"No."

"Who prepares the food?'

"Butch is our line cook. He puts everything together. Mom is the head chef. The classic Armenian, Lebanese, and Greek food is all prepared by her."

The detective drummed his fingers. "So your mom prepares the hummus?"

"Yes."

"Who has access to the kitchen?"

"All the members of the staff. It's unrestricted." At his frown, Lucy rushed to add, "It's not FBI Headquarters. Wait staff has to go into the kitchen to make coffee, tea, get supplies, and take dirty dishes to the dishwasher." Lucy wondered what information the detective was after. Why all the questions?

Clemmons reached for the folder and flipped it open. Lucy was surprised when he removed a paper.

Hadn't he just told her that he wasn't at liberty to reveal anything?

"The medical examiner ruled out salmonella, botulism, or anything that would result in food poisoning or a severe allergic reaction resulting in death," he said.

Her hopes blossomed. "That's good, right?"

"Yes and no. Heather Banks was a young, healthy woman in her thirties. The medical examiner is ruling it a suspicious death until the toxicology results are final. He believes Ms. Banks was poisoned."

"Poisoned? On what basis is he making that call?" Even though Bill had warned her, it was still distressing to hear that the medical examiner had completed his autopsy and included it in his report. She tried to swallow the lump in her throat.

"The ME's report states he detected a bitter-almond odor during the autopsy. The victim's skin color was a deep pink, almost cherry red in color. And she'd vomited before she died."

"What does that mean?"

Clemmons's flat unspeaking eyes prolonged the moment. "Have you ever heard of cyanide poisoning?"

Now Lucy's shock was real. "Cyanide! You think she was poisoned with cyanide?"

"The telltale signs are there. Cyanide poisoning suffocates its victims. Her abnormal color was due to oxygen staying in her blood and not getting to her cells. It explains the strange odor, skin color, and vomiting, as well."

Lucy listened with mounting dismay. "That's ridiculous. There's no cyanide in the restaurant."

"You certain about that?"

What possible use could her parents have for cyanide? None. Nada. The thought was absurd and, under any other circumstances, she would laugh. "Heather must have eaten it before she came to Kebab Kitchen."

Clemmons drew his lips in a tight smile. "The thing about cyanide is that it works fast. The medical examiner suspects Ms. Banks ingested the deadly dose within a short window of time."

"How short?"

"Very short. We'll know for certain when we get the tox results."

Lucy recalled that Heather had seemed restless and had been sweating and breathing heavily. She had forgotten to tell Clemmons that detail when he interrogated her at the crime scene, but something held her back from mentioning it. Goosebumps rose on her arms, and she felt sick to her stomach. "Your team collected everything she ate from the restaurant, even the trash."

"That's right. Everything we took will be tested."

"You won't find anything. There's no cyanide at Kebab Kitchen."

"We interviewed your line cook, Butch. Other than seeing Ms. Banks around town, he has no connection to the victim. He also mentioned that Ali Basher had arrived in the kitchen with a delivery the day Heather died. I've since interviewed Mr.

Basher. He claims he never knew Ms. Banks, that he remained in the kitchen the entire time he was there, and he never saw her in the dining room."

Lucy wasn't surprised. Butch and Big Al were longtime family friends and trusted by her parents. She couldn't fathom why either had a reason to harm Heather. "That should confirm it then. No one at the restaurant would harm Heather."

Clemmons ignored her and put the autopsy report back in the folder. "What was your relationship with her?"

"I already told you. We didn't have a relationship. We were in the same high school class."

"Witnesses saw you arguing with Ms. Banks at Mac's Irish Pub."

Lucy stiffened her spine. "I mentioned that as well. We never argued. We just exchanged a few words." She realized how ridiculous that sounded as soon as the words left her mouth.

A smirk crossed Clemmons' face. "Is that what you would call it? Exchanging words?"

Since that wasn't much of a question, Lucy didn't answer. "You can't seriously believe I had anything to do with her death, do you?"

He withdrew another sheet of paper from the folder. Lucy instantly recognized the pink carbon paper as the health inspection report. Heather's signature was ominously scrawled on the bottom of the page. Lucy's insides froze, but to her credit, she was able to keep her expression bland. For the first time since coming home to Ocean Crest, her years of legal training came to her aid. Her civil trial professor's voice rang in her head. S*how little emotion to an adversary, no matter how bad the facts.*

Detective Clemmons was quickly becoming an adversary. If that hadn't been clear before, it was now.

She was a prime suspect.

"Do you recognize this?" he asked.

"Let me see," she said, reaching out for the paper. She feigned reading the report for several seconds before looking up to meet his gaze straight on. "It's the restaurant's most recent health inspection report."

His beady eyes narrowed. "Don't you mean its most recent *failed* health inspection report?"

"It wasn't a failed inspection, but violations that require reinspection. They're all minor infractions—"

"Issued by Heather Banks," he pointed out.

"The violations are inconsequential," she argued.

"I wouldn't call any health violation inconsequential. The restaurant could be shut down if the problems aren't remedied."

"What I meant to say is that it's no big deal. A quick call to a handyman and we're good to go." She knew it wasn't that simple. The additional sink Heather wanted in the kitchen would cause plumbing and structural problems and could cost a significant amount. The numerous other items were enough to give her and her parents headaches, as well.

"You were there the day Ms. Banks inspected the restaurant, correct?"

"Yes."

"That must have upset you and your parents."

She shifted forward in her chair. "Now wait a minute, Detective. Are you suggesting that I had a reason to harm Heather because of this?" She jabbed a finger at the inspection report.

"I'm not suggesting anything. I'm just interviewing the last person to see the victim alive."

The interview was not progressing well. Her first day back, witnesses had seen her arguing with Heather. Lucy was also the person to deal with Heather when she arrived to inspect the restaurant. And Lucy was unlucky enough to serve Heather her last meal.

Lucy didn't have to be a genius to know she was in big trouble. "You're calling Heather a victim now? Do I need a lawyer?"

"That's up to you."

She took a deep breath. "Let me assure you that I didn't slip anything into Heather's food or harm her in any way." She pushed back her chair and stood. "Now if you're finished questioning me, I'd like to be on my way."

"Of course." Calvin Clemmons stood, the smooth smile back in place.

She shook his hand and hurried to the door.

"One more thing, Lucy."

Her hand grazed the doorknob as she turned. "Yes."

"How long will you be visiting us in Ocean Crest?"

"A month or so until I can go back to work."

"Really? Your Philadelphia law firm confirmed that you're no longer employed there."

Oh, no. She winced. Clemmons had done more investigating than she'd thought. "I never said I planned to return to my old firm, but that I'm here temporarily until I can find legal employment."

He nodded curtly. "Fine. But don't leave town anytime soon."

He'd done his research, all right. The problem was he was focused on the wrong suspect.

Me! He thinks I poisoned Heather.

Lucy recalled her dad's order to find the killer. She thought of Katie's offer to help. She'd already taken notes, thought of suspects, and even questioned Azad. But things had gotten even worse.

Not only was the future of the restaurant at stake, but her family's livelihood, her parents' pride—and most frightening of all—her own freedom.

By the time Lucy left the police station it was after five o'clock. She headed straight for Katie's house. She opened the door and was blasted with loud, pounding music. Katie was in the family room, absorbed in imitating the movements of a fit male trainer on the TV, furiously punching, jabbing, and kicking the air.

"Katie," Lucy called out.

Katie spun around and clutched her chest. "Jeez! You scared me to death."

"Sorry, but you can't hear anything over that." Lucy pointed to the TV.

Katie reached for the remote and turned off the kickboxing DVD. One glance at Lucy's face and she stilled. "Whatever happened with Calvin Clemmons, it can't be good."

As Lucy paused to catch her breath, her fears were stronger than ever. "The autopsy is complete. The medical examiner thinks Heather died from cyanide poisoning."

Katie blew a strand of blond hair that had escaped her ponytail. "Cyanide? Like in the old spy movies when the villain is caught and he commits suicide by biting into a cyanide capsule that was hidden in his mouth?"

Katie really did watch too many police and espionage movies. "I guess."

"What else did Clemmons say?"

Lucy's stomach churned with anxiety and frustration. "He thinks I poisoned Heather."

Katie's jaw dropped. "What? Why?"

"Witnesses saw us arguing at Mac's Pub. Clemmons found the health inspection report listing numerous problems and knows I was with Heather when she inspected the restaurant. Plus, he knows I served Heather her last meal. Why wouldn't he think it was me?"

"How does it he think the cyanide was delivered?" Katie asked.

"He said it works fast, but it also depends on the dose. We won't know how much was in Heather's blood until the toxicology results return. But the poison had to have been delivered within a short amount of time—either soon before she arrived at the restaurant or during her meal. Clemmons must think I poisoned Heather's hummus."

Katie placed her hands on her hips. "Clemmons is thick-headed and stubborn about his theories. He's also under pressure from the mayor and every business owner in town to figure out what happened before Memorial Day. *And* he dislikes your family."

Lucy felt a moment of panic as the truth of Katie's words rang true. How much effort would Calvin Clemmons put into seeking the real killer, now that she was his prime suspect?

"I have an idea." Lucy went to Katie's laptop on the coffee table and typed in cyanide poisoning in the search engine. A long list of sites came up on the screen.

"Good idea," Katie said as she hunched over Lucy's shoulder to see the screen.

"Here's a site with info," Lucy said. "It says cyanide poisoning is rapid-acting and potentially deadly. It can be a colorless gas, a crystal, or a white powder. It mentions a bitter almond smell, but not everyone can detect the odor." Lucy glanced at Katie over her shoulder. "Clemmons said the coroner smelled bitter almonds."

"How can it be ingested?" Katie asked.

"It's strictly regulated by the government for manufacturing purposes. But it can also occur naturally in some foods and certain plants such as lima beans and almonds. Also apple seeds and cherry and peach pits." Lucy drummed her fingers on the coffee table. "Clemmons thinks Heather ingested it quickly. If it was in her food or drink, it would probably be delivered as a powder. The site also says how fast it works to kill depends on the amount of cyanide a person is exposed to."

Katie propped a hip against the sofa and folded her arms across her chest. "What else can you remember from when Heather came into Kebab Kitchen?"

Lucy let out a breath as she thought back. "Heather was uneasy and restless when her cell rang. She was also sweaty and breathing rapidly. I know she vomited before she lost consciousness."

Katie confirmed what Lucy was afraid to hear. "They're all listed as symptoms of cyanide poisoning."

"Heather's boyfriend was closest to her and could have slipped her something in her drink. Do you know where Paul Evans lives?"

Katie shook her head, then reached for the laptop and started typing. "It's not a problem. I can easily find out. Real estate taxes are public record in the county." She pulled up the county website and typed in Paul Evans' name. "Nothing's showing up." She turned to look up at Lucy. "Wait a minute. Paul said he only came back to Ocean Crest six months ago. He probably doesn't own a home, but is renting a place."

Lucy tapped her foot. "That makes sense. His name wouldn't appear in the real estate tax records. I can ask Max. He handles almost all the rentals in Ocean Crest."

"Good idea," Katie said. "Meanwhile I think I know where we can find him."

"Where?"

"I stop at Lola's Coffee Shop on my way to work every day. I always see Paul in a corner table writing on his laptop."

"You think he'll be working so soon after Heather's demise?" Lucy asked.

"It's worth a try."

"I'll head there early tomorrow morning," Lucy said.

Katie shook a finger. "Not without me you won't. Lucky for you, I don't work Fridays."

"Pushy, aren't you?" At Katie's expectant look, Lucy grinned. "The truth is I'm glad to have a Watson."

"Just like old times." Katie said brightly. "I'll drive."

CHAPTER 7

Bright and early Friday morning, Lucy's eyes were wide as saucers as Katie's jeep sped down Ocean Avenue. "Slow down! We have to be alive to question Paul Evans, remember?" She clutched the handle above the passenger side door as the jeep screeched to a stop at the town's first of three stoplights. She'd forgotten about Katie's aggressive driving.

Katie shot Lucy a sidelong glance before the light turned green and she stepped on the pedal with a lead foot. "Relax. I always drive like this."

Lucy's right hand tightened on the door handle as she pulled her seat belt an inch tighter with her left. "It must help that your husband is a cop. No one in town would give you a ticket for reckless driving, would they?"

"Hey! I don't drive reckless," Katie protested. "And I wouldn't use Bill to get out of a ticket."

Lucy never had a chance to argue. The jeep whizzed into the coffee shop's parking lot in what she was certain was record time. The vehicle came to a screeching halt, and Katie put it in PARK.

"See?" Katie said. "Safe and sound."

Lucy exhaled. "How about I drive next time?"

Katie gave her a sidelong glance. "Suit yourself."

When they entered the coffee shop, Lola Stewart, the owner, was busy behind the counter. She was a tall, thin woman with pronounced cheekbones, a sharp chin, and steel-gray hair she always wore pulled tightly back into a bun. She was working an espresso machine which hissed and spat clouds of steam as it turned milk into frothy foam. Sunlight from the shop's front window caught her glasses, sending flares of light across her face, and her friendly smile softened her otherwise harsh features.

A customer with a caffeine-deprived look on his face waited by the counter for Lola to complete his order. Other customers sat at colorful bistro tables in wire-backed chairs drinking coffee, lattés, and cappuccinos as they read the newspaper, checked e-mail on their smartphones, or worked on their laptops. Framed photographs of the beach during the busy summer season with sunbathers, colorful umbrellas, and sandcastles decorated the walls. The aroma of freshly ground coffee beans made Lucy's mouth water.

"Sure smells good in here," Katie called out.

Lola looked up. "Hey, there, Katie." Her gaze slid to Lucy. "Hi, Lucy. I heard you're back for good."

Why on earth did everyone in town think she'd

permanently returned? And more important, did the small town's rumor mill *have* to include her? Lucy hoped Lola wouldn't mention what had happened at Kebab Kitchen.

"I heard what happened at your parents' restaurant," Lola said. "Are they all right?"

So much for hoping. "My parents are upset, but fine." Lucy said. "Thanks for asking."

"We're looking for Paul Evans. Have you seen him this morning?" Katie asked.

Lola handed a mug to the eagerly waiting customer before turning back to Katie and Lucy. "Funny you should ask. I was wondering where he was this morning. Paul always sits over there"—she pointed to a cozy table in the corner—"but he's not here today."

"Do you know where he could be?" Lucy asked.

"Check Cutie's Cupcakes. That writer has a serious sweet tooth," Lola said.

Five minutes later, and with two large coffees in the jeep's cup holders, Lucy and Katie continued farther down Ocean Crest toward Cutie's Cupcakes. The air from the open window was warm and pleasant and hinted that summer was approaching. Soon dozens of tourists would be packing the sidewalks carrying beach chairs and sand toys, and heading for Ocean Crest's beautiful beach. Lucy pushed the thought aside.

Katie turned into a small shopping strip, parked the jeep, and they hurried to open the door of Cutie's Cupcakes. Inside, a refrigerated glass case displayed a delectable assortment of calorie-packed desserts—homemade apple, blueberry, coconut custard, and lemon meringue pies, huge chocolate chip cookies the size of Frisbees, red velvet cupcakes, and the baker's house specialty of salted caramel cupcakes. Lucy gazed at the lemon meringue longingly and imagined the extra pounds on her hips.

Susan Cutie, a pretty woman with a shoulder-length bob and a quick smile, looked up from a birthday cake she'd been decorating with pink and blue balloons which read *Happy First Birthday Emily!* "Hey you two! I've been wondering how long it would take before you visited. Lemon meringue, right?"

Lucy religiously dropped into the bakery at every holiday visit, no matter how brief, to buy a lemon meringue pie to take to her family gathering. "Hi, Susan. I'll take a slice of pie to go, but that's not why we're here today."

"Oh?" Susan set down a pastry bag and a good tablespoon of icing oozed out onto the counter.

Lucy licked her lips. Butter cream was another weakness. "We're looking for Paul Evans."

"That writer has a thing for my red velvet cupcakes. Comes in a couple times a week, but he still stays as thin as a rail. Who knew writing could burn so—"

"Was he here today?" Katie said hastily.

"What? Oh, sorry. No, not today. Try the barber shop next door," Susan said.

Lucy doubted Paul would get a haircut or shave so soon after his girlfriend's demise. Maybe coffee and a pastry—a guy had to eat after all—but grooming?

"He hangs out with Ben Hawkins, owner of the barbershop," Susan continued. "An unlikely friendship, a barber and a famous writer, but it's true." It made sense that Paul would seek the support of a friend. It's what Lucy would do. She glanced at Katie standing beside her. Correction. It's what Lucy had done the same day she'd come back to Ocean Crest.

Susan removed a lemon meringue pie from a refrigerated case, cut a piece and wrapped it in a Styrofoam container and handed it to her. Lucy knew from experience that Susan's lemon filling was rich and tart with fresh lemon juice and lemon zest, the meringue light and sweet, and the crust just perfect, and Lucy couldn't wait to eat it. After she paid, Susan picked up her pastry bag and went back to the birthday cake.

Leaving the bakery, Lucy and Katie headed for the spiraling red and white barber pole next door. Ben Hawkins was in his early forties, with a lightly pockmarked face, bushy eyebrows, and thinning brown hair. A draped customer reclined in a chair while Ben smoothed shaving cream over his cheeks and chin with a large bristled shaving brush.

"Hi, Ben," Katie said.

Ben looked up. "Hi, Katie. Is Bill coming in today for a cut?"

Katie shook her head. "Not today. We were wondering if Paul Evans was here."

"I haven't seen him today. I'd think he's broken up about his girlfriend. A real tragedy." Ben picked up a sharp-looking razor and began to shave his customer.

"Do you know where he could be?" Lucy asked. She didn't know Ben Hawkins. It wasn't as if she or Emma had ever needed the services of a barber. Ben's movements were sure as he skimmed over his customer's prominent Adam's apple. Lucy wondered how he didn't nick the man.

"Why the interest in Paul?" Ben asked.

Katie didn't miss a beat. "We both went to high school with Heather Banks. We want to check on Paul and offer our condolences."

Lucy looked at Katie. When had she become such a good liar? She had a feeling she'd need to follow Katie's example if they were going to get to the bottom of this mess.

Ben rinsed the razor in a bowl of water. "Why didn't you say so? Did you check Lola's Coffee Shop?"

"We did," Lucy said.

"How about Cutie's Cupcakes?"

They both nodded.

"Do you know where he's staying?" Lucy held her breath.

"Sure do," Ben said. "Paul's renting a nice house

at the edge of town on Sandstone Street. It's a stone's throw from Cape May."

Katie had been right. Paul was renting.

Ben picked up the razor, shook it off, then resumed shaving his customer. "Paul likes to work at Lola's in the morning then takes a break and visits here, but he hasn't stopped by today so I assume he's at home."

"Thanks, Ben," Katie said. "I'll tell Bill to visit soon. He's in need of a close shave."

"I didn't know they built such grand houses in Ocean Crest," Lucy said.

"They've been building on the undeveloped land in town. They think it will bring in more wealthy tourists, but I think this one is grossly oversized and out of place," Katie said.

They'd parked down the street from Paul Evans' rental home and made their way up the winding driveway of the McMansion on foot. The sprawling white stone façade, towering pillars flanking the front door, numerous gabled roofs, and replicas of seminude Roman statues appeared gaudy and excessive to Lucy—as if too many details were borrowed from different historical periods and mashed together in a builder's blender. But no matter how garish the design, it was the magnificent ocean view that proclaimed the house was worth a small fortune.

They reached the top of the driveway where a

bubbling fountain with nude mermaids gurgled. The front yard boasted well-tended hedgerows, flowering shrubs, rosebushes, and an impressive lawn.

Lucy knew it was difficult to grow grass that close to the beach, and it cost money to maintain. "The rent must be a small fortune. His suspense novels must be paying good royalties," she said as they climbed the steps to the front porch.

"No kidding. I suspect that was a huge part of his appeal for Heather. She always was high maintenance," Katie said as she reached for the brass doorknocker.

Lucy was expecting a maid or a butler, but Paul Evans opened the door himself. He looked down at them, a blank expression on his face. Once again, she was taken aback by his nondescript looks. With his slender build and brown hair and brown eyes, people must walk past him all the time without recognizing him as the famous writer. Dressed in khakis with a white collared shirt, he looked similar to when she'd seen him at Mac's Pub. The only difference was the dark circles beneath his eyes. Had he been recently crying?

"May I help you?" Paul asked.

Lucy stepped forward. "I'm Lucy Berberian and this is my friend Katie Watson. Do you remember meeting us at Mac's Pub the other day?"

Paul's brows drew together for a moment, then

he nodded. "Of course, I remember you. You both went to high school with Heather."

Katie cleared her throat. "We may not always have gotten along with Heather, but we're truly sorry for your loss."

Paul rubbed swollen, red eyes. Expecting him to burst into tears, Lucy held her breath.

"Would you like to come inside?" he asked.

"Yes, thank you," Lucy said.

They followed Paul past a marble foyer and down a carpeted hall. He halted just outside a room and opened the door. Sunlight streamed through large windows to illuminate what had to be his office. A large oak desk was situated beneath the window. Stacks of paper were all over the desk, a laptop was in the corner, and a laser printer off to the side on an end table. A large white board with sticky notes labeled with chapter numbers hung on the wall. It was clearly a writer's cave, no doubt where Paul produced his *New York Times* bestselling novels.

Lucy still found it hard to believe this mild-mannered man wrote edge-of-your-seat, nail-biting thrillers. She glanced at the computer screen where a document was open. Had he been working on his next novel when they interrupted?

"Please sit," Paul said, motioning to the two empty chairs before his desk. "Can I offer you something to drink?"

"No. Please don't go to any trouble," Lucy said as

they occupied the chairs "We know it's a difficult time, but we were hoping to ask you a few questions."

He frowned as he pulled up a leather armchair and sat across from them. "I thought you were here to pay your respects."

"Yes, well. The truth is we're looking into Heather's death." Lucy said.

Paul looked taken aback. "You two? The police were already here, and I told them everything I know. Why are you getting involved?"

Lucy supposed it was good news to learn the police had already questioned Paul Evans. At least Clemmons had interrogated the boyfriend. But, on the other hand, she suspected the detective was more interested in her as a suspect than Paul since she'd served Heather her last meal and cyanide worked quickly.

Lucy took a breath. "Mr. Evans, are you aware that Heather died in Kebab Kitchen's parking lot? My parent's restaurant?"

"Yes, the police told me."

Heaven only knew what he thought. Did he also believe the food Heather ate killed her? Lucy cleared her throat. "I was waitressing the night Heather came into the restaurant. She received a call on her cell and was arguing with someone pretty fiercely. Do you know who she was talking to?"

Paul's gaze narrowed. "What are you saying? You think she was fighting with me?" It was clear the question had made him defensive.

"We're not accusing you. We're just asking

questions. The police took Heather's cell phone and will soon have access to her phone records," Katie said.

"It wasn't me. I have nothing to hide." A tense silence enveloped the room as Paul leaned forward in his chair. "Why are you two really here? Do you think I had something to do with her death? Or are you desperate to point a finger away from your parents' restaurant?"

Lucy had expected this argument and was prepared. "I know it wasn't from the restaurant's food, and I'm confident everything will be revealed in the toxicology results. Still, we thought it wouldn't hurt to ask a few questions of our own."

When Lucy met his eyes, pain flickered there. "I know how this works. I'm a suspense writer. Everyone suspects the boyfriend. Well, I didn't do it. I loved Heather. We weren't fighting that night, or any other night either." He stood and went to his desk, opened the drawer, and pulled out a black box. Flipping open the lid, he revealed a large square-cut diamond. Sunlight from the window reflected off the exquisite diamond in a kaleidoscope on the wall. "I was going to propose to her."

Lucy's eyes were riveted on the impressive ring. The diamond was at least two carats. She looked up at Paul. "I'm truly sorry."

His face crumpled as he nodded. He closed the lid and dropped the box back inside the drawer. "I saw her before she finished her rounds that day. I stopped by on my way to Lola's for a cup of coffee, then came home to write. I wish I had told her I loved her one more time."

If he'd returned home to work after visiting Heather, he didn't have an alibi for the time she'd been at the restaurant. Still, his grief seemed genuine.

"Do you have any idea who may have wanted to harm her? Did she have any enemies?" Lucy asked.

Paul met Lucy's gaze, his eyes hardening like bits of stone. "I'll tell you the same thing I told the police. There is one man."

"Who?" Katie asked.

"Guido Morelli, the owner of the Hot Cheese Pizzeria. Heather had repeatedly cited his restaurant for health violations. The day she died, she'd planned on delivering inspection reports to some restaurants and Guido's place was on her list. Guido hated her. I remember one night we took an evening stroll on the boardwalk and ran into him. That hot-tempered Italian flung a string of curses at Heather. He claimed she was corrupt and the town would be better off without her. If that's not motive, I don't know what is."

An hour later, Katie and Lucy were at Kebab Kitchen in time for Lucy's shift.

"Well, that was fruitful," Katie said as she chose a maple booth in the corner.

"We need to talk about what we learned, but I

won't have time until my shift slows down. Can you stay for lunch?"

"You bet. I'm starved."

Lucy handed Katie a menu just as Sally came around the corner, crying. "Where's my tabbouleh salads?"

Emma hurried out of the kitchen, carrying a tray that held plates of tabbouleh salad. "Here they are. Mom made a trip to the famers market yesterday for fresh mint and parsley."

Sally took the tray from Emma. "Good. I have tables waiting."

Lucy jumped into action and helped Sally deliver the food. The refreshing salad of chopped mint, parsley, tomatoes, and cracked wheat in a savory lemon and olive oil dressing was a customer favorite.

The rest of the lunch menu featured traditional Mediterranean cuisine of *madzoon* soup, a yogurt based soup; white snapper, a firm and flavorful Mediterranean fish; lamb chops marinated in olive oil, lemon, and fresh herbs; and delectable almond cookies for dessert.

Lucy took orders, delivered food, and cleared tables. It wasn't a busy lunch service, and soon there was a lull. She was able to join Katie and slipped into the maple booth opposite her. Katie was already enjoying a *mezza* appetizer platter of tabbouleh salad, falafel, and stuffed grape leaves for lunch.

"This is delicious," Katie said as she bit into a stuffed grape leaf.

"Thanks. I'll be sure to tell my mom you like it. She'll probably send you home with a dozen."

Katie's fork hovered in midair. "Really? I'll have to hide them from Bill."

Lucy played with her apron strings. "Do you believe Paul's story?"

Katie chewed slowly. "He seemed quite sincere. He had that huge diamond ready to go."

"We still don't know who Heather was arguing with on her cell that day. Maybe they're one of those couples who thrive on arguing and then making up."

Katie chuckled. "You mean like your sister, Emma, and her husband, Max?"

Lucy rolled her eyes. "They're a perfect example. But even if Heather was fighting with Paul, it doesn't necessarily make him a murderer."

Katie set down her fork. "I think we should talk to Guido Morelli. But first, let me confirm Paul's story by checking the township records when I go back to work on Monday to find out if Heather did cite the Hot Cheese Pizzeria for violations in the past as well as the day she died."

"Good idea. We should also find out what other establishments Heather inspected that day. Paul said she was supposed to go to others. Any one of them had opportunity to slip her poison," Lucy added.

"I'll see you back at the house." Katie took one

last mouthful of food, grabbed her purse, and headed toward the door.

With nothing much to do, Lucy set to rolling silverware in cloth napkins when the kitchen doors swung open and her parents entered the dining room. Angela stopped short, a dismayed expression on her face as her gaze swept the empty tables and booths. "Where are all our regular customers?"

"I don't know, Mom. We only had a light lunch service." Lucy didn't feel the need to point out that within two days of Heather's untimely demise, most of the town residents had already heard the news, and as a result were afraid to eat there.

The phone rang and Angela hurried to answer it at the hostess stand. She pulled the black reservation book from the shelf and started to scribble in it. After hanging up, she came over, a frown marring her brow. "Another cancellation. The third one for this evening. What are we going to do?"

"We'll think of something," Raffi said.

Angela stiffened and looked out the window. "*Asvads!* Dear Lord! A news truck is outside." Her face was pale as she clutched the reservation book tight to her chest.

Lucy raised the blinds to get a better look out the window. A white van with a sign in bold, black letters, proclaiming OCEAN CREST TOWN NEWS, was parked in the restaurant's lot. She took one look at her parents' horrified faces and made a quick decision. "Let me handle them."

Angela pointed a trembling finger toward the

van. "You don't understand. That's Stan Slade. He used to work at a fancy New York City paper, but came here a couple years ago. He loves town gossip and is always looking for a good story. There hasn't been a murder in Ocean Crest in the forty years we've lived here. If he prints anything bad about the restaurant, we'll be ruined!"

Lucy resisted the urge to cover her ears at her mother's screeching. "Let me handle Mr. Slade, Mom." She didn't want to put her parents through even more stress. If what they said was true and the reporter was hungry for a story, it was better for her to deal with him. Her parents often slipped back into an incomprehensible and confusing mixture of Armenian, Greek, Arabic, and English when they became nervous. The reporter could easily misinterpret anything they said.

Lucy didn't have much experience with reporters, but she did have years of dealing with adversarial attorneys. How different could it be?

CHAPTER 8

Lucy met the reporter outside the front door of the restaurant. "May I help you?"

"Stan Slade of the *Town News*," the reporter said in a brusque, nasally voice. A middle-aged man with black-rimmed glasses, he had a stocky, muscular build and a head that appeared to rest directly on his broad shoulders.

"I take it you're not here to eat?" Lucy asked.

"Not today. I want an interview, Lucy Berberian." Slade pulled out a notepad and pen from his jacket pocket.

Lucy blinked. "You know my name?"

"It's my job to know whom I plan to feature. And this isn't a large town." He shot her a smug look. "Not until tourist season, that is. A murder in Ocean Crest is big news."

Lucy bristled at his tone. "It wasn't a murder. The police haven't officially announced a cause of death."

Slade snorted and clicked his pen. "Not yet, they

haven't. But I have a source that tells me it's just a matter of time before the police go on record and call it a suspicious death. And we all know Heather Banks croaked immediately after she ate at Kebab Kitchen."

So much for handling adversarial attorneys. Lucy didn't have luck with Detective Clemmons, and she had a bad feeling her success wasn't going to be much better with Stan Slade. Still, it was better than if her parents were subjected to his brash manner.

"The truth will be proven once the toxicology results are in." Lucy didn't add that it could take weeks for the tox results, or that the tourist season would be underway by then.

"You served Ms. Banks the night she died, right? I want an exclusive interview with you," Slade said.

No way was she sitting down and subjecting herself to questioning by the slick reporter. He'd twist her words and print anything to sell papers. "There's nothing I can tell you that you won't learn from an official police statement."

"Is that a no?" he asked.

"Look. I just ate here and I feel fine," Lucy pointed out.

"Good for you. Is that really what you want me to print?" Stan's lips twisted into a cynical smile.

"No. I would hope you would print the truth."

"The truth is subject to interpretation, Ms. Berberian."

This was turning out bad. Lucy realized how damaging his article could be. HEALTH INSPECTOR

DIES AFTER EATING AT KEBAB KITCHEN. RESTAURANT REFUSES INTERVIEW.

"Tourist season is only three weeks away. What do you have for me?"

Lucy met his beady eyes straight on. "Nothing." She needed to follow up and speak with Guido Morelli. She needed leads and fast from the hungry look on the reporter's face. The restaurant was already suffering. What would happen after Slade's article came out? "But I suggest you wait before printing anything damaging to the restaurant. You wouldn't want a lawsuit for libel against the paper, would you?"

It wasn't a real threat, but it was all Lucy had. The paper could go to print with what they believed to be true from the facts and Lucy couldn't do much to stop it.

Slade's brow furrowed above the rim of his glasses. Clearly he was thinking of the pros and cons of her question. "Fine. Tell you what—I want an exclusive from you in exchange for waiting a few days. But once the police issue an official statement, all bets are off and I go to print."

"Is that blackmail?"

"No. It's the news business."

"That didn't go well, did it?"

Back inside, Lucy turned to see Sally approach. Tall and slim, she set a stack of trays on the waitress station. She'd wiped down the trays and they would later be used to deliver drinks and food.

"Am I that obvious?"

"No, I've been waiting tables a long time and I have a sixth sense about people. Plus, I've heard all kinds of stories about the lead reporter of the *Town News.*"

Lucy grimaced. "I take it they're not all flattering."

"Mostly that he can be aggressive and obnoxious. Do you remember Beatrice Snyder?"

"The head librarian in town?" Lucy recalled taking Niari to the library for story time when she was a toddler. Beatrice had run the program. She was a kind lady who'd never married, loved the local children, and had worked at the library for years.

"Beatrice packed up and moved after Stan Slade printed a story saying she misappropriated funds from the library's overdue fines account. It was never proved to be true, but she quit and left in shame to live with family in Pennsylvania."

"That's awful." Lucy's heart hammered. If Slade could print an article and run a kind spinster and longtime librarian out of town, what could he do to her and her family?

Lucy helped Sally arrange the trays in stacks. "You've been with my parents a long time. How hard are they taking everything?"

Sally had worked there for years and knew her parents well. She was also observant. She hesitated as if contemplating whether to tell the truth or not, then nodded. "Your parents tend to worry. Especially your father."

"I thought my mom would take it harder."

"Nah. She's more vocal, but your dad handles the finances, and he tends to brood in his office." Sally picked up a waitress pad from the counter and tucked it into her apron.

Lucy worried her bottom lip. "I'm concerned about them."

"What about you?"

Lucy blinked. "Me?"

"You're under a lot of pressure. I know they asked you to find out who killed that nasty health inspector. How are you handling everything?"

"I'm managing." Lucy was managing, just not fast enough. Slade's appearance hadn't helped.

Sally propped a hand on her hip and regarded her. "You take care of yourself, Lucy. I'm glad you're back and it's not just because Millie left to have another baby and we're short staffed. If you ever need to talk, I'm always around."

"Thanks," Lucy said.

Sally winked. "I mean it. You may have been away for a while, but you have friends here, and you can always talk to me in confidence."

Lucy swallowed as Sally returned to the kitchen. She hadn't expected Sally to offer reassurance and friendship. She was the only female staff member who wasn't a family member.

Someone she could talk to.

Despite everything that had happened, it sounded like a very nice offer.

"Mokour Lucy!" Niari called as she opened the front door and threw herself into Lucy's open arms. Lucy loved being called "mother's sister." Dressed in an Ocean Crest soccer uniform with the number 99 printed on the front and back, Niari's dark hair was pulled back in a ponytail. A glittery red headband read *Go Strikers!*

"How's soccer?" Lucy asked as she stepped into her niece's home.

"Great! I'm on a travel team now. Our last game was an hour away."

Lucy could just imagine Emma and Max driving all over Southern New Jersey for weekend soccer games. Lucy pulled out her cell phone. "I liked your last selfie and text. But I couldn't understand everything you wrote."

"Let me see," Niari said as she took the phone from Lucy.

A picture of Niari making a silly face with crossed eyes and tongue sticking out was accompanied with illegible text. Niari read out loud, "2gtbt ur here! See u 2mor vbg bfn." She glanced up at Lucy. "It's simple."

"No, it's more complicated than Morse code."

"What's that?"

"Never mind. What's it say?" Lucy asked.

"Too good to be true you're here! See you to-morrow. Very big grin. Bye for now." Niari gifted Lucy with a big smile. "See. It's easy."

"If you say so."

Niari handed the cell phone back to Lucy. "I want Instagram, but Mom says I'm too young."

"Your mom is right. Where is she anyway?"

"She's in the kitchen. Mom and Dad are excited you're babysitting so they can go out." Niari jumped up and down once. "So am I."

"We're going to have a blast. I brought you something." Lucy held up a bag.

Niari pulled a box out of the bag in record speed. "Legos!" Her face lit up like a Christmas tree. "They're my favorite."

"I know. Please take them into the family room. I need to talk to your mom."

Niari raced away, her ponytail bouncing behind her.

Lucy went into the kitchen to find Emma opening a box of macaroni and cheese on the counter. A pot of boiling water steamed on the stove.

"There's no need to cook. It's your Friday date night and I planned on ordering pizza," Lucy said.

"I know. But I want to make sure there's extra food for both of you."

"You sound like Mom," Lucy pointed out.

Emma turned away from the counter and gave her a bug-eyed look. "Just great. Am I getting that bad?"

Lucy grinned. "Don't worry. You haven't reached the point of no return. You're cooking from a box. Mom would have a heart attack before she ever did that."

Emma placed a hand on her chest. "Thank goodness. I don't want to be *too* much like her."

Her sister was dressed in a colorful blouse and black pencil skirt with flats. Lucy had always envied Emma's slim figure and good taste in clothes. It came easy to Emma, but Lucy always felt like she had to work at it. She preferred business suits—very little matching was required.

"How are things with Max?" Lucy asked.

Emma poured the box of pasta into the boiling water and stirred it with a spoon. "He's busy. Tourists are calling for last minute seasonal rentals."

"That's good, right?"

Emma set the spoon down and leaned against the counter. "Yes . . . I suppose. Although I wish he was around more often."

"Well I hope tonight's date night will help with that." Lucy removed a stray Lego from the kitchen chair and sat.

"Sorry," Emma said. "Niari's obsessed with them. She's building an Eiffel Tower from leftover Legos."

"Maybe my niece will be an engineer."

"I'm worried about Dad," Emma said, abruptly changing the topic.

"Heather's death would stress out any business owner," Lucy said.

Emma shook her head. "It's not just that. You haven't been around to notice."

Lucy swallowed the guilty knot that rose in her throat. Did Emma harbor bitterness that Lucy had left Ocean Crest and her sister had stayed behind? Or was Emma just concerned for their father? "Tell me."

"He keeps eating high fat foods despite Mom's constant nagging to eat healthier. He's overdue for a visit to his physician for an annual checkup. And he's put on at least twenty pounds in the past six months. It puts him at risk for things like diabetes."

Lucy knew her father was mulishly stubborn, and he disliked going to the doctor. He had always been a large man, but how could she not have noticed that much of a weight gain? Fresh guilt settled in her gut. "Twenty pounds? Are you sure?"

"At least." Emma turned her attention back to stirring the boiling pasta. "Both Mom and Dad are aging and under a lot of stress lately. Why couldn't that health inspector have died elsewhere?"

That's the million dollar question, Lucy mused. She took a breath. "Emma, what can you tell me about Calvin Clemmons?"

The spoon rattled on the counter. Emma blinked and her expression shuttered. "What do you want to know?"

"Well for starters, how hard did he take your breakup all those years ago in high school?" Was it her imagination or did Emma's face pale slightly?

"Uh . . . well . . . it ended badly."

"You cheated on him, didn't you?"

"It wasn't my fault. It was high school, and I had a preference for . . . well, bad boys."

"You cheated on Calvin with Max?"

Emma's shoulders fell. "No."

Lucy looked at her in surprise. She'd always known her sister had a wandering eye, but she'd believed it was Max who'd tempted her away from Calvin. "Then who?"

"Calvin's best friend, Will Thomas."

"Jeeze, Emma." In Lucy's mind, it wouldn't have been as bad if it had been Max. At least Emma had married him. But for her to cheat on Calvin with his best friend . . . well, that was just downright selfish and mean.

"Max and I dated on and off in high school and college, but it wasn't him. Will Thomas had that bad boy thing I couldn't resist. He used to steal his dad's cigarettes and smoke in the boys' lavatory. He was fun back then, and Calvin was more straight-laced and geeky."

Lucy's earlier concerns were justified. "Calvin called me into the police station for additional questioning. He wasn't very nice."

Emma folded her arms across her chest. "You think he still holds a grudge?"

"I'm worried he does."

"It makes sense. Mom and Dad never liked him and Calvin knew it."

"Great." Clemmons had good reason to dislike Emma and her family.

Emma closed her eyes for a second, then opened them. "There's more. Calvin hit on me at the fall festival. I told him I was a married woman, but he said he didn't think that would stop me. I slapped him."

Lucy sat up straight. "The jerk deserved it."

Emma lowered her eyes to her hands. "Sorry. I never meant to cause trouble."

Lucy sighed. "I know. I just need to find out what we're up against. Go out with Max. Don't worry about anything. Niari and I have a Lego Eiffel Tower to finish."

Emma hugged her.

As Lucy watched Emma and Max pull out of the driveway, she was worried about Clemmons' impartiality. Things just kept getting worse—the additional stress from Heather's death on her aging parents, a pushy former New York City reporter who was salivating over the first murder in Ocean Crest's history, and Detective Clemmons who had good reason to hate her family and want to pin a murder on Lucy and close the restaurant's doors forever.

What was next?

CHAPTER 9

"I'm glad you came," Azad said as he held out a chair for Lucy.

"I can never turn down a cup of Lola's coffee." Lucy sipped the brew she'd ordered at the counter and stared at Azad over the rim of her cup.

He looked especially handsome today dressed in a navy golf shirt that accentuated his dark eyes and skin. A lock of hair brushed his brow and her fingers itched to smooth it back. She bit her lip and looked away.

The coffee shop was busy Saturday mornings, and Lola Stewart was occupied serving a steady stream of customers at the counter. Mouthwatering pastries from Susan Cutie's bakery filled the glass display case. Lucy scanned the glass for a slice of lemon meringue pie and experienced a pang of disappointment when she didn't see any. She'd have to settle for chocolate chip muffins instead and would buy them for Katie and Bill on her way out.

Azad cradled his cup. "How are your parents holding up? I've been meaning to visit, but haven't had a chance."

"They're okay."

"I hate that they're upset."

"They've been in business for thirty years and they're tough."

He chuckled. "You're right about that. Especially your dad. I remember my first day working there as a busboy and dishwasher. He lectured me on the art of washing dishes."

She smiled as she pictured the scene. Her father took every duty seriously.

Azad sobered. His stare was bold as he watched her. "Even after all these years, I know it's awkward between us."

Awkward was an understatement. Every minute she was in his company the feelings she'd fought so hard to bury resurfaced.

"How'd it go with Calvin Clemmons?"

Her nerves tensed. Azad had known she'd been summoned to Clemmons' office the day he'd stopped by Katie's house to ask her to go for a cup of coffee. "It wasn't pleasant."

Azad's lips thinned with displeasure. "Don't let him bully you. He struts around Ocean Crest like it's his town. He forgets we have a mayor. He came around and asked me questions, too."

"He did?"

"Yeah. I told him everything I knew, which isn't much, and he left."

She looked at him curiously. "About that day . . . I know we already talked about you knowing Heather, but there's more I want to ask you."

He nodded. "Shoot."

"You were in the restaurant when Heather came in to eat. Did you see anything unusual?"

"No. You were busy taking her order, and I went into the kitchen to say hello to Butch when I saw Big Al making a delivery. I helped Al unload his truck, then left."

"No one else wandered into the kitchen?"

"Not that I saw. Sorry I can't be much help."

She looked down at her coffee before meeting his gaze straight on. "Do you still want to buy Kebab Kitchen?"

"I do."

"Even though the town health inspector died in the parking lot after eating there?" she asked.

"My intentions haven't changed. I've wanted my own place for a long time. I know the business. I'd like to make a few changes, of course, starting with a computer system that will bring the place into the twentieth century."

Lucy grinned. She couldn't blame him. Emma had battled her technology-deficient parents over the same issue for years.

"How will you pay for it?" It was unlikely the local bank or any bank would give Azad a loan without collateral.

"I talked to your dad. He agreed to give me a mortgage. I'd pay him monthly with interest until the place is paid in full. We'd have to use a real estate specialist like Max to establish fair market value first, then a real estate lawyer to draw up the papers."

Lucy was surprised her father hadn't mentioned anything about this to her. He kept referring to her as a lawyer for everything else—most recently investigating a crime. So why not ask her about giving Azad a mortgage? It was risky. The proceeds of the sale were the only retirement her parents had other than social security.

Lucy leaned back in her chair, mulling over this information. The arrangement made her realize one thing—the fair market value of Kebab Kitchen would plummet if they had no business. And business would surely suffer if everyone thought the health inspector died after eating at the restaurant. Azad could buy the business for a dime on the dollar and would luck out at her parents' expense.

It sounds like great motive, she thought.

"I know what you're thinking," he said.

Lucy felt her face heat. "You do?"

"There was never anyone else after we broke up, Lucy."

Whoa. That wasn't what she'd been thinking about at all. The conversation just took a turn she wasn't sure she wanted to follow.

"I know you thought I ended things between us because I was dating someone else."

She did. He'd led her to believe it after college. "You insinuated it."

"I lied. Freaked out. Your parents were pushing for us to marry right out of college. We were twenty-one. Remember when your dad sat us down at the kitchen table in your house? If he had the authority, he would have married us then."

Lucy squirmed in her seat. It was true. Her father had never been tactful. "Why didn't you just tell me the truth?"

"Would you have understood back then?"

If she were honest with herself she didn't know. She'd been hurt and it was possible she would have pushed him away. "So you just weren't ready?"

"That's right, but now I am." He reached across the table to squeeze her hand.

She was the one panicking now. She pulled her hand from his grasp and set it on her lap. "Azad . . . um . . . I'm flattered, but it's s not a good time for me."

"You're still angry. You have a right to be."

"No. It's not that." *Not entirely.* She had her hands full with Heather's murder, panicked parents, and a nosy reporter. "There's a lot going on right now."

"Do me a favor. Promise you'll think about us, okay?"

She stood and pushed back her chair. "All right. But no other promises."

He rose and grinned. "I'll take it."

Later that night, Lucy locked the back door of the restaurant and headed to her car. She averted her gaze from where Heather had been found dead on the asphalt parking lot. The image was imprinted in her brain. She took a deep breath and focused instead on the chirping of locusts and the distant sound of ocean waves echoing in the alley. A meow sounded and Gadoo came from around the corner to rub against her legs.

"Hello, Gadoo. Out prowling tonight?"

He looked up, his yellow eyes glowing in the twilight.

She checked that the cat had fresh water. Her mother must have fed him extra cat food and it remained uneaten in his bowl by the back door. She reached in her purse and pulled out a bag of cat treats she'd purchased from Holloway's grocery. She tossed a few chicken-flavored treats shaped like little chicken legs to the cat. Gadoo ate them quickly.

His second meow was cut short and rudely drowned out by the roar of a motorcycle. Lucy jumped and nearly dropped her keys. Gadoo took off down the alley like a shot.

The ear-piercing noise was close. Curious, she walked to the edge of the fence separating the restaurant's property from the business next door—Citteroni's Bike Shop. The shop should be closed at this late hour, but the garage door was open and brightly lit. Bicycles, tricycles, and surreys were parked in neat rows inside the space.

A helmeted man dressed in a black leather jacket and jeans was parking a motorcycle. A tall, lean, muscled biker dismounted from the bike. Reaching up, he removed his helmet and hung it on the handlebars.

Her pulse did a double take. He was sinfully handsome, with the kind of dark hair and classic features that could be found on the cover of a men's magazine. His faded jeans were molded to long, muscular legs, and he took off the leather jacket to reveal a tight, black T-shirt. He bent to check something on the motorcycle, and the cotton stretched across broad shoulders.

Sweet Lord.

She must have made a noise because he turned his head and looked directly at her. "Hi, there. You plan on standing behind that fence and watching all night?"

Busted. Caught peeking like a girl looking through a hole in the boy's locker room. Lucy's heart hammered and her cheeks grew hot. She stepped out from where she stood half hidden behind the fence. No sense running back inside the restaurant. She'd been caught.

She crossed the short expanse of sidewalk separating the two businesses and stepped into the garage. "Sorry. I wasn't sneaking. I heard your motorcycle. I work next door."

He grinned a slow sexy smile that made her all too aware of her plain work clothes—an unflattering white collared shirt and simple black slacks. "Ah, the fancy place next door."

The garage light fully illuminated his face. His eyes were a striking ocean blue and he was even better looking up close.

She swallowed. "I suppose you can call it fancy although we aim for just above casual." She eyed his motorcycle. "I thought you just rented bicycles?"

"I have a weakness for fast rides."

Goodness—what a cheesy line!

He extended a hand. "I'm Michael Citteroni."

She blinked in surprise. "You're Anthony Citteroni's son?"

"I'm helping my dad out with the bike shop this summer."

Mr. Citteroni was notorious in Ocean Crest. If rumors were to be believed, he had mob connections several beach towns north of Ocean Crest in Atlantic City, and his many businesses—bike shops, Laundromats, and trash trucks throughout town—were how he laundered money.

According to her parents, Anthony Citteroni was also interested in buying Kebab Kitchen and opening an Italian restaurant.

She realized she was staring, and quickly shook his extended hand. His fingers were long and tapered, his palm a bit calloused, and her skin tingled at the touch. "I'm Lucy Berberian. I'm helping my parents with the restaurant this summer."

"Well, Lucy. We have something in common then, don't we? Family obligations."

Something in his tone told her he wasn't that

pleased to have taken over responsibility of the bike shop. She could commiserate.

"Have you ever ridden a motorcycle?" he asked.

She eyed the black machine. It was a sleek Harley-Davidson, polished to a shine with large handlebars and a leather saddlebag on the side. "No. I never had a chance to ride one of those." She wasn't sure she wanted to either.

"I'd like to take you. You haven't lived until you've ridden one of these babies." He rested a hand on a seat that was big enough for two. "I have an extra helmet in the garage."

"Maybe another day."

He chuckled. "Nervous?"

"A little."

"Okay, but you're not off the hook. I'll ask again in the future." She didn't miss his obvious examination and approval.

She regarded him curiously. "Is your dad here?"

"Why? Don't tell me you stopped by to see him?" Michael asked in mock disappointment.

"No. I came because I heard your bike, remember? But I would like to talk with him in the future. He expressed an interest in buying my parents' place."

"That so? I'm not surprised."

"You didn't know?"

"Dad's always looking to expand. He doesn't spend much time at the bike shop, though. Tell you what, I'll ask him when I see him. How about I take you on that ride after I hear and we can talk shop?"

After a long dry spell like the Sahara, she'd come home only to have two very attractive men express interest in her on the very same day.

CHAPTER 10

"It's true. I checked the township records this morning and Heather Banks issued citations to Guido's Hot Cheese Pizzeria, not twice, but *three* times over the past six months for health violations," Katie said.

Lucy looked up from where she was slicing eggplant on a prep table. Katie had burst into the restaurant and tracked Lucy down in the kitchen. Cutting vegetables wasn't part of Lucy's waitressing duties, but the mundane activity gave her something to do to keep her mind from the fact that the restaurant had had only a handful of customers for lunch. Besides, she needed to feel helpful and knew Butch planned to make a vegetarian eggplant bake for dinner service.

Lucy whistled through her teeth. "Three times? That's enough to make anyone furious. When was Heather's last visit to the pizzeria?"

Katie flipped through a stack of papers in her hand. "She visited Guido's the day she died. According to Heather's reports that I found at the township office, she was to deliver reports to two restaurants, the Hot Cheese Pizzeria and Mac's Irish Pub, before she came to Kebab Kitchen."

Lucy's heart pounded as she set down the knife on the cutting board. "That would fit the time frame of poisoning. Maybe Paul Evans was right and Guido Morelli hated Heather enough to kill her."

Katie shifted from foot to foot. "When is your shift over?"

"Didn't you notice the empty dining room on your way to the kitchen? The last customer left a half hour ago. I can leave any time. Are you thinking of paying Guido a visit?"

"Absolutely."

"How? It's Monday. Don't you have to go back to work?" Lucy asked.

"Nope. I took the rest of the day off. I don't feel well." Katie shot her a sly wink.

"Katie Watson! What if someone sees you running around town and word gets back to your supervisor?"

Katie covered her mouth and starting hacking. "Don't I sound believable?"

"Well . . ."

Katie's eyes flashed. "Forget work! I can't let you have all the fun."

Lucy held up a hand. "Okay. The truth is I'm

glad you're coming with me. Wait here a minute, and I'll be ready to go."

Lucy took off her apron and went in search of her father. She found him in his office at his desk, pencil in hand. He rubbed his chin as he pored over an accounting ledger. Paperwork, order sheets, and invoices littered the surface of the oak desk. A tall metal shelf held spare parts for the dishwasher as well as payroll sheets and the samples of canned and boxed food suppliers often gave him.

"Dad?"

He swiveled in his chair to see her in the doorway. "Is everything all right out there?"

"Everything's fine." Lucy felt a tug in her chest. He was a hard worker, a man who'd arrived as an immigrant with little and had become a successful businessman and a proud American. He'd never had the opportunity to go to college. During her youth she may not have always agreed with his old-world attitude or his plans for her future, but she'd always admired him.

"Katie's here and we have to go somewhere." Lucy couldn't bring herself to explain her plans. She didn't want to give him false hope.

She also didn't want him to ask questions.

But he was intelligent and caught on. "Ah, you're investigating. Good girl. Go and do right by the family."

Her chest tightened. What if she didn't find anything and the restaurant's reputation was never cleared? She swallowed. "Thanks, Dad. I'm working tomorrow's lunch and dinner shift."

She shut the door and met Katie outside by her jeep. Lucy frowned as she opened the passenger door. Of all the luck. She'd walked to work this morning. The restaurant wasn't far from Katie's house and Lucy had enjoyed the fresh ocean air. Now she wished she'd driven. She buckled her seatbelt and pulled it tight.

Katie chuckled. "You're a nervous Nellie."

"Anyone would be. Try to take it slow today, okay?"

"Sure."

Fifteen minutes later, which included three handle-clutching and wheel-squealing turns, they arrived at their destination. The Hot Cheese Pizzeria was in a shopping center tucked between a surf shop and a used bookstore. Katie parked in a metered spot and they got out of the jeep.

Lucy started fishing through her purse for quarters.

Katie stopped her. "Meters are still free. It's not officially the season yet."

Lucy zipped her purse closed. "Don't remind me." The tourist season starting on Memorial Day was like a ticking time bomb hovering over her head.

Together, they stepped inside the pizzeria. A few customers eating pizza sat at tables with checked red and white plastic tablecloths. A teenage couple, heads bent together, sat in the corner whispering to each other. A family with twin girls in booster chairs was seated by a window. The place smelled of tomato sauce, melted mozzarella cheese, and garlic. Nobody was minding the hostess station.

Lucy waved down a young, skinny waiter with several tattoos on his bony arms carrying an empty pizza tray. "We're looking for the owner, Guido Morelli. Is he here?"

"Sure. Let me call him from the back."

The waiter disappeared behind swinging doors. A split second later they heard him loudly shout out, "Guido! Two ladies want you out front."

"Goodness," Lucy said. "Is Guido hard of hearing?"

Katie scanned the restaurant. "The place doesn't look dirty. I wonder why Heather failed it?"

"The front may be clean, but you never know what goes on in the back of a restaurant. The kitchen or storeroom could be a mess," Lucy pointed out.

Katie wrinkled her nose. "Please don't tell me. Bill and I like to eat out."

"Sorry. It's not Kebab Kitchen. My mom and dad are clean freaks. I'm just telling you what I heard about other places when I was growing up."

They waited another five minutes before a heavy-set man with slicked-back dark hair and a walrus-shaped mustache hurried toward them. "I'm Guido Morelli. How can I help you?" he asked in an Italian accent.

"I'm Lucy Berberian and this is Katie Watson. We'd like to talk to you about Heather Banks."

"What about her?" Guido asked, instantly on guard.

"We understand she inspected your pizzeria," Lucy said.

"So?" Guido said.

"And that she cited you for health inspection violations, not once but three times," Katie said.

Guido's eyes narrowed. Lucy wanted to haul Katie outside. She meant well, but her straight-to-the-jugular tactics didn't put Guido at ease. They weren't the police. They didn't have a warrant, and they needed him to voluntarily offer information.

"Heather Banks was an evil woman," Guido said tersely. "She said my kitchen was dirty. Dirty!" He pointed to his chest. "I've been in business for over fifteen years and no one has ever said my kitchen was dirty."

"You said she *was* evil. You know she's dead?" Lucy asked.

He looked at her as if she was a simpleton. "Of course. Everyone knows. It's a small town."

Guido then started to wag his finger at Lucy. "She should never have taken over her father's position. Mr. Banks was fair and honest. His daughter was corrupt."

"Corrupt? That's a harsh accusation," Lucy said.

"It's true. She accepted bribes from other restaurants to overlook *their* dirty kitchens. Everyone in the business knows this. Why do you think she never fined Mac McCabe's Irish Pub?" Guido said sharply.

Lucy was startled by the name. Mac's Irish Pub was the bar she had gone to on her first day back to Ocean Crest. It was also the pub where she'd first seen Heather and Paul. And Katie had said Heather had delivered health notices to both Guido and Mac the day she died.

"You think Mr. McCabe paid Ms. Banks to overlook health code violations?" Lucy asked.

"I don't think so, I know so."

"Why would she risk her job and do that?" Katie asked.

"Because she had a nasty gambling habit," Guido said. "She needed money to keep going back to the Atlantic City casinos. She kept demanding more and more cash from McCabe in order to keep his pub in business. Maybe McCabe had enough of her blackmail and *he* wanted her dead."

Lucy was startled. No one had ever mentioned that Heather was a gambler.

But who would know? One name kept coming to mind—Paul Evans. Heather's boyfriend hadn't said anything about her gambling addiction. Why would he keep it a secret?

"You think Mac McCabe had something to do with Ms. Bank's death?" Katie asked.

Guido nodded and pointed to himself once again. "It wasn't me. And a man can only pay so much. I wouldn't blame McCabe. He did all of us a favor."

* * *

Outside, Lucy turned to Katie. "Guido gave us a lead. Heather was a gambler? Who knew?"

"Paul Evans had to know and he never said a word."

Lucy halted at Katie's Jeep. "I was thinking the same thing."

"Maybe they were arguing over the phone because she was gambling away all their money," Katie said.

Lucy thought back to Heather's cell phone conversation the day she died. She'd been arguing heatedly with someone. If it wasn't with her boyfriend, could it have been with a moneylender? "If Heather wasn't fighting with Paul, maybe she owed money to a scary bookie. But I think we're forgetting something else here."

Katie frowned. "Like what?"

"You said Heather visited Guido the day she died to deliver an inspection report?"

"That's right," Katie said.

"She ate at Kebab Kitchen's hummus bar even though she complained about it in her written report. Maybe she also ate or drank something from the pizzeria that day."

Katie's eyes widened. "Good thinking."

The pair hurried back inside the pizzeria. Guido wasn't in sight. Lucy stopped the same tattooed waiter they had flagged down when they first entered the restaurant. "I'd like to get a pizza to go."

"Sure." The waiter pulled out his pad and pencil.

He was chewing a large wad of pink bubble gum. "What size?"

"A large pizza. By the way, were you working the afternoon the health inspector came in the other day?" Lucy asked.

"Tall, red-haired woman with a tight outfit and a bad attitude?"

"That would be the one."

"Sure. I remember her. Why?" he asked.

"Did she eat anything here that day?"

The waiter chewed his gum and shook his head. "Nope. Just an iced tea to go. I remember because she'd insisted it had to be fresh and unsweetened. She was a picky lady . . . a real pain in the butt."

Katie and Lucy were back in the Jeep with a steaming pizza on Lucy's lap.

"Heather ordered iced tea to go from the Hot Cheese Pizzeria after she inspected the place. That's also what she drank at Kebab Kitchen the day she died," Lucy said.

Katie turned onto Ocean Avenue and accelerated as they drove down the main street. Lucy cringed as the car hit a pothole. A block later, they passed a police car and Katie waved. The blond officer wasn't her dark-haired husband, but instead of turning on his lights and attempting to pull her over for speeding he waved back.

"You think someone slipped Heather a lethal dose of cyanide in her iced tea?" Katie asked.

"We won't know what was in her system until the tox results. But what if?" Lucy asked.

"It's a good theory. It's not like Guido Morelli is upset she's dead."

CHAPTER 11

"The pizza's really good." Katie took a bite out of a slice as cheese and sauce dripped onto her paper plate. "Are you sure you don't want any?"

Lucy's stomach grumbled. "I was saving my calories for later, but you've convinced me," she said as she helped herself to a slice. Her first bite of warm pizza crust topped with homemade sauce and cheese was heavenly. Katie was right. It was delicious. Lucy quickly finished her slice.

Sitting at Katie's kitchen table, the small flat screen TV on the counter was turned to a cooking channel. A handsome male chef was demonstrating how to cut open a ripe avocado, remove the pit, and make guacamole. Prominent muscles were visible beneath his apron, and Lucy wondered how many hours the young chef spent in the gym versus the kitchen. Her mother loved to watch cooking shows, and Lucy had never understood the fascination. After cooking all day in the restaurant, how could she want to go home and watch someone else cook? Or was her mother just tuning in to watch the cute TV chefs?

Lucy frowned as a sudden thought occurred to her. "I need to search Kebab Kitchen."

Katie lowered her pizza. "For what?"

"Cyanide, of course. I should have thought to search the restaurant before. Sodium cyanide and potassium cyanide are both white powders. If Heather was poisoned, it makes sense that it would be a white powder, not a gas. A powder could be mixed into her drink or sprinkled on her food."

"Do you think you'll find rat poison?"

Lucy wrinkled her nose. "I doubt my parents keep rat poison in the place."

"It would be a waste of your time," Katie said.

"Why?"

"The police have already searched the restaurant and took everything they wanted from that night, remember?"

"Maybe they missed something. I have to check."

"How do you plan to search the place? Your parents, Emma, or Butch are always around."

Lucy had already thought of a good time. "I'll go bright and early before anyone gets there."

Katie eyed her, then went back to her pizza. "Suit yourself."

The wind chimes from the front porch tinkled and swayed from the afternoon breeze. Moments later, the scrape of a key in the lock alerted them that Bill was home from his shift.

The front door opened and Bill stepped inside, dressed in his policeman's uniform. He removed his hat and ran his hand over his buzz cut.

Lucy pushed back her chair and stood. Every time she saw Bill, she struggled with the urge to interrogate him to find out if he'd learned anything, however small, about the investigation into Heather's death.

"Hey," Katie said, her tone dry, but her eyes lit up as they traveled up and down Bill's muscular frame in his uniform. "Any news you'd like to share with us?"

Bill's jaw tensed. "You know I'm not supposed—"

"It would be nice to hear it before it's in print, Bill," Katie said.

"You're not going to let it go, are you?" Bill asked.

"Not a chance," Katie said, "But my stubborn nature is one of the reasons you love me."

"Fine. I suppose Lucy does have a right to know and be prepared," Bill said. "We looked into Heather's cell phone records. She received a call during the time when she was in Kebab Kitchen."

"Just like I told you," Lucy said.

"It was a burner phone and untraceable," Bill said.

Disappointment settled in Lucy's chest at the dead end.

"Anything else?" Katie asked.

"All I can tell you is that the department sent the food and trash it collected from Kebab Kitchen from the night Heather Banks died to the state lab for testing. The results take time." He hesitated, then took a deep breath before continuing. "But after the coroner's report, Detective Clemmons is convinced what Heather ate caused her death. He wants to go on record and announce it as a suspicious death and call in the county prosecutor."

Lucy's stomach dropped. "Kebab Kitchen might as well close its doors!"

Bill's gaze snapped to Lucy's. At her dismayed expression, his jaw eased. "He won't say *how* he thinks Heather died, only that her death is suspicious."

Clemmons' announcement would have terrible consequences for the restaurant. And summoning the county prosecutor could cause even more trouble. "He doesn't have to spell out how. People will assume it was from the food."

"You can't be serious?" Katie asked, hands on her hips. "Isn't Clemmons jumping the gun?"

"It's out of my hands," Bill said.

Lucy swallowed her panic. There had to be something she could do. "What about Heather's gambling habit?"

"That's right. Heather needed money to support her addiction," Katie chimed in.

"What are you two talking about?"

Lucy didn't know if she'd made a grave error in telling Bill what they'd learned. Maybe the police knew about the gambling already. But if they didn't, the police had the resources to confirm whether it was true.

The cat's out of the bag now, Lucy thought. She

might as well tell Bill everything they'd learned and hope the police and Calvin Clemmons would investigate every lead.

"We talked to ah . . . someone who said Heather had a bad gambling habit and may have been accepting bribes in exchange for giving certain restaurants a pass for health violations," Lucy said.

Bill's eyes narrowed and he pinned them with a cold glare. "You two aren't supposed to get involved. Promise me you are not messing with police business."

Katie smiled sweetly. "Just look into it, okay?" She took a plate from the counter, put a large piece of pizza on it, and handed it to her husband.

Bill wasn't entirely pacified, but his wife's smile—combined with the hot pizza—had the intended effect. He accepted the plate and sat at the table to eat.

At five o'clock sharp Tuesday morning, Lucy walked into Kebab Kitchen prepared for some serious snooping with a flashlight and a pocket full of plastic baggies.

She hit the storage room first, shining the flashlight into every dark corner. Nothing looked suspicious. Bags of flour, yeast, and salt were the closest items that resembled white powder, but she could tell by their scent and texture that they were not cyanide. Not surprisingly, she didn't find any rat poison. She walked away empty-handed from the kitchen and dining room as well.

She headed back into the storage room but walked straight to her parents' office in the corner. Turning the knob, she stepped inside the small room. The surface of the oak desk was clear except for a desk blotter and a stack of time cards. The tall metal shelves in the corner were packed with small boxes and canned food samples from different salesmen that visited the restaurant. If her mother liked a new product, her father would order it for the restaurant. Her mother was picky, and as a result, the shelves were full of unopened cans and boxes of food samples that they would donate to a local food kitchen.

The only two items that resembled white powder was a glass jar of generic seasoning salt and a box of dishwashing detergent. Lucy opened the box of detergent and sniffed the contents, when an all-too familiar voice pierced the silence.

"Lucy, what are you doing here so early?"

Lucy jumped in surprise and dropped the box of detergent. It landed on the tile floor with a solid thud that split the box open. White powder spilled out on her sneakers and the floor in a cloud. Her hand flew to her chest, and she whirled to see Angela standing in the doorway.

"Mom! You scared me half to death."

Her mother's brow furrowed and her eyes lowered to the mess on the floor. The scent of the dishwashing detergent—strong lemon and chlorine—filled the room.

"Sorry about the mess. I was hoping to come in early and start on the payroll to help you and Dad out." Lucy crossed her fingers behind her back at the little white lie.

Her mother eyed her curiously as she repinned a loose lock of hair back into her beehive. "I have a large catering order. You can help me in the kitchen instead."

Lucy was relieved her mother didn't ask more questions. She already felt guilty for her clandestine search of the place. "Sure. I'll clean up and meet you in the kitchen."

Lucy found a mop in the storage room and cleaned the office floor. Her yoga pants and sneakers were another matter entirely. She brushed her pants off with her hands, but remnants of white powder could still be seen on the black fabric and between the laces of her shoes. She may have been discovered, but at least she hadn't found cyanide in the restaurant. Katie was right. Since the police had taken all the leftover food Heather had eaten, Lucy's family would just have to wait for the results.

By the time Lucy finished cleaning and entered the kitchen, her mother was kneading dough on the wooden prep table. Her oversized apron swallowed her five-foot frame. The industrial mixer that could hold fifty pounds of dough sat in the corner. The ovens behind her were set on PREHEAT. A small TV was mounted in the corner and an infomercial for wrinkle cream was playing.

The smell of yeast and flour wafted over to Lucy. "What are you making?"

"I'm filling a catering order for an out-of-town wedding. They want five dozen choreg, twenty trays of baklava, and ten tubs of hummus. Thank goodness for our catering business. Out-of-towners don't seem concerned like the locals."

Choreg was a type of bread that was flaky and slightly sweet, and traditionally served warm with Munster cheese. Baklava, the dessert with layers of buttered and flaky sheets of phyllo dough and walnuts and cinnamon, was Lucy's favorite. On the side of the prep table sat a bowl of chick peas soaking in water and a large jar of tahini—sesame paste delivered by Big Al—which would be used to make different varieties of hummus.

"When's the wedding?" Lucy asked.

"I have three days to fill the order."

"That's a lot of food and not a lot of time. Where's Butch?"

"He has his regular days off to spend with his family. You're here now."

Lucy didn't want to point out that she wasn't supposed to be there that early, but held her tongue. Her mother clearly needed help. Three days wasn't much time to prepare all that food, but Lucy knew the large order would keep her mother busy and her mind off their troubles.

Angela stopped kneading dough and pointed with a finger coated in flour to where the aprons hung on hooks in the wall. "Pick an apron and wash your hands, Lucy."

Just a week ago, Lucy never would have wanted

to, but today she found she wasn't dismayed to spend time with her mother in the kitchen. Her mother was an exceptional cook—self-taught by her own grandmother and mother-in-law. Lucy hadn't inherited her mother's talent. Emma, on the other hand, could cook well, but sadly Max didn't love Mediterranean cuisine. He preferred his hamburgers and steaks grilled without any seasonings or spices.

Lucy tied her apron and rolled up her sleeves while Angela cut a large piece of dough and put it on the work surface in front of her. "The dough is cold," Lucy pointed out.

"It's supposed to be. I prepared the dough yesterday and let it rise in the refrigerator overnight."

Lucy realized how little she knew about her mother's recipes and cooking in general. She'd never cared in the past when she'd worked late nights in the city. All that had been important to her then was memorizing every good take-out restaurant phone number by heart. But things had changed now that she'd returned to Ocean Crest and Kebab Kitchen. Watching her mother, Lucy was surprised that she *wanted* to learn.

A lively tune sounded from the TV, and Lucy looked up at the screen. The infomercial had ended and a young, handsome chef with blond hair and a dazzling smile stood in a high-tech kitchen with stainless steel appliances. He was the same celebrity chef Lucy had noticed while watching the cooking channel at Katie's house.

"Ah," Angela said. "It's Cooking Kurt. I like his recipes."

Looking at the appreciative expression on her mother's face, Lucy didn't think it was only Kurt's recipes she liked. Lucy bit her cheek to keep from chuckling.

"What next?" Lucy asked as her mother's attention returned to the prep table.

Together they kneaded small fistfuls of dough, rolled it into three pieces, and braided it into a small personal sized loaf. Lucy then brushed each choreg with egg wash to make it shiny, and they put the full trays into the oven.

Her mother wiped her hands on a towel. "The police think that Banks woman was poisoned from my hummus," she said, her voice troubled.

Lucy looked up startled. They'd been working side by side for a half hour without a word. "The truth will come out when the toxicology results are final. Remember what Bill said?"

"The police are pressured to quickly place blame," Angela said.

It was true, but how did she know that? Her mother always had a sixth sense that had driven Lucy crazy as a kid. It was one of the reasons she could never sneak out of the house as a teenager, drink beer underage, or get involved in mischief.

"I'm doing what I can, Mom. I promise."

"I know. You're a good girl, Lucy. We need to find you a husband."

"Mom," Lucy said, a note of whining in her voice.

"Do you have to talk about men every time we're alone?"

"It's my job as a mother to see you happy." She kneaded the dough with a bit more force.

"I *am* happy."

She was, wasn't she? Had she been happy at the law firm? Looking back, she couldn't say she was. The stress of working long hours in hopes of achieving partner status hadn't worked out for her. But the truth was since coming back to Ocean Crest, she'd been more relaxed, even with finding a dead body and becoming an amateur sleuth. She valued the time she'd spent with Katie, her sister, Sally, and her parents . . . even Azad.

Good grief. Her mother must never know she'd met Azad for a coffee date. And it had been a date of sorts even if they'd talked business. But if her mother learned the truth, she'd rush out and pick out china patterns and linens.

Lucy decided to quickly change the topic of conversation. "I'm glad the catering end is doing well since the restaurant is slow." She pulled on an oven mitt and took a tray out of the oven. The baked choreg smelled delicious and her mouth watered. How long had it been since she'd had one?

"How soon do you and Dad want to sell?" Lucy asked.

"Within the next year assuming we have a buyer. But who would make an offer now?"

"Don't think of it, Mom."

"How can I not? I only hope Azad hasn't changed his mind."

Lucy held the tray in midair as a nagging thought returned. Azad would benefit if the value of the restaurant plummeted by thousands. He could buy it cheap, afford to modernize the place, then make his money back in record time.

"Set that down before you burn yourself," Angela chided.

Lucy dropped the tray and it rattled on the counter. "You said Azad went to culinary school?"

"That's right. He's always wanted his own place, and he's been saving." There was a clear note of pride in her voice.

"Culinary school is pricey. He must have debt," Lucy said.

Angela shrugged as she kneaded fresh dough. "I guess so."

"Then how can he afford to buy the restaurant?"

"I'm the chef. Your father handles the finances. Ask him if you want details."

Her explanation didn't put Lucy's mind at ease. Azad had already told her that he hoped her father would give him a mortgage for fair market value. Whether that was true or Azad received a business loan from a bank, money and greed were motives for murder. If Azad wanted to buy the restaurant, he'd have to pay not only for the building, restaurant equipment and all the supplies, but for the business as well. If the business was suffering, her parents would most likely lower their price.

Lucy already knew Azad had motive, but for some reason she'd never truly thought of opportunity. She thought back to that fateful day when Heather came to eat at the hummus bar. Azad had been in the dining room. He claimed he went into the kitchen to say hello to Butch, but found Big Al making a delivery. Lucy had been preoccupied waiting on Heather. Azad could have easily gone back to the dining room to slip something into the hummus bar.

The result—Heather would die, business would plummet, and the value of the restaurant would dramatically decline.

Azad would luck out.

CHAPTER 12

Later that afternoon, after helping her mother in the kitchen, Lucy decided to go for a run. There was nothing better than a jog on the boardwalk. Lucy's running shoes seemed to fly across the wooden boards as she breathed in the salty ocean air. Running in Center City Philadelphia had never been as pleasurable. Skyscrapers, stores, and city traffic offered plenty for a jogger to take in, but it couldn't compare with the breathtaking view of the Atlantic Ocean and the steady, rhythmic pounding of the waves on the shore. The cry of seagulls circling above added to the sea sounds.

The Ocean Crest boardwalk was an eclectic mix of shops, restaurants, and entertainment. She passed a fudge and salt water taffy shop; a clothing store that offered novelty T-shirts, bikinis, beach cover-ups, and boogie boards; a burger joint; a pizzeria; and an old-fashioned ice cream parlor. She jogged past the sole amusement pier, which boasted the thrilling wooden roller coaster and

Ferris wheel. She kept running, passing an arcade, a tattoo parlor, a fortuneteller.

No matter how much fun the boardwalk was, it was all dwarfed by the stretch of beach and the endless ocean. Reaching the end of the boardwalk, she jogged down the steps onto the beach and kept going. It was harder to run on the sand and sweat quickly beaded on her brow. The sand was still slightly damp from high tide and her running shoes left imprints behind. As she grew tired, childhood memories of building sandcastles on the beach and body surfing in the sea arose in her mind.

Eventually, Lucy left the beach and came to the street leading back to Katie's house. Two blocks later, she could hear loud music blaring from Mac's Irish Pub. A cover band was warming up to play for happy hour.

Making a snap decision, she jogged to the pub's front door.

Once again, Sue was behind the bar. "Good to see you're still in town, Lucy. Draft beers are only three dollars during happy hour."

"No thanks. Can you tell me if Mac McCabe is here?"

"Sure is. I'll get him for you."

Five minutes later, McCabe greeted Lucy at the bar. He was tall, in his early fifties, with a substantial beer belly and brown hair tied back in a ponytail. His handshake had a strong grip. "What can I do for you?"

"My name is Lucy. I was a friend of Heather Banks. I know she used to come here with her boyfriend. Can I ask you a few questions?"

"I heard about her death. I'm sorry for your loss, but I don't know what I can help with," Mac said.

"Did you know her?"

"Not on a personal level. She was the town's health inspector, and occasionally came here with her boyfriend, some famous author."

"Paul Evans," she offered.

McCabe nodded. "That's the guy."

"I heard that Heather delivered an inspection report to your pub the day she died."

Mac blinked, then focused his gaze. "I came in just as she was leaving."

Lucy took a deep breath, then decided to just go for it. "I also heard that Heather abused her position as a health inspector and accepted bribes to overlook restaurant violations."

Something flickered across McCabe's face—suspicion? fear?—but it was quickly replaced with a flash of anger in his blue eyes. "You've been talking to that Italian buffoon, haven't you?"

"Pardon?"

"Guido Morelli. He's always been jealous of my success. He'll say anything to hurt my business, especially since his daughter has been following my son around like a lovesick puppy."

Well, McCabe was turning out to be an interesting source of information.

"Are you saying Guido's daughter has romantic feelings for your son?" Lucy asked.

"I'm not saying. I know. They're kids in high school. His daughter, Maria, asked my son, Connor, to the senior prom. It threw Guido into a fit. I have nothing against his daughter, but I admit I enjoyed how he went crazy. We're in competition. Always have been."

"How? He owns a pizzeria and you own an Irish pub. I can't imagine you compete for the same clientele."

But as soon as she said the words, she knew better. The busy summer season didn't discriminate. All the restaurants in the small beach town competed for business during the summer. And if you counted the other close-by Jersey shore towns, then the number of restaurants fighting for business increased to hundreds. The three main vacation months—from June to August—comprised a lion's share of profits for everyone that had to last throughout the year.

"Did that lying Italian tell you I paid off Heather Banks in order to pass inspection? No one can prove it. Ever," McCabe said sharply.

He had a point. How could anyone prove that McCabe had paid bribes to Heather in order pass inspection or that McCabe got tired of Heather's blackmail scheme?

"The Hot Cheese Pizzeria failed health inspections over and over because his place is a cesspool and he deserved to fail. He's just bitter that I didn't."

Lucy decided to change tactics. "Do you know of anyone who wanted her dead?"

"Other than Guido Morelli?"

"Yes. Other than Mr. Morelli."

Mac pursed his lips. "Heather Banks had a gambling problem. That author boyfriend of hers knew about it and he didn't like it."

"How do you know that?" Did everyone in town know that Heather was a gambler? Lucy had already wondered why Paul hadn't mentioned Heather's addiction. She could only assume he wanted it kept secret. But that didn't make sense if others in town knew about it, including Guido Morelli and Mac McCabe.

"Because I saw them fight over money. They came in here one night and drank too much. I happened to be behind the bar and heard their fight. She was a seasoned veteran of the Atlantic City casinos. He complained that she'd blown his entire royalty check of twenty thousand dollars and he wasn't happy about it."

Twenty thousand dollars! Lucy gaped. Paul had definitely lied to them when he said he rarely fought with Heather. Not only had he been aware of her gambling problem, but she'd spent his money and they'd argued.

What else wasn't Paul telling them?

Lucy eyed Mac McCabe. "One more question. Did Heather happen to eat or drink anything when she came in to deliver the inspection report that day?"

He scowled as he thought back. "Yeah, so? You don't think I harmed her do you?"

"Of course, not. She didn't die in *your* restaurant." Mac didn't know Lucy's family owned Kebab Kitchen, and she saw no reason to enlighten him.

McCabe relaxed. "She didn't eat anything. She just had iced tea. Unsweetened."

Lucy's blood ran cold. It took every ounce of control not to let her emotions show. Heather had drunk unsweetened iced tea at each establishment she'd inspected the day she died. What if someone poisoned her favorite beverage?

Despite Mac's adamant denial, she wasn't sure she believed the wily bar owner any more than she believed the hot-tempered pizzeria owner. If Heather had demanded more and more money from Mac to pass inspection, there was motive for murder. Combined with the iced tea, there was opportunity.

Just like Guido.

Lucy forced a smile. "Thanks for your time."

As she jogged back to Katie's home a single unpleasant thought kept turning over and over in her mind. *If someone had poisoned one of Heather's drinks that day, why did she have to die outside of Kebab Kitchen?*

Lucy walked into Katie's kitchen and found her cutting a tray of freshly baked brownies. "What took you so long?" Katie asked.

"I took a detour and ended up at Mac's Pub talking to Mac McCabe."

Katie's eyes widened. "You questioned him?"

"I told him I was a friend of Heather's."

Katie put a brownie on a plate and handed it to Lucy. "And?"

Lucy eyed the brownie. Chocolate was one of her weaknesses. She justified the calories by reminding herself that she'd just jogged. She took a small bite and nearly groaned out loud as the chocolate melted on her tongue.

Katie was patiently waiting. Lucy set down the plate and quickly summarized what Mac had revealed.

Katie whistled through her teeth. "Heather delivered reports to the Hot Cheese Pizzeria and Mac's Pub right before arriving at Kebab Kitchen. She also ordered iced tea to go at each place. We know cyanide works quickly depending on the dose, but if Heather only spent a few minutes at each place, it's possible someone at either of them could have slipped cyanide into her drink before she went to your restaurant and ate at the hummus bar."

"I'm thinking the same thing. They have motive. Guido hated Heather because she continually cited his pizzeria for violations. Mac denied paying Heather bribes to overlook violations, but my gut tells me that both are hiding something."

Katie bit into her own brownie. "Guido blames Mac, and Mac blames Guido. The only thing they agreed upon was that Heather Banks had a bad gambling problem."

"And Paul Evans knew about it." Lucy rubbed her chin in thought. "It's possible we're overlooking something else."

Katie blinked. "What?"

"Paul is a thriller and suspense writer. Maybe all that research about killing people came in handy."

"Please hand me the chopped walnuts," Angela said.

"Coming right up." Lucy pressed the pulse button on the food processor and watched as the sharp blade chopped the walnuts into small pieces. She poured them into a large bowl and handed it to her mother. Lucy had arrived at five-thirty sharp Wednesday morning to help only to find that five trays of baklava were already in the oven.

She stood behind a long work table in the kitchen with her mother, helping her finish the trays of baklava to fill the catering order for the upcoming wedding. The corner-mounted TV was turned on and Cooking Kurt was looking exceptionally manly holding a pair of long tongs and flipping a steak on a large grill.

"I heard he has a book signing at Pages Bookstore this summer," Angela said.

Lucy's lips twitched with amusement. "Really? Will you go with Dad?"

"Posh! He has no interest. I'll take Emma or you."

Lucy didn't think she'd be around by the summer, but stayed quiet. "What's next with the baklava?"

"Unroll the phyllo dough and spread the first sheet in the tray," Angela instructed.

Lucy gave an anxious little cough. She'd never had luck working with the thin pastry dough in the past. Each sheet had the thickness of a piece of newspaper and was easy to tear. If one didn't butter it quickly enough or left it exposed to the air too long, it would dry out and crumble.

The trays of baklava were almost finished baking in the oven. The delicious smell of buttered pastry filled the kitchen and made her mouth water. She couldn't wait to taste the flaky pastry with the walnut and cinnamon filling as soon as it was finished baking and topped with her mother's special recipe of simple sugar syrup with cloves.

"You should have been here by my side years ago," Angela said.

"I wasn't lounging around. I was practicing law, remember?"

"I was always proud of you, Lucy, even though you hardly ever visited. When you did, it was only for short bits of time and you avoided the restaurant. I always thought you would get your worldly experience at that firm and then come back home."

Lucy stayed silent. She wouldn't have come back home for this long if she'd made partner instead of Stanley Upton. She'd carefully mapped out her entire life. Work at the Philadelphia firm for eight years, make partner, and move up the law firm ladder until she was promoted to managing partner.

It hadn't been that long ago since she'd quit the firm, yet it seemed much longer than the nine days she'd been home.

Family had always been overwhelming to her— *big, bold, loud, opinionated,* and *overbearing*—were just a few adjectives she'd used in the past to describe her ethnic family. She hadn't been wrong. They had turned out to be even more overwhelming upon her return, but in a different way. She'd never imagined finding a dead body in the back of her parents' restaurant.

Despite everything, if she was truthful to herself, she *was* glad to be home.

A sudden thought clicked in her mind.

She didn't miss the law firm, she realized, or her Philadelphia apartment. She was relieved to be home. True, there'd been a murder, but there was a lot more going on since coming back to Ocean Crest. She'd spent time reconnecting with Katie, Emma, Sally, her parents . . . even Azad.

She'd miss all that if she'd made partner. She glanced at the pastry brush in her hand, then at her mother's profile as she worked beside her. *She'd miss this.*

She chuckled to herself. Maybe she should send Stanley Upton a thank-you card.

A loud buzzing sound made Lucy jump. The oven timer announced that the next batch of baklava was ready.

She pulled on oven mitts, removed the hot trays from the oven, and set them on cooling racks, then licked her lips. "It smells delicious. What about the sugar syrup?"

"I won't add it until after I deliver the baklava. The pastry has to cool so it doesn't get soggy," Angela said.

Lucy swallowed her disappointment. She wasn't going to get a chance to taste the finished pastry after all.

Her mom patted her hand. "You don't think I'd keep it all from you, do you?" She cut a large piece from one of the trays and put it on a plate. "I always have extra sugar syrup." Reaching for a glass jar on a shelf, she poured the simple sugar syrup over the baklava and handed it to Lucy. "Eat."

Lucy didn't need further encouragement. Her eyes slid shut as she bit into the hot pastry. The crunch of the thin layers of buttered pastry, the sugar, cinnamon, and walnuts, blended together in a sweet ballet. She devoured the piece and licked her fingers. "Oh my gosh. That was *so* good."

Angela started to cut another piece. "You want another?"

Lucy was sorely tempted, but was stopped from answering when Butch walked into the kitchen. "Butch! You're back." She was happy to see him after his few days off.

"Hi, Lucy Lou." Butch halted and pointed to her face. "You have something on your chin."

"Oh, thanks." Lucy wiped a flake of pastry from her chin.

"Big Al is here with a delivery," Butch announced.

Angela set down the knife and wiped her hands on her apron. "Send him back."

Lucy frowned as Butch disappeared around the bend into the storage room. "Why is Big Al here? The restaurant's slow. Do we still need our regular delivery?"

Angela sighed. "Your father can be stubborn, and he sees no need to limit our deliveries. He's convinced you are going to figure out what happened to that Banks woman."

Lucy stiffened. "I hope the police figure it out before me."

"Bah! The police know nothing. They think it was from something she ate, don't they?"

They also suspect that I had something to do with it. But Lucy would never voice those concerns to her mother. She'd fly into a rage and march into the police station if she thought Detective Clemmons suspected her daughter.

Lucy was saved from answering the question when Big Al, carrying two boxes stacked upon each other, entered the kitchen. "Hello, ladies!"

Angela kissed the air on both sides of his cheeks. "What do you have for me today?"

Big Al began unpacking one of the boxes. "The tahini, red lentils, chick peas, and some other items you wanted."

"Wonderful. Just in time for my next catering order."

Lucy picked up a box containing a ten pound bag of bulgur. "Where do you want this?"

Angela pointed to the storage room beyond the kitchen. "You'll find all the bulgur on the second shelf."

Lucy nodded as she headed into the storage room and tried to find space on the second shelf. It was full of grains, canned goods, and spices. She put the bulgur next to a sack of rice and set the empty box aside.

On her way back to the kitchen, Lucy heard Big Al say, "I noticed the bike shop is open next door. Mr. Citteroni must be getting ready for the season."

Her mother's voice was strained. "Yes, it's coming fast, isn't it?"

"I'm sorry about what happened here with the inspector lady. Could this bring business down by a lot?" Big Al asked.

"Don't be ridiculous. We've survived recessions and multiple hurricanes pummeling the Jersey shore over the years. This is no different," Angela said.

Lucy's head swirled with doubts. She hoped her mother was right.

CHAPTER 13

Big Al kissed Lucy and her mother good-bye and headed back outside. Lucy picked up her pastry brush just as a thought occurred to her. "I left the empty box in the storage room."

Angela looked up for her tray. "Al likes to take the empty boxes with him. If you hurry, you can catch him."

Lucy fetched the box and hurried outside. Big Al was about to close the doors of his delivery truck.

"Al!" Lucy called out as she hurried to the truck. "Do you want this empty box or should I recycle it?"

"Thanks, Lucy." He took the box from her. "I reuse them. I like to think it helps keep the earth green." He loaded the box into the back of his truck.

Lucy waited until he closed the double doors and locked them. "Can I ask you a question?"

He turned back to her. "Of course."

"You were here the day the health inspector died." She knew Detective Clemmons had already questioned Big Al. Clemmons had told her when he'd interviewed her at the police station.

"I was. I made a delivery and stayed longer than I planned. I ended up talking to Azad in the kitchen."

She remembered. She'd also felt annoyed that everyone knew everyone in town, especially in the restaurant business. "Did you know Heather?"

"No. She had never been in a restaurant when I happened to make a delivery."

It made sense. Al delivered to restaurants throughout the Jersey shore, not just Ocean Crest. He didn't own a restaurant and, as such, he had no reason to deal with Heather in her capacity as a local health inspector. His statement confirmed what Detective Clemmons had already told her. Big Al had no connection to Heather.

Still, it couldn't hurt to ask him additional questions about that day.

"Did you see anything unusual when you were here?"

He shook his head. "Nothing. I would have told the police if I had. I'm sorry, Lucy. I've known your parents since they opened this place. I consider them family. I hope everything works out."

"Thanks. So do I."

After Big Al left, Lucy worked side by side with her mother until Cooking Kurt's show had long ended and almost all of the twenty ordered baklava trays were finished. She felt like she'd buttered endless layer after layer of phyllo dough sheets, spread the finely chopped walnuts, cinnamon, and sugar mixture between the layers, then buttered everything all over again. Her back hurt from bending over the prep table, her shoulders were stiff, and her feet ached. She marveled at her mother's stamina.

Lucy rubbed a knot in her lower back. "How do you do this day after day, Mom?"

"Now you see why your father and I want to retire," Angela said, placing a tray from the oven onto a cooling rack.

"I just can't imagine you selling the place. It makes me sad."

"We never wanted to sell. It's a good living. We wanted you to take it over with Azad by your side."

There it was again—the not so subtle request for her to marry Azad, pop out half a dozen kids, and raise them to take over the family business. Why on earth did *she* have to be the one to keep everything together? They still didn't pressure Emma, even though she was older. Whether it was because Lucy had attended law school or because she was never boy obsessed like Emma, she didn't know.

Lucy's voice was hoarse with frustration. "You know *he* was the one who broke it off with me."

Her mother huffed. "That was years ago. He's changed. Matured. I still want him for you. Spending all your child-bearing years laboring at that law firm is a waste. You're not getting any younger and I want more grandchildren."

Lucy rolled her eyes. They had spent a pleasant and productive morning together, and she was determined not to argue. "You should be pressuring Emma and Max to have more kids."

"I'm hopeful that Niari will have a sibling soon. But you," she said, pointing a buttered pastry brush at Lucy, "need a little push."

A mischievous gleam in her mother's eye made Lucy nervous. In the past that look usually meant meddling or matchmaking was soon to follow.

Taking a step closer, Lucy plucked the raised pastry brush from her mother's hand. "What do you mean by a little push?"

Angela averted her gaze. "Nothing to worry about."

The scrape of footsteps behind Lucy made the hair on her nape stand on end.

"Hello, ladies."

At the sound of the familiar masculine voice, Lucy whirled to see Azad walk into the kitchen.

"Azad! What a wonderful surprise," Angela said in a tone that suggested she was anything but surprised.

Azad halted. "You left a message on my cell phone that you needed help, Mrs. Berberian."

Lucy shot her mother a withering gaze that her parent completely ignored. *Nothing to worry about.* Who was she kidding? Her mom knew she would be helping her with the catering order this morning, and she'd purposely asked Azad to come at the same time.

Azad turned to Lucy and smiled. "You look good in the kitchen."

Lucy felt her face redden and struggled with the urge to smooth her hair and strip off her butter-stained apron. She was highly conscious that she wasn't wearing a speck of makeup and her army-green T-shirt was the most unflattering item in her wardrobe.

"What can I help you with?" he asked.

Angela washed and dried her hands, then smoothed her beehive. "A large catering order. I also need help loading our truck and delivering the food."

"No problem. I'll help load the truck," Azad offered.

"What would we do without you?" Angela said, then shot Lucy a pointed look. "Do you mind helping Lucy finish the baklava? I want to feed Gadoo out back, and then I have paperwork to do in the office."

"Sure." He reached for a clean apron on the row of hooks on the wall and tied it behind him.

Lucy gaped at her mother's back as Angela hurried out of the kitchen and toward the office. *Could she be more obvious?*

"She's not very subtle, is she?" Azad said.

Lucy turned to him. "No kidding. What are you doing helping my parents anyway? You don't work here anymore."

"Not officially, but I told you that I never stopped coming by. I also have today off from work. My mom and dad have been gone a long time and yours are like my adoptive parents. Always have been."

"Fine," she said, her voice tense.

Azad placed a hand on his chest. "And I thought we were getting along nicely at the coffee shop the other day."

"We did, but let's just think of this as a work day, okay?" She picked up her pastry brush and started dabbing globs of butter on a sheet of phyllo.

His lips curled in a smile. "Easy there. You don't want to tear the dough. It's fragile."

Lucy watched him out of the corner of her eye as he worked. If she was thinking straight, she would have found the sight of him in one of her mother's aprons funny since it was too short and too tight for his muscular frame. Instead, she couldn't tear her gaze away. He had an easy, confident way about him, and there was definitely something sexy about a competent male in the kitchen. It was clear Azad was in his element, and she could see why he'd gone to culinary school.

For the first time, Lucy understood her mother's fascination for the hot celebrity chef. Azad's muscles bunched beneath his shirt as he lifted hot trays from the oven, and she had to turn away. Last thing she wanted was to get caught gaping at him like a horny high school girl.

"I still can't believe you want to buy this place," she muttered.

"Why? Just because you don't want it doesn't mean it's worthless."

Lucy glared at him. "That's not fair."

The thought of her parents selling Kebab Kitchen to Azad, or Mr. Citteroni, or *anyone,* made Lucy's nerves tense. It seemed so wrong. For as long as she could remember, her father had said the place was in their blood. She'd never understood until now.

Why after all these years? Why after a murder in the parking lot? Why did she finally understand what her father meant?

It *was* in her blood. And she'd be sad to let it go.

But was she sad enough to stay?

"You're right. I'm sorry. It's just that you've been gone a long time. I never thought you'd come back for good," Azad said.

Lucy blinked. "I never said I'm back for good."

He hesitated, his expressive eyes traveling over her face. "Well, it's good to have you even for an extended visit. You may decide you want to stay."

Her breath caught and her pulse quickened. She didn't want to think about how he would convince her.

Her grip on the pastry brush tightened, then she gasped as a painful cramp pierced her hand. "Ouch!" Lucy dropped the brush. Melted butter splattered on her apron.

Azad's brow furrowed. "What's wrong?"

She cradled her hand. "Nothing serious. Just a cramp from too much buttering."

"Let me see."

"No, I don't think—"

Azad ignored her protests and took her hand in his larger one. His thumb pressed gently in the center of her palm and started massaging the tight, cramped muscles.

Ah. The painful ache subsided, and she glanced at him through lowered lashes. They were standing close, too close, and she felt the heat from his body. An unwanted tingling began in the pit of her stomach.

Careful Lucy! her inner voice warned. *You're growing weaker by the second.*

He kept massaging her hand, and the tingling traveled up her arm.

"Do you think there's a chance we can start over?" His voice was low, husky. He was still cradling her hand in his.

"Why the interest?"

"Isn't it obvious? I like you."

"Do you? Or are you simply looking for an easier way to get your hands on the restaurant?" She nearly recoiled at the bitterness in her voice. Now where did that come from? She didn't really believe he would stoop so low, did she?

A flicker of anger crossed Azad's face, and he dropped her hand. His tone was clipped. "I would hope you know me better than that."

She studied his features. She'd known him half her life. He may have broken her heart when he ended their relationship without providing the closure she'd desperately needed, but that had been ten years ago. A person could change a lot in ten years.

She'd changed, hadn't she?

Her heart skipped a beat at the heated look in his eyes. The irony was not lost on her that she would have given anything to see that interest years ago.

Uncomfortable beneath his scrutiny, she walked away. "We need more butter." She headed for the walk-in refrigerator. Pulling open the insulated stainless steel door, she stepped inside and flipped on the light.

Azad was right on her heels. "Hey. Don't run away."

"I'm not running," she fibbed. "I'm looking for butter." She scanned the wire metal shelves and tried to remember where the butter was stored. It was a cool forty degrees, just like any refrigerator except this one was a large room with tall shelves on each side holding everything from eggs to milk to meat to homemade bread and rice pudding. The door automatically closed behind them to save energy, but the florescent lights kept the room well-lit. For safety reasons the door didn't lock, and there was no handle on the inside. Kitchen staff with full armloads of cold food could easily push the door open with a hip or foot to exit the refrigerated room.

"It's right here," Azad said, brushing her arm as

he reached up to the second shelf to pull down a tub of butter.

"Thanks." Lucy trailed Azad as he made his way to the door.

He pushed the door with his side. It wouldn't budge. He tried again. Nothing. "What the heck?"

"Let me try." Lucy pushed, then *really* pushed. The door stayed closed.

Lucy banged on the door with a fist and called out. Her mom had purposely left them alone in her matchmaking efforts and was probably in the office. She wouldn't hear anything until she decided to wander back out.

Azad placed the tub on a nearby shelf. "Looks like we're stuck in here until someone comes along."

Gooseflesh rose on her arms. Her T-shirt and thin slacks weren't sufficient to stay warm for long. The space was frigid. Her stomach churned with anxiety and frustration. "What are we going to do?"

"Don't panic. We just have to wait it out."

She rubbed her arms. "Wait it out? We're going to slowly freeze."

His lips curled in a grin. "No, we won't." He stepped close and wrapped his arms around her.

She sucked in a breath and inhaled the scent of soap and the sweetness of pastry. Her head spun, and a different type of panic traveled down her spine. "What are you doing?"

"You're cold. We have to share body heat until we're found."

Body heat!

He cocked his head to the side, his smooth olive skin stretching over his cheekbones. "It's scientifically proven."

She glared at him, but held her tongue. She was cold and soon would be freezing. "I'm beginning to think you did this on purpose."

His lips parted in a display of straight, white teeth. "Impossible. The door is jammed from the outside. But if I could have figured out a way to lock us in together, I may have done it."

She laughed. "You're outrageous."

"I prefer *charming*." He began to rub her back, causing her nerves to tingle. It felt good.

She looked up at him. Fluorescent light glimmered over his handsome face. She felt a stab of guilt that she'd considered him a suspect. Her gut told her he couldn't kill anyone, even for monetary gain. Or was her brain chilled and her traitorous body influencing her judgment?

"Do you think someone intentionally locked us in here?" Lucy asked.

"No. Something must have fallen and blocked the door. That's all."

Maybe it was the murderer. Maybe he found out she was investigating on her own and was trying to turn her into a Popsicle to stop her efforts.

"Relax," Azad said. "Your heart is racing. You need to conserve your energy to stay warm."

"I can't help it."

"Think of something else."

"Like what?"

"I can think of something pleasant to distract you."

Out of the corner of her eye, she saw his hand come up to cup her cheek. His palm was blessedly warm, and she fought every instinct roaring to life not to lean into his touch. He inched closer, his eyes pinned to hers as his lips slowly descended.

Her heart leaped. *He's going to kiss me!*

His breath fanned her cheek, then his lips lowered another inch.

"Lucy!"

They jumped apart just as scraping sounded outside the door.

Lucy flew to the door and pounded on the stainless steel. "We're stuck in here!"

Seconds later, the door swung open.

Her mother stood there with a confused expression and a broom in her right hand. "What happened?"

Lucy and Azad hurried out of the walk-in refrigerator. The warmth from the kitchen ovens felt like a blast furnace on her face.

"We were locked inside," Lucy said.

"This broom was wedged against the door handle and the drain pipe. It must have fallen," Angela said.

"Thankfully you found us, Mrs. Berberian." Unlike Lucy, Azad looked perfectly composed. His complexion wasn't red.

Lucy suspected hers was, first from the cold, then from the rush of heat when he'd come close to kissing her. And she would have allowed it. Correction. She had wanted it.

Angela's shrewd eyes traveled from Lucy to Azad, then back to Lucy. "You two got along well in there?"

"I don't want to talk about it, Mom. I'm too cold to argue with you." Lucy plucked the broom from her mother's hand, then studied the drain pipe and the refrigerator's handle. Was it possible? If the broom was leaning against the wall, could it have fallen and become wedged between the pipe and the refrigerator's handle?

Or had someone sneaked inside the restaurant's back door with the intention of foul play?

It was late-morning by the time all the baklava trays were finished and they'd cleaned up. Lucy slipped out while Azad was loading the truck under her mother's supervision. She knew it was cowardly not to say good-bye, but she was confused by her feelings. She still couldn't believe how close she had come to letting him kiss her.

Thank goodness she'd parked out front and not in the back next to the restaurant's catering van. Her mom couldn't attempt any more matchmaking. Gadoo sauntered up to her as she hurried to her car. He stopped in front of her, looked up, and gave her a look that said *coward*, before continuing around the corner.

"Thanks for that," Lucy mumbled beneath her breath as she shut the door of her Toyota. She settled in the driver's seat, then noticed a flyer tucked beneath her windshield wiper. She disliked the abundance of paper advertisements on car windshields that ended up littering the beach. She opened the door and reached across the windshield to grasp the ad and crumple it in a ball when the top line of print caught her eye.

NY TIMES BESTSELLING AUTHOR
PAUL EVANS BOOK SIGNING

She quickly read the rest of the flyer. Paul was having a book signing for his latest suspense novel, *Killer Status,* at Pages Bookstore. Lucy checked the date.

Today.

Her mind whirled. Paul was promoting his new book? Shouldn't he have canceled the book signing, only days since his girlfriend had died?

She looked at the advertised time. Twelve noon. It was only eleven-thirty. If she hurried, she could make it.

CHAPTER 14

Lucy rushed back to Katie's from the restaurant to change and ran into her friend who was arriving home for her lunch break.

Lucy held up the book signing flyer and quickly explained where she was going.

"I want to come with you," Katie said, folding her arms across her chest.

"I want you to, but it's Wednesday. Don't you have to return to work?" Lucy asked.

"I'm on my lunch break. If I run late, I can stay late and make up time."

It only took a minute for Katie to convince Lucy. "It's best if we can observe Paul before he recognizes us," Lucy said.

"He's a big draw. The bookstore will probably be busy and he won't see us."

Lucy tapped her foot as she thought. "Still, I think we should try to disguise ourselves."

"Okay. I'm in. What are you thinking?" Katie asked.

After a quick debate, they settled on something fast and easy—an Eagles cap and wraparound sunglasses for Lucy, and a wide-brimmed sun hat and vintage Jackie O-style specs for Katie. Lucy drove to Pages Bookstore, and they parked and hurried inside.

Pages Bookstore was a quaint establishment nestled between Cutie's Cupcakes and Magic's Family Apothecary. The cozy bookstore took advantage of every inch of space. Wall-to-wall shelves were crammed with books, magazines, and DVDs for its customers' reading and viewing pleasure. The owner of the store, Candace Kent, was an attractive young widow with tortoise-shell glasses and blond hair pulled back in a tight bun.

A tall pyramid of Paul's latest release, *Killer Status*, was set up at a table by the front door. Paul sat at a table, greeting a long line of fans waiting to get signed copies. A tall, gaunt assistant with a brooding expression opened each book to the title page, inserted one of Paul's bookmarks, and handed it to the author to personalize. Candace fluttered around, chatting with customers in line, an eager expression on her face at the good turnout.

Katie and Lucy paced in the back of the shop, browsing in the cooking section and picking out a few books while they kept an eye on the line. The last time they'd seen Paul he was the grieving boyfriend. But how would he act at a crowded book signing so soon after Heather's death?

"He doesn't look like he's grieving at all," Katie said, peeking out from behind a Betty Crocker cookbook. Her sun hat and oversized sunglasses made her look like an old-fashioned Hollywood star.

"You're right. He looks like he's *enjoying* himself." Lucy tugged on the rim of her Philadelphia Eagles baseball cap and lowered a slow cooker recipe book to glance at Paul. A young blonde with big breasts and a tight T-shirt that read I'm AN EVANS ÜBERFAN, hugged the author and had her picture taken with him.

"Where's the broken-up boyfriend we visited the other day?" Katie scoffed.

Paul smiled at the blonde and signed the back of her T-shirt by her shoulder.

Lucy smirked. "I guess fans like that busty blonde help with the grief."

An hour later the line finally seemed to slow down. When Lucy was certain she'd be the last customer in line, she selected a cookbook on comfort foods written by Cooking Kurt that came with a pair of checked oven mitts. No doubt her mother would be thrilled at the large, glossy picture of the celebrity chef on the cover. Lucy then picked up a copy of Paul's new thriller, handed Katie her sunglasses and baseball cap, and headed straight for him.

Paul's assistant barely looked at her before he took the book from her, opened it to the desired page, and stuck a bookmark inside.

Paul looked at the page, pen poised in hand, not bothering to glance at Lucy. "To whom should I inscribe the book?"

"That depends."

Paul's brow furrowed and he glanced up. Surprise registered on his face. "Lucy! I apologize. I didn't recognize you. After signing books for two straight hours, I'm quite tired."

Lucy pointed to her copy of *Killer Status*. "I hope you're not too tired to sign one for me?"

"Of course not."

As Paul scrawled his signature, his cell phone buzzed once and lit up with a calendar alert. Lucy read the text reminder that flashed across the screen before Paul swiftly turned over his phone. **Meet Mr. C at 10 pm tonight.**

She feigned interest as he pasted a SIGNED BY AUTHOR sticker on the front cover and handed it to her. Thoughts flitted through Lucy's mind. *Who was Mr. C?*

The only two people she could think of with that initial were Calvin Clemmons or Anthony Citteroni. If Paul was meeting someone tonight, she needed to find out who it was.

"I hope you enjoy the book. I'm always grateful for online reviews by readers," Paul said.

The book cover featured a young brunette woman,

glancing behind her as she ran, and a dark shape of a man looming behind her. Lucy wanted to read the book, but made a mental note to only do so when Katie or Bill was at home.

"Congratulations on the new release. I'll be sure to post a review," Lucy said.

Paul smiled politely. "Thank you. I wasn't certain I wanted to do this book signing so soon after I lost Heather, but my editor insisted. She didn't want me to let down the fans."

"I'm not here to judge you."

At least not about promoting your book, Lucy thought. She glanced at his hovering assistant and lowered her voice. "About Heather . . . something came up. Is there a place we can speak privately?"

Apprehension crossed Paul's features before he nodded. He stood and spoke quietly to his assistant, then motioned for Lucy to follow him to the back of the store by the restrooms. The spines of the books said they were in the self-help aisle.

"It's the closest we can get to private back here," Paul said.

Lucy decided to get right to the point. "You never told me that Heather had a gambling problem."

Paul's brows drew downward and he glanced down the aisle to the door. "I didn't think it was relevant. We didn't fight over it or anything."

"That's not what Mac McCabe told me."

"Who?"

"The owner of Mac's Irish Pub. He said he

overheard the two of you at the bar arguing over her gambling debts. Something about Heather spending your royalty earnings," Lucy said.

Paul shifted from foot to foot. "Wait a minute. Now you think I killed Heather over her gambling habit?"

"That's not what I'm saying, but the police will find out."

"The police already know. Detective Clemmons showed up again to question me, and I told him everything."

Lucy knew for a fact that the police had no idea about Heather's gambling addiction until she had mentioned it to Bill in passing. So the police had used her tip and questioned Paul. "Why didn't you tell the police from the beginning?"

"For the same reason I didn't tell you. It's not relevant," Paul insisted.

Bull. Lucy thought he must be hiding something. Only when his hand was forced, did he tell the police and Clemmons.

"I disagree. It's important for the police to know everything," she insisted.

Paul pressed his lips together. "Don't be hypocritical. I learned something about you as well. After talking with Detective Clemmons, he thinks Heather's death had something to do with the food she ate at your family's restaurant."

A shiver ran down Lucy's spine. Not only that, but the detective thought *she* had administered the deadly dose. How soon was Clemmons going to pin the murder on her, then head to Cutie's Cupcake Bakery and celebrate with a fresh doughnut?

But that wasn't something she'd admit to Paul.

"Clemmons' theory is wrong. I want to find the real killer." Lucy tilted her head to the side and regarded him. "What about the day she was killed? She was fighting with someone over the phone. It *was* you, wasn't it?"

Paul shook his head. "No. I told you it wasn't me and who I thought had motive—Guido Morelli, the owner of that pizzeria."

"I already spoke with Mr. Morelli. He admitted to disliking Heather for citing his pizzeria for health violations, but he swears he didn't kill her. You knew Heather best. Who else do you think wanted to harm her?"

Paul hesitated for a long while and Lucy thought he wouldn't answer, but then he ran his hand through his hair and sighed. "Heather borrowed money from numerous people, but only one loan shark. Someone who truly worried me. He didn't strike me as the kind to overlook a late payment. Ever."

"Who?"

"Mr. Citteroni."

Lucy felt her gut clench tight. Anthony Citteroni's name kept coming up. Was that who Paul was meeting tonight? The more she thought of it, the more convinced she became.

An unbidden image came to mind of Mr. Citteroni's son, Michael, and his Harley-Davidson. Handsome as sin—and if she ignored her hormones and listened to her brain—he was dangerous in a different way. He'd also said he'd speak with his father about his interest in buying Kebab Kitchen.

Anthony Citteroni gave her pause. She knew he owned the bicycle rental shop next to Kebab Kitchen, as well as a major linen supply company and private trash trucks throughout Ocean Crest. If the rumors were true, he had his fingers in everything.

"You make Mr. Citteroni sound ominous," Lucy said.

Paul glanced at the front entrance again as if the mobster was expected to stroll through the door. "Have you ever seen the guy?"

"No." The bike shop may be next to the restaurant, but Mr. Citteroni always had managers run the shop during the season. This year it was his son, Michael.

"I've written plenty of villains in my thrillers, and he would be a perfect one. You have to meet him for yourself," Paul said.

Lucy couldn't agree more. She rummaged through her purse for her business card and a pen. She scribbled out her former law firm's phone number and wrote her cell phone number above it. "If you think of anything else, will you please call me?"

"Sure. But there's nothing else to tell." Paul said.

Lucy wasn't convinced. "Just in case. By the way, good luck with the book."

* * *

"What do you think? Do you believe Paul?" Katie asked.

Lucy pulled her car into Katie's driveway and put it in PARK. She'd already told Katie about the calendar reminder she'd seen on Paul's cell phone. "No. He's lied to us before and the only reason he told the police about Heather's gambling debt was because we leaked that tidbit to Bill. Also, Paul didn't mention the twenty grand of his money she spent. I think he's holding back information."

"From the police, too, it seems."

"Paul was acting funny. He kept glancing at the front door as if he expected Heather's ghost to walk inside."

"Hmm. That would make for some entertaining news in Ocean Crest. Stan Slade of the *Town News* would be in his element."

"The more I think about it, Paul could easily have poisoned Heather. He admitted to seeing her during her shift the day she died. Maybe he slipped cyanide into one of her iced teas or offered her a poisoned beverage?"

"It's a solid theory," Katie said.

"His meeting tonight at ten offers a good opportunity. I'm going to follow him."

"A stakeout?" Katie asked.

"I guess you can call it that. I want to know who he's meeting. He's our primary suspect so far."

"I'm in. Sounds exciting," Katie said.

They got out of the car, and Katie was opening her mailbox just as the unmistakable rumble of a motorcycle sounded down the street.

A shiny Harley-Davidson and a black leather-clad figure came into view. Lucy's pulse leaped as he turned into Katie's driveway.

Michael Citteroni removed his helmet and hung it on the handlebars. He was a bad boy personified with his leather jacket, black jeans, and motorcycle. His blue eyes were vivid in the afternoon sunlight. He grinned at Lucy.

"Well, well," Katie drawled. "Aren't you full of surprises, Lucy? I'll leave you alone with the biker hunk."

Lucy rolled her eyes as Katie went into the house.

Michael walked forward and stopped before her. "Hey, Lucy. I've come as promised."

"You spoke with your father about the restaurant?"

"Sure did. Are you free tomorrow? There's no better time to go for a ride than a pleasant Jersey shore evening."

She eyed the motorcycle warily. "You're not going to tell me anything unless I agree to get on that black beast of yours, are you?"

"Nope."

Lucy laughed. She should be annoyed, but she couldn't muster any anger. She couldn't figure out why he was so damned persistent that she ride on his motorcycle with him when he was good-looking enough to have girls fight for the chance.

"All right," she agreed.

"Great. I'll pick you up at seven tomorrow."

He turned to leave, then stopped to look back at her. "Oh, and wear jeans. You're gonna love it."

CHAPTER 15

"I've always wanted to go on a stakeout," Katie said.

They were parked in Lucy's car at the bottom of Paul Evans' driveway. The lights from the fountain on the lawn cast the nude mermaids in an eerie white glow. Smaller lights illuminated the Roman statues of gods and goddesses scattered across the grass. The front room was lit and Paul's shadow crossed the large bay window.

"It looks like after hours at a gaudy museum," Lucy said.

Katie chuckled. "Maybe we should knock on the front door. We know he's home."

"What do we say? We know you're a liar and we're watching you to see who you're meeting and what you're up to?"

"You're right. That imbecile Clemmons should be conducting a surveillance of Paul tonight, not us. We should get paid for doing his job," Katie said.

Lucy's brow furrowed as she glanced at Katie. "Don't forget we're not to engage, okay? Even if it turns out to be a woman visiting Paul and we see them strip and get sweaty, we're not to confront him."

"We should be so lucky. If he did have a secret lover, it might explain why he'd want Heather out of the way. She was clingy when we saw them together at Mac's Pub, and she struck me as the jealous type."

It was close to nine o'clock and the text message she'd read had said Paul was meeting someone at ten. Lucy wanted to be early just in case Paul's meeting wasn't at his house and he planned to leave. It could easily be a long night.

She yawned. Her day had started early at the restaurant preparing baklava with her mother. Thankfully, Emma, and Sally had taken over the dinner shift tonight. "I brought sustenance." She handed Katie a Styrofoam cup of coffee from Lola's Coffee Shop. "It's black, just the way you like it."

Katie cradled the cup in both hands. "You're a good friend."

Lucy was yawning again forty-five minutes later when one of the three garage doors opened. "Katie." She nudged Katie just as a white BMW backed out of the driveway. She caught a glimpse of Paul in the driver's seat.

"What now?" Katie asked.

"We follow."

Lucy stayed three car lengths behind as the BMW drove down Ocean Avenue.

"Don't let him see us," Katie whispered as if Paul could hear.

Lucy wrinkled her nose. "I know."

It wasn't as easy at it looked in the movies. Paul turned down no fewer than four different streets, and Lucy's fingers tightened on the steering wheel as her eyes were glued to the BMW.

"Don't lose him."

"I'm trying not to, but I don't want to be obvious about it either."

Fifteen minutes later, the BMW pulled into a parking lot of a strip mall. Only one shop was open and the sign was lit.

"Ultimate Massage Parlor?" Katie read out loud.

They watched as Paul hurried into the building and the door closed behind him.

"Who would get a massage this late at night?" Lucy asked.

"No one. These places aren't legit. They're known for a different type of massage for their male clients," Katie said.

It took a second before the meaning of Katie's words registered. "Ugh. So Paul was cheating on Heather with a hooker posing as a masseuse?"

"Maybe she found out and threatened to spill. It could tarnish Paul's career as a respected *New York Times* novelist. His fans wouldn't like it," Katie said.

"If Heather's addiction was gambling, maybe Paul's was paying for sex in dirty massage parlors," Lucy said.

"I wonder what an ultimate massage includes."

"Ewww. Please stop."

"Do we wait until he's finished and keep following him?" Katie asked.

Lucy was contemplating the same thing when Paul stepped out of the massage parlor. "That was fast."

"Too fast for a massage," Katie said.

Stuffing his hands in his coat pockets, Paul lowered his head as he walked around the storefront, turned the corner, and then disappeared into the alley between buildings.

Katie leaned forward in her seat. "Where's he going?"

"I don't know, but we're going to find out." Lucy opened the car door.

Katie grasped her arm. "Wait! You're going to try to get close enough to eavesdrop?"

"Yes."

Alarm crossed Katie's features. "It could be dangerous. We don't know who Paul's meeting in a dark alley this late at night."

It was the first time Lucy had seen Katie express any type of hesitation or anxiety about their investigative efforts so far.

"You're right," Lucy said. "You stay here. I'll go."

Katie swallowed, then shook her head. "No. I'll come, too."

"You sure?"

"Not really. But you may need backup."

Lucy wasn't sure how much backup Katie could provide, but she stayed silent. Together they crossed the street and crept along the side of the building toward the alley.

They made it to the entrance of the alley without being seen. The streetlights were bright enough to illuminate a third of the way down the alley, and Lucy could see Paul pacing.

The side door opened into the alley, casting a beam of light on the blacktop. A man in dark clothing stepped out. For a brief moment before the door closed, she made out that he had a goatee and was in his early-thirties. A swath of tawny hair fell casually on his forehead. His expression was grim.

"What's going on?" Katie whispered.

The man's fair hair gleamed in the fluorescent light a moment before the door closed and he was cast in shadows. Gathering her courage, Lucy peeked down the alley. She couldn't hear a thing. She needed to get closer.

She scanned the alley. The Dumpster offered a place to hide in the shadows if they could make it that far without alerting the men to their presence. Lucy motioned with her hand, and Katie's eyes widened in fear, but she nodded to let Lucy know she'd understood.

Heart pounding, Lucy sprinted into the alley. Katie was right behind her.

Lucy resisted gagging as they were forced to plaster their backs to the Dumpster, their breathing ragged. The stench of rotten eggs and garbage filled the air around them.

Crouching low, Lucy shifted forward and peered

from around the Dumpster. Katie glimpsed over her shoulder. Lucy recognized Paul Evans, but the second man remained cast in eerie shadows. A shiver prickled up her spine.

"Who is he?" Katie whispered.

Lucy shook her head.

"You're late again." The strange man's gravelly voice shot through the clear night air and made Lucy jump.

"I'm grieving. Heather's dead," Paul said.

"I've heard. You should be grateful. That broad caused you a lot of trouble."

"How can you say that about her? You're a bastard."

Hoarse laughter. "I've been called worse. But you're not off the hook, remember? Mr. C wants his cash."

"Your boss could just let it go," Paul said, a note of whining in his voice.

"Why would he do that?"

"He doesn't need the money."

"You're right. Mr. C doesn't. But being generous is not how he got to where his is."

Were they talking about Mr. Citteroni? Was the man Paul was meeting one of Mr. Citteroni's henchmen? Lucy recalled what Paul had said about the mobster and a tremor of unease slid down her spine. Shuffling forward, she tried to get a better view. Despite the cool evening, sweat trickled down her brow.

"You're no better than the bully you work for," Paul said.

Crude laughter again. "Don't be a hypocrite. You're not as upstanding as you'd like others to believe, are you, Mr. Evans? You knew about her gambling all along. I'd know better than to stay with that broad."

Paul took a step back and turned. In the dim lighting, Lucy saw him flinch. He withdrew an envelope from his jacket pocket and tossed it to the man. "Here. Take it."

The man opened the envelope, glimpsed inside, and gave a terse nod. "This is good for now. Now get out of here."

Lucy panicked. She'd wanted to get close enough to hear, but she never considered how she was going to leave undetected. She turned to Katie and saw similar alarm reflected in her eyes. If Paul passed them on his way out of the alley, he would spot them.

Just as Lucy was going to signal they make a run for it, Katie snatched a rusted can from the ground and tossed it far into the alley. It landed with cacophony of noise in the silent night and bounced several times.

"What the hell was that?" the man snapped.

"Sounded like an animal knocked something over. Maybe a cat or rats?" Paul said.

Lucy and Katie didn't hesitate. Scrambling from behind the Dumpster, they sprinted to the street and ducked behind a parked car. Hearts pounding, they waited.

After a minute passed, Katie whispered, "It worked. I don't think they saw us."

Moments later, Paul emerged from the alley and climbed back into his white BMW.

Lucy let out a held-in breath. "We did it."

"Thank God. It scared the crap out of me," Katie said.

"You thought fast on your feet back there," Lucy pointed out.

Katie blinked. "I did, didn't I?"

"Let's get out of here before that man comes out of the massage parlor or anyone else spots us."

They made it to their car and drove back to Katie's house. Lucy collapsed on a kitchen chair while Katie rummaged through the cabinets. She returned with a victorious smile and bag of chocolate chip cookies.

"I can think of nothing better to calm ourselves with than junk food." Katie opened the bag. "Who do you think that man was?"

Lucy reached for a cookie. It was crisp and chocolatey and was just what she needed after their harrowing escape. "He called his boss Mr. C. It has to be Mr. Citteroni."

Katie munched on a cookie and spoke with her mouth full. "What do you think was in the envelope Paul gave him?"

"Money. Probably to pay off Heather's gambling debts," Lucy said.

Katie swallowed. "You're probably right. Paul is hiding information from the police. And you know what the police say about suspects who continuously lie—they're most likely guilty of the crime."

At precisely seven the following evening, Michael Citteroni knocked on the door.

Lucy stepped onto the porch and eyed the Harley-Davidson warily. "I'm still not sure this is a good idea."

He took her elbow and led her to the bike. "There's nothing to it. You sit, hold on, and I'll do the driving."

It would help if he wasn't so attractive. His wavy, dark hair brushed the collar of his worn leather jacket and his blue eyes were fringed with thick lashes that any woman would envy.

She felt a stirring of guilt after being locked in a walk-in refrigerator with Azad yesterday and sharing his body heat.

Ridiculous.

She didn't owe either man her loyalty. Azad may want to be more than friends, but Lucy wasn't convinced. Although she had her doubts that he was capable of murder, she couldn't dismiss the obvious. He had motive and opportunity. As for Michael Citteroni, he may ooze sex appeal and portray the enticing bad boy motorcycle image that had lured plenty of good girls to their doom, but the only reason Lucy had agreed to meet him tonight was to glean some information about his father's true interest in her family's restaurant.

And after the adventurous stakeout last night, she wanted to learn about Michael's father.

Michael held out a black helmet. The side was inscribed with a scull and crossbones. "This is yours." When she didn't immediately reach for it, he placed the helmet on her head and fastened it under her chin. He sat on the bike. "Ready?"

Lucy took a breath, then climbed on the seat behind him. She'd waitressed for most of the day, and had changed from her uniform to a pair of jeans and boots.

"You're going to love this," he said. "There's nothing like your first ride. Now hold on tight."

Uncomfortable with touching him, her fingers brushed both sides of his jacket. The leather creaked as he gripped the wide handlebars, then the engine roared to life beneath her like a powerful beast.

Lucy's heart thudded as they rode down Ocean Avenue toward the Atlantic City Expressway. Soon they were on the highway and picking up speed. She forgot all about comfort and plastered herself to his back and held on for dear life as he sped down the highway in what felt like breathtaking speed.

She knew they weren't going much over the speed limit gauging by the few cars that were on the road, but it felt like she was flying. After a few minutes, she got the nerve to open her eyes, lift her head, and took in her surroundings. He was right.

It was *exhilarating*.

The wind, the road, the scent of the ocean, the power of the engine all combined in an unforgettable experience. She felt a sense of freedom she'd never quite experienced before, and she wanted it to last. Her overheated skin cooled from the rush of air, and she loosened her death-grip from around his waist.

Too soon Michael turned back. The bike slowed as they reached Ocean Avenue. He passed Katie's street and stopped the bike by a ramp that led to the boardwalk. After dismounting and removing their helmets, his blue gaze studied her.

"Well?" he asked.

Lucy felt a little breathless. "Thank you. It was fantastic."

The corner of his lips curled in a knowing grin. "I knew I could turn your opinion around."

They started up the ramp and soon were on the boardwalk. Lucy breathed in the salty ocean air. Several of the shops had opened early for the season and Michael bought her an ice cream cone. They enjoyed their cones as seagulls squawked and circled overhead. It was low tide and the steady, rhythmic pounding of waves on shore was calming. Lights from ships far out to sea blinked on the horizon, and the deep call of a foghorn sounded from afar.

"I held up my part of our bargain. Now it's your turn," Lucy said as she licked her ice cream.

"You were right. My father wants to buy the

restaurant, but not for the business. He wants to tear down the building and expand the bike shop."

Lucy lowered her cone. *Tear down Kebab Kitchen?* She experienced a mix of perplexing emotions. Would her parents allow such a thing? She'd rather sell to Azad or even the prospective buyer her parents had mentioned on her first day back, who wanted to turn it into another Jersey diner. The restaurant had so much meaning to all of them.

To her.

Damn. When had that happened?

She'd spent years in Philadelphia, working at the firm and trying to distance herself from the family business. After only ten days home, she found herself more emotionally invested than ever before. The nagging was back. Just like when she'd been baking with Azad, the uncomfortable feeling centered in her chest.

She didn't want to see the place go. But if her parents wanted to retire and Emma and Max didn't want it, then it was up to her to take over.

Could she do it?

Could she stay in Ocean Crest and give up her future practicing law?

"From your expression, I take it you think this is bad news?"

Lucy's gaze snapped back to Michael. "It's just that . . . I don't know if . . ." She took a deep breath. "My parents were under the impression Mr. Citteroni wanted to convert Kebab Kitchen to a high class Italian place. I don't think they would sell it knowing it would be torn down."

I don't think I'd want them to.

Maybe she was wrong. Maybe her parents were tired and wouldn't care if their labor of love of thirty years was bulldozed to the ground?

"No, my dad was pretty clear when we talked," Michael said. "He's only interested in the property."

She felt a trickle of annoyance and wanted to argue, but held her tongue. Michael had done her a favor by being truthful. She may not like what she'd heard, but it wasn't his fault. "Thanks for telling me."

"You're welcome. He's not the easiest parent to talk to."

"I'm sorry." She wondered what it would be like to have a father like Mr. Citteroni. From what Lucy had heard ever since she was a kid, he was a gangster. Last night's spying episode in the dark alley didn't change her opinion. She had no desire to appear on Mr. Citteroni's radar. "What about your siblings?"

"I have one younger sister. Teresa and I are opposites. She idolizes my father and takes after him. She involves herself in his business enterprises as much as he'll allow her."

Lucy was getting the picture. Michael was different, wanted to be different. "What about your mom?"

"She died when I was a teenager. They never got along. My dad has a temper, and my mom learned to stay away from him. I never blamed her. Most grown men are apprehensive around him."

Lucy wondered if poor Mrs. Citteroni and a young Michael had born the brunt of his father's temper while the younger Teresa escaped his wrath. "Why did you agree to run the bicycle shop for your father this summer?"

His face shuttered. "He's not easy to say no to, but for different reasons now. I'm no longer afraid of him, but the truth is, he knows how to elicit family guilt."

"Hey, if it's any consolation, my dad's not easy to say no to either." She recalled when her father had asked her to step up and help the family business by waitressing on her first day back. Raffi Berberian could be just as manipulative when he truly wanted something.

"Then we have something else in common. Hot-blooded and hotheaded ethnic families."

"I guess you can say that."

"I like you, Lucy. You're easy to talk to."

Michael Citteroni may be handsome enough to make most women swoon, but Lucy felt kinship blossom between them. He got up to throw away his ice cream cone in a nearby trashcan.

"Hey! You shouldn't throw that out. The end of an ice cream cone is the best part."

"Sorry," he chuckled. "I don't want to get ice cream on this fine leather jacket."

Lucy rolled her eyes. "Then hand it over."

They settled on a bench facing the ocean and

chatted for another hour. Soon it was dark, and he stood and offered his arm. "Are you ready to go home?"

As he walked her to the ramp leading off the boardwalk, moonlight illuminated the single pier with the Ferris wheel and old-fashioned wooden roller coaster. "Too bad the pier isn't open yet. We could have ridden the coaster."

"I used to love that coaster. It reminds me of my high school dates," Lucy said.

"Sorry. You'll just have to be content with a ride on a Harley."

"You converted me. I just may buy my own motorcycle."

It was his turn to roll his eyes. "Heaven forbid. Just don't buy one with more horsepower than mine. I don't think I could live *that* down."

CHAPTER 16

Lucy slowed from a jog to a brisk walk on the beach. She swept the sand off the stone of a jetty overlooking the Atlantic Ocean and sat. A breeze cooled her heated cheeks and blew stray wisps of hair that had escaped from her ponytail. The ocean was calm this morning, and sunlight glistened off the sparkling surface like glittering diamonds. In the distance, two sailboats coasted along. She spotted a seashell, picked it up, and held it to her ear. The distant sounds of waves pounding against the shore echoed in her ear. Lowering the shell, she breathed in the ocean air.

The magnificent view was tranquil and so vast it made her feel insignificant in the scope of the universe. It was easy for someone to forget all their troubles.

She sighed. If only she *could* forget. But Heather's murder could not easily be ignored. The family business had already suffered consequences and lost customers. Calvin Clemmons considered her a prime suspect and Stan Slade could put another nail in the coffin by printing a fantastic story in the *Town News* about a dead health inspector, a hummus bar, and a former high school rival turned killer.

If only she'd unearthed something useful . . . but the current list of suspects hadn't changed. She thought back to who had been in the restaurant the day Heather died.

Her parents were in their office working on payroll.

Butch was cooking. He had opportunity when he prepared the pita, but no motive. Clemmons had questioned him, and as far as Lucy knew, he wasn't a suspect. Plus, she had known him since she was in pigtails, and he was trusted by her parents.

Azad was in the dining room when Heather arrived, then he moved into the kitchen to talk with Big Al. Azad had motive *and* opportunity to slip something into the hummus bar. But would he go to such lengths, killing the food inspector in order to lower the value of the business so he could turn around and purchase it cheaply?

Big Al was in the kitchen. He had opportunity, but he did not even know the victim and had no motive. The police had questioned him, as well.

Guido Morelli and Mac McCabe both had motive for Heather's blackmail schemes, and they had opportunity to slip cyanide into her iced tea when she'd delivered inspection reports.

Paul Evans admitted to stopping by during her work shift to see Heather which meant he had opportunity. He'd held back information from the police about Heather's gambling addiction and that she'd gambled away an impressive chunk of his last royalties. Lucy wondered what else he was hiding. He was her prime suspect to date.

Anthony Citteroni was another possibility. Could he somehow be responsible? He may want the property, but he seemed an unlikely suspect. Michael said his father rarely visited the bike shop and the chances were slim that he'd been there the night Heather died.

Lucy stood and stretched her legs. Frustration roiled inside her. She was no closer to finding the killer.

Maybe she should shift her focus. Look at it from a different angle. Maybe she was overlooking the obvious. If she could figure out exactly *how* Heather was poisoned, then she would know *who* did it. Lucy suspected Heather's iced tea was laced with cyanide, but what if she was wrong? What it if was delivered differently?

After draining her water bottle, she decided to stop at the restaurant on her way back to Katie's home to get a refill.

Lucy was sweating again by the time she made it to Kebab Kitchen. Gadoo was eating from his food bowl outside by the back door and he looked up long enough to give her a welcoming *meow*. She made a mental note to buy more cat treats on her next visit to Holloway's.

As soon as Lucy stepped inside, Emma rushed to

her side, her face flushed. "Lucy, thank goodness you're here."

"What's wrong, Em?" Lucy set her water bottle on a table and turned to her sister.

"See for yourself," Emma said.

Lucy's fingers twisted by her side as her parents walked into the dining room alongside a slender woman with short cropped hair in a stylish bob, a classy beige suit, and respectable heels. She was clutching a briefcase. Even without the briefcase, Lucy recognized the very air around the woman— confidence and a touch of arrogance.

Perhaps it took one to know one—a fellow lawyer.

The hair on Lucy's nape rose on end. Why would her family meet with an attorney?

Lucy's mother rubbed her gold cross between her thumb and forefinger. Not a good sign. Her dad swiped a hand over his thinning pate. Another bad sign.

Her parents spotted her beside Emma and relief simultaneously crossed their faces.

"See," Emma muttered. "I knew they'd be happy to see you."

Lucy approached the trio who were standing by the hummus bar.

"Lucy, this is Ms. Marsha Walsh, the Ocean County Prosecutor," Raffi said before he motioned to Lucy. "And this is our younger daughter, Lucy Berberian."

The county prosecutor. Warning bells went off in

Lucy's head. If the prosecutor was in Ocean Crest, that meant Detective Clemmons had summoned her.

Her father touched her arm and his chest puffed a few inches in his button down shirt, "Lucy's a lawyer, as well."

Lucy knew her father didn't mean to put her in an awkward position. She also knew what her parents were thinking. They were intimidated by the prosecutor, and they believed if they pointed out Lucy had a law degree, Ms. Walsh would be more cautious around them.

Lucy forced her lips to curl in a smile. Dressed in sweaty running clothes and sandy sneakers, she felt anything but confident. Her stomach churned with anxiety.

Was the woman going to pull out an arrest warrant from her purse for murder or accuse her of meddling with an active police investigation?

Marsha Walsh's eyes were dark and unreadable. "Hello, Lucy. May we have a word in private?"

Lucy swallowed and assumed a look of ease she didn't feel. "Sure."

Her parents didn't move. Clearly they were torn about leaving her alone with the prosecutor.

"It's okay, Mom and Dad," Lucy said in her most reassuring voice.

Angela elbowed Raffi and they turned and disappeared into the kitchen. Emma trailed behind them.

Lucy and the prosecutor remained standing by the hummus bar.

Lucy motioned to a table. "Would you like to sit?"

"No, thank you. Right here's fine," Walsh said, glancing at the hummus bar where bins of different varieties of hummus awaited the lunch shift, then meeting Lucy's gaze straight on.

Lucy tried to swallow a lump that lingered in her throat.

Walsh folded her hands before her. "As your father pointed out, you're an attorney so I assume you know why I'm here."

If Lucy had a dime for every time someone assumed that just because she'd passed the bar she was an experienced police detective she'd be richer by now. "Not really, no. And I'm a patent attorney."

"I see. So I'll be sure to explain everything nice and simple." Walsh turned her attention to the bins of hummus. "I never knew there were so many varieties."

"I like to think of my mom as a culinary genius. She has over a dozen varieties of homemade hummus, although only eight are out at one time," Lucy said.

"I recently tried hummus for the first time. I was pleasantly surprised. I buy it at my supermarket."

What was Lucy to say to that? *That's nice. Good for you. Why are you staring at our hummus like you want to try it but you're afraid you'll die if you do?*

Walsh cleared her throat. "Detective Clemmons contacted my office. He believes Heather Banks' death is suspicious. Upon a brief review of the facts, my office agrees."

Lucy looked up at her with an effort. "I see. Has Clemmons made any progress then?"

Walsh held Lucy's gaze. "You mean have the police found the source of the suspected poison that resulted in Ms. Banks' death?"

If anything, the woman was blunt. "Well, yes."

"You and I both know nothing official can be announced until the toxicology results are in." The prosecutor pointed to one of the bins. "What variety is that?"

Lucy was having trouble keeping up with the woman. She glanced to where Walsh pointed. "That's sweet basil hummus."

"Sounds interesting. My supermarket doesn't carry it."

"Like I said, my mother comes up with her own varieties." Lucy gave an anxious cough. "If the tox results aren't back yet, why are we even speaking?"

Walsh raised an eyebrow. "Because you are a person of interest. Heather Banks died in the parking lot of your family's restaurant."

Lucy watched her warily. "Is that the only reason?

"Detective Clemmons told you the coroner suspècts cyanide poisoning as the cause of death," Walsh said.

Lucy raised her chin. "No one at Kebab Kitchen would poison anyone."

"But you served Heather Banks her last meal here, correct?"

Lucy shifted. She knew how bad *that* sounded. "You already know the facts."

"True."

The anticipation was killing Lucy. "If you had enough evidence, you would have made an arrest," Lucy challenged.

Walsh's eyes narrowed. "That's not something I'd talk to you about."

"What about my family's restaurant? Can you talk about that?"

"Let's just say if we wanted to shut the place down, we could do it overnight."

Was that a threat? "Will you?"

"Not yet."

Not yet. Lucy's fingers twisted at her sides. The prosecutor's words weren't very reassuring.

"What flavor is that one?" The woman pointed to another bin.

Lucy's brows snapped together. The woman was a complete mystery. One minute she's discussing how the victim ate at the restaurant and then died, and the next minute she's asking about the food.

"That's black bean hummus. No chick peas, but it still contains garlic, lemon, and tahini, which is sesame paste."

"Hmm. Interesting choice." Walsh turned back to Lucy. "We're aware you're residing with an Ocean Crest police officer and his wife."

Lucy blinked at the change in topic. What was the wily prosecutor's intent?

"Yes. I'm staying with Bill and Katie Watson," Lucy said.

Marsha Walsh pinned her with a hard glare. "You

wouldn't happen to be questioning people on your own about Ms. Banks' demise, would you?"

Trepidation coursed through Lucy. It was as if the woman could read her deepest secrets. "Of course not," she lied.

"Good thing. I wouldn't want to arrest you for obstruction of justice. And if I learn that Officer Watson has leaked pertinent information about an active investigation to you, that could result in ruining his career."

Good Lord. That was the last thing Lucy wanted. She already felt indebted to Bill. Harming his career would be devastating. Why couldn't Calvin Clemmons investigate other subjects like Paul Evans, Guido Morelli, or Mac McCabe to name a few? If the stubborn man would look past his long nose, maybe he could find the real killer.

The prosecutor leaned forward. "Am I being clear enough for you now, Ms. Berberian?"

Lucy met the woman's gaze straight on. "Yes."

"Good." Marsha Walsh reached into her jacket pocket and pulled out a business card. "If you need to speak to me."

Lucy took the proffered card with the raised county seal. Did the woman think she'd call her and confess?

"I'm glad we have an understanding." Walsh eyed Lucy and raised a finger. "Oh, and one more thing. I'd like a take-out container for the hummus bar."

* * *

As soon as the prosecutor left, Emma and their parents rushed out of the kitchen and bombarded Lucy with questions.

Lucy held up a hand. "All's fine." *For now,* she kept to herself. "The prosecutor is not shutting down Kebab Kitchen. It's business as usual. Just like we already knew, the police are waiting for the lab results before making any decisions."

Angela pinched her lower lip with her teeth. "Meanwhile, business is slow. Maybe that's what they really want. For us to close on our own."

Raffi's cheek muscles stood out when he clenched his jaw. "I don't like it. That woman makes me nervous."

"The prosecutor loaded a take-out container with hummus from the hummus bar," Emma said. "She must not think it's poisoned."

"Or she doesn't think it's poisoned any longer," Angela said.

"Let's not overreact," Lucy said. "It could have been worse. Let's be grateful the restaurant stays open."

That seemed to pacify her parents, and they went back to their office, leaving Lucy alone with Emma.

"Did you tell Mom and Dad the truth?" Emma asked.

"I did. Marsha Walsh isn't planning on shutting down the place any time soon."

Emma threw a dishtowel on the counter of the

waitress station. "The thing is, maybe it's best if we did close."

Lucy glared at her sister. "Good grief, Em. How could you say such a thing?"

"We've all had it with the business. Mom and Dad are exhausted from working nights and weekends. Combined with diminishing profit margins and increasing overhead and the rising cost of inventory, the restaurant business is one of the toughest around. Maybe this is an omen and the push our parents need to let the business go."

Lucy blinked in surprise. "You can't mean that." The time back home had truly changed her point of view. The business was in her blood, in *all* of their blood. She couldn't imagine her parents fully retired. They just needed someone else to take over and then they could cut their work hours.

The only chance her parents had to keep the place in the family was if she stayed and saw it through. Was that something she wanted to do?

"I'm quite serious about this," Emma said. "When Mom and Dad announced they wanted to sell, I wasn't opposed to it. Max feels the same way."

"But you're the dutiful daughter who stayed behind, married a town resident, and popped out a kid. You're the one who has always worked here."

"That's just it. I've stayed and it gives me a perspective different from yours."

It hit Lucy then. "You're bitter I left, aren't you? If I had married Azad all those years ago, I'd be here alongside you."

"I won't lie and say I wasn't bitter. You had an exciting life in Philadelphia making good money. I never pursued a career. But lately I'm fortunate for the way things worked out. You wouldn't have the worldly experience you do now. You wouldn't be able to help us by investigating Heather's murder."

Lucy was flattered, but then logic took over. "I'm not sure how much help I am, Em."

"If anyone can crack this case, you can," Emma said. "I know Calvin Clemmons has a grudge against me. I didn't exactly treat him nicely back in high school."

"It's not your fault. He should be unbiased in his duties," Lucy said.

Emma hugged Lucy. "Well, Max and I are glad you're back. And not just because we need you after what happened to Heather. So many people are happy that you're back. Sally, Katie and Bill, Mom, Dad, and Azad. Even Susie Cutie and Lola Stewart told me they're excited that you're here."

"Thanks." Her sister's words struck her. Since returning home, Lucy realized she had more friends in town than she'd made in all the years she'd worked in Philadelphia.

Maybe Ocean Crest wasn't so bad after all.

CHAPTER 17

"Mind if we both leave early tonight? Niari is at a sleepover party and Max and I are going out," Emma said as she tallied a check for a party of two sitting at a cozy table.

"And it's my bowling night," Sally added as she untied her waitress apron.

Lucy waved a hand. "No problem. You two have fun."

The three of them had worked the dinner shift together, and Lucy was glad to help out by staying until closing. Since she had no husband or children—as her mother was fond of pointing out—and no other social plans for the night, she didn't mind. For obvious reasons, Kebab Kitchen had been slow. She could easily handle the rest of the evening as the sole waitress.

"Thanks bunches," Emma said as she kissed Lucy's cheek and sailed out the door with Sally.

Lucy waited on a couple of stray customers, then cleaned up the waitress station and prepared the tables with white linen tablecloths, matching napkins, and flatware for the next day before wandering into the kitchen to find Butch.

He was busy chopping tomatoes, cucumbers, parsley, and scallions for tabbouleh salad, and the fragrant scent of the herbs filled the kitchen. She took off her apron and hung it on the row of hooks in the kitchen. "I locked the front door and finished cleaning up. Will I see you tomorrow?"

Butch smiled and his gold tooth flashed in the fluorescent kitchen lighting. "You bet. Good night, Lucy Lou."

"I'll take the trash on my way out." Lucy opened the back door and stepped into the parking lot. Clouds passing over the moon cast the parking lot and the Dumpster in shadows. She looked around for Gadoo, but didn't see the calico cat anywhere. His water bowl was full, but he'd eaten whatever her mother had set out for him. She took a few steps forward, then halted.

For a heart-stopping moment, she experienced déjà vu. She'd been in the process of carrying out the exact same task—dragging a trash bag to the Dumpster—when she'd tripped over Heather's body. She vividly recalled Heather's sprawled limbs and her red hair spread out across the asphalt like blood.

Gooseflesh rose on Lucy's arms.

Don't be such a ninny.

Lucy heaved the trash bag across her shoulder and marched toward the Dumpster. Halfway across the parking lot, a dark figure stepped into her path. Lucy dropped the bag and screeched.

The figure stepped forward into a swath of moonlight to reveal a short, stocky man dressed in a black trench coat. His head rested directly upon his shoulders, giving a no-neck appearance. He had a square wall of a forehead with heavy brows, black eyes, dark hair, and a thin, carefully clipped mustache.

"I didn't mean to scare you," the man said in a deep, gravelly voice.

"Who are you?" Lucy demanded.

"My name is Anthony Citteroni. I own the business next door."

Good grief. This was the mobster? Lucy scanned the parking lot. She could understand why Paul Evans feared him.

"I assume you are Lucy Berberian?"

"Yes."

"My apologies again if I frightened you."

Sure. That was probably what he said to all his friends before he gunned them down. Did he know she had followed Paul Evans? Or that she'd witnessed Paul hand over a fat envelope of cash to the young, tall henchman who worked for Mr. Citteroni?

Jeeze. She hoped not.

"I heard a tragedy happened here . . . to the health inspector. I was at my bike shop next door. I would have helped if I'd known."

His words piqued Lucy's curiosity. "You were? Did you hear anything?" She wasn't aware that Anthony Citteroni had been next door the day

Heather died. Michael hadn't mentioned it. Maybe he didn't know. But if Mr. Citteroni had been so close, couldn't he have slipped inside the back door and somehow poisoned the hummus bar or Heather's iced tea?

He certainly had opportunity and his motive would be the same as Azad's. Both men wanted to buy the property and the business, but for different reasons. One wanted to keep it a Mediterranean restaurant, the other wanted to tear it down and make a glorified parking lot.

But would the mobster go to such lengths to get the property?

Or was she being paranoid?

"It's been a while since I've seen your parents." Citteroni shook his head. "I'm sure the health inspector's death is the last thing they need."

What was that supposed to mean? "You know my parents?"

"We used to talk often. We are neighbors."

Her parents had never mentioned any type of friendship with Anthony Citteroni. From what Lucy understood, he didn't visit his property often, and he certainly didn't participate in the day-to-day running of the business.

So why was he talking to her in the dim back parking lot? "Is there something I can help you with, Mr. Citteroni?"

"My son, Michael, told me about you. It's a pleasure to finally meet you, Lucy." He extended his hand.

Lucy swallowed as she glanced down at his

proffered hand. The fact that Michael had spoken about her to his father was as unexpected as Anthony's Citteroni's appearance. She watched him warily as she shook his hand. It was firm as it engulfed hers.

"My son says you are a charming lady. He doesn't speak favorably of many women. I had to see for myself who had captured his interest."

"We are just friends." Her nerves tensed. She didn't want the man to think her relationship with Michael was serious.

"My son is turning thirty-five next week. I'm having a surprise birthday party for him in Cape May tomorrow night. I'd like you to attend."

It was more of a statement then an invitation. If her nerves hadn't been strained she might have made an excuse. But she considered Michael a friend—and his father was a bit frightening—so she agreed. "Thank you for the invitation."

He nodded once as if her acquiescence had been expected.

"Eight o'clock. Black tie affair. I'll have an invitation sent with the address."

"I'm looking forward to it," Lucy said.

He turned to leave by the opening of the fence that led to the small patch of sidewalk separating the restaurant from the bike shop. Lucy exhaled, but her relief was short-lived when Mr. Citteroni halted and looked back at her. "Don't forget it's a surprise party." He grinned. "Michael may try to ask you, but I trust you'll keep it secret. After all, I know everything that happens in this town."

Lucy let out a held-in breath when he was out of view. She headed toward her car where she planned to lock the doors before starting the engine. A meow sounded as soon as she reached for the car door handle.

Gadoo sauntered past.

"Now you show up. Some guard cat you are."

Gadoo blinked.

She picked up the cat, held him close, and buried her fingers in his soft fur. The tension in her shoulders eased a notch. Mr. Citteroni had invited her to his son's party, but she couldn't help but wonder if his ominous farewell warning was the true purpose behind his visit.

"You're going to want to see this," Katie said, handing Lucy the newspaper the following morning.

Lucy choked on her coffee as she glanced at the front page of the *Ocean Crest Town News*. The headline jumped off the page. COUNTY PROSECUTOR DECLARES DEATH OF HEALTH INSPECTOR SUSPICIOUS. A large picture of Kebab Kitchen was right below the article. Her gaze homed in on the first paragraph.

> Heather Banks, Ocean Crest's new health inspector, eats her last meal and dies at local restaurant. Bad food? Bad service? Or both. It was all a killer to Ms. Banks.

Lucy crumpled the paper in her hands. The article cinched the noose around her family's neck as neatly as if the prosecutor had shut down the restaurant herself. Business had already been slow and now it would be dead. Even her mother's catering business could be affected.

Anger simmered in Lucy's veins. She felt like a volcano on the verge of erupting. "I can't believe this! Stan Slade went too far."

"I agree," Katie said. "The police haven't officially said anything about poisoning or cause of death. All they said on record was that it's a suspicious death."

"Stan Slade filled in the gaps. A picture is worth a thousand words. Everyone will assume it was from the food at Kebab Kitchen." The slimy reporter had told her that he'd wait before printing anything in exchange for an exclusive interview. Apparently, the prosecutor's announcement had voided their agreement. "This is nothing but Slade's attempt to sell papers. I'm not a murderer, but he may turn me into one."

Katie's eyes widened. "What are you going to do?"

Lucy reached for her car keys. "Have words with him."

"In person?"

"I can't think of a better way." Lucy headed to the door. "At least I want to know what else he has planned."

Lucy got in her car and drove to her destination. Her anger grew with each passing block. Ten minutes later, she walked into the office of the *Town News*. "I want to see Stan Slade."

A young Asian woman sat behind the receptionist desk. "Do you have an appointment?"

"Yes," Lucy lied. "My name is Lucy Berberian, and he wants an exclusive interview with me."

The woman pointed down the hallway. "Stan's office is third from the left."

Lucy thanked the lady and marched down the hall until she spotted the plaque with Stan's name outside one of the offices. She didn't bother to knock.

The door hit the wall with a loud bang. Stan looked up from his desk where he was holding a cigarette in one hand and typing on a computer keyboard with the other. His eyes widened behind his black-rimmed glasses.

"You call this reporting?" She waved the paper madly in the air.

Stan placed his cigarette in an ashtray and stood. He seemed even more stocky and muscular than the first time she'd seen him. "Lucy, what a pleasant surprise."

She stalked forward and felt a glimmer of satisfaction when he tensed. She tossed the crumpled newspaper on his desk. "This is nothing but cheesy tabloid reporting."

"Untrue. I printed only the facts."

"The facts! You know damned well this article is only ten percent truthful at best."

He snorted. "Seventy-five at least."

She quoted the damaging lines out loud. "'Bad food? Bad service? Or both. It was all a killer to Ms. Banks.'" Lucy glared at him. "That plus an enormous picture of Kebab Kitchen on the front page is downright dirty reporting if you ask me. You know everyone will link the prosecutor calling it a suspicious death to the food Heather Banks ate at Kebab Kitchen. It's slanderous and I'm going to sue—"

"Don't be ridiculous." He smirked. "You'd never win. It's freedom of the press."

She wanted to wrap her hands around his thick neck and squeeze. "You're completely untrustworthy. You told me you'd wait a few days in exchange for an exclusive interview."

"That was before the prosecutor went on record and called Banks' death suspicious."

"You went farther than the prosecutor. You insinuated she died from something she ate at the restaurant."

He reached for his cigarette. "So? She did, didn't she?"

"No! You need to wait for the toxicology results before you can put that in black and white." Business was already slow. She didn't want to guess how much worse this article would make it. She prayed her parents didn't read the paper.

The cigarette dangled from one side of his mouth, the smoke curling across his face. "How about that exclusive now? You can point out all the reasons why Heather didn't die from the food."

"You've got nerve!"

"My article didn't mention you by name as serving Ms. Banks' last meal. Maybe my next one will."

"And you were a former New York City investigative reporter? Did you leave of your own free will or were you fired?"

His eyes narrowed to slits. "What's that supposed to mean?"

"You're overlooking the obvious," Lucy snapped.

"It can't get more obvious to me. Heather ate at Kebab Kitchen. You served her. Heather died."

"You never bothered to look at other suspects, did you?"

His arrogance slipped for a second, but it was enough to give Lucy hope. "There are other people who will gain from Heather's death. Did you know she had a gambling problem and that she blew a large chunk of her boyfriend's last royalty paycheck?"

"The writer, Paul Evans?" Stan asked.

Lucy took a step forward. "Have you looked into him?"

Stan picked up a pen and pad of paper on his desk. "I'm listening. Who else?"

Prosecutor Walsh's warning not to get involved in the murder investigation pierced Lucy's haze of anger. *Watch your mouth, Lucy!*

Stan Slade couldn't be trusted.

She could cause more harm than good with loose lips around him. "That's enough, isn't it? I would hope any reporter worth his salt would follow up on *every* lead."

Stan tossed down his pencil and the smugness returned to his beady eyes. "Well, if that's the only lead you can offer and you're not prepared to give me an exclusive interview, I must get back to work."

Lucy stormed out of his office and headed straight for her car when her cell phone rang. She dug into her purse and glanced at the screen to see Emma's name. "Hello?"

"Lucy! Thank God you answered."

"What's wrong?"

"It's Dad. He's having chest pains and we called the ambulance. Come quick. He's at the hospital."

The emergency room of the Ocean Crest Medical Center smelled of antiseptic and bleach. Rows of examination rooms were divided by curtains and the constant sounds of machines beeping and humming accompanied the voices of doctors and nurses as they rushed from patient to patient. Lucy hurried down the hospital corridor to see Emma, Max, Butch, and even Sally huddled in the hallway outside a curtained partition.

"What happened?" Lucy asked.

"We're not sure yet. They won't let us all in the room at one time. We're taking turns. Angela's with him right now," Max said.

"They'll let two in at one time. You go in with Mom, Lucy," Emma said.

Lucy didn't waste a second. She pulled back the curtain to find her mother sitting by a hospital bed. "Oh my gosh. How is he?" Lucy went to the bedside and clutched her father's hand, careful of the IV line in his vein.

"I'm fine now. I keep telling them I want to go home." Her father didn't look sick. He looked mad.

Angela's lips pursed. "Stubborn as ever! Your father grabbed his chest and had difficulty breathing. He didn't want us to call the ambulance, but of course we did anyway. We're waiting for the doctors."

To her mother's exasperation, Raffi Berberian hadn't been to the doctor in over ten years. Stubborn was too nice a word to describe her father when it came to doctors. He had an Old World view and had often said the hospital was a place to die, not to get better. Lucy could just picture the struggle when Emma and her mother had called the ambulance.

The curtain parted and a doctor in blue scrubs with gray hair and a slight limp entered the room.

Angela jumped to her feet.

"What can you tell us?" Lucy asked.

"After numerous tests and blood work results, we believe it wasn't Mr. Berberian's heart, but rather that he suffered a panic attack."

"A panic attack? But he was having chest pains," Angela said.

"Heart attacks and panic attacks can feel frighteningly similar," the doctor said. "Both can exhibit symptoms of chest pain, heart palpitations, shortness of breath, dizziness, sweating, fainting, and numbness of hands and feet."

Angela let out a held-in breath and sat back in her chair. "Thank the Lord that's all it was."

Lucy stared in surprise. "But why would he have a panic attack? What would cause it?"

Her mother sniffled. "It started after he saw this morning's newspaper."

Raffi struggled to sit. "That imbecile. He prints lies. All lies. Business is already bad, and now it will be worse."

Anxiety coursed through Lucy. She'd just left Stan Slade's office, but she wanted to go back and scream at him anew.

The doctor placed a hand on her father's shoulder. "Lie down, Mr. Berberian. No sense getting upset. You'll set off the monitors."

"I feel fine now," Raffi insisted. "How soon before I can go home?"

"A nurse will arrive to go over your discharge instructions. You can go home soon after. But if anything else happens, chest pains or shortness of breath, you have to come back in, all right?" the doctor said.

"Fine."

The doctor turned to Lucy and her mother. "His cholesterol is high, and we're prescribing a medication to lower it." He tore off a sheet from his prescription pad and held it out. "See that he takes this twice a day with meals."

Lucy took the prescription from the doctor

before her mother had a chance to reach for it. "I'll fill this at the pharmacy and deliver it to you. You have enough to worry about."

As soon as the doctor left, everyone else filed into the examination room. Relief was evident on all their faces when they learned he'd be going home.

As Lucy watched everyone huddled around her father, an emotion tightened in her chest. For years, she'd purposely lived away. She'd helped her clients with their legal issues when her own family needed her help. She couldn't change the past and deep down she knew she didn't want to. Her experiences away made her the person she was today, and that wisdom was not something she'd have had if she'd married Azad straight out of college, skipped law school, and stayed at the restaurant. But now that she was back home her goals had somehow changed. She no longer felt a burning desire to find another law firm job quickly and leave Ocean Crest and the restaurant. She'd found another purpose, to help those most important to her—her family and her friends.

Maybe . . . just maybe Kebab Kitchen wasn't something to flee from, but something to fight to hold on to.

"Lucy!"

Lucy halted in the hospital parking garage and turned to see Sally waving from the end of the aisle. Sally's long legs quickly closed the distance between them.

"Is everything all right?" Lucy asked. She'd just left her parents after receiving discharge instructions from the nurse. Her mother insisted on driving her father home.

Sally adjusted the strap of her handbag on her shoulder. "Don't worry. Everything's fine. I just wanted to see how you're holding up."

"I'm okay. Just worried about my dad. He's mulishly stubborn."

Sally cracked a grin. "That's true. But I think stubborn can be a good thing."

"You do?" Lucy wasn't so sure. If her father had gone for yearly physicals to the family doctor, he would have had blood work and would have known of his high cholesterol. It may not have prevented his panic attack, but it would have helped with his overall care.

"He'll recover faster. Mr. Berberian hates being here, and he certainly doesn't want your mom fussing over him. Those two bicker enough already."

Lucy smiled for the first time that day. "You're right." Her parents frequently quarreled at home and at work. They never had outright screaming matches, but they had mastered the art of bickering. Raffi would call something black and Angela would protest it was white. Gray was never a possibility. Growing up, it was clear they loved each other, and Lucy and Emma had come to realize that the squabbling was just how they communicated. If there was a day their parents didn't exchange a few words, Lucy would worry.

"Thanks for coming to the hospital, Sally."

Sally cocked a head and looked at her. "Are you kidding? I wouldn't be anywhere else. You're family."

Lucy experienced a warm glow, similar to how she'd felt when everyone had gathered around her father's bedside.

Sally wagged a finger. "Now, don't feel guilty about your dad."

Was it that obvious? "How can I not? Dad asked me to help with the case, but I haven't been very successful."

"For goodness sakes, even the police haven't been able to find the culprit yet. You can't blame yourself for what that glory hungry reporter prints in the paper"

Lucy let out a held-in breath. "I know. You're right."

"Then don't let guilt weigh you down. I've been with your family long enough to see the kind of pressure they put on you. You're a good daughter, Lucy."

Lucy hugged her "Thanks, Sally. You're the best."

CHAPTER 18

With her father's prescription in hand, Lucy entered Magic's Family Apothecary, a small pharmacy nestled between Holloway's Grocery and Cutie's Cupcake Bakery.

Shelves of over-the-counter medicines, cosmetics, and quick snack bags of chips and candy bars were situated in the store's front. The cashier greeted Lucy as she headed to the back of the store where the pharmacy was located.

Theodore Magic, a short, thin man in his early seventies, was filling a customer's prescription behind the counter. His plethora of wrinkles, brown spots on his face and arms, and shock of white hair made him look like a mad scientist. He'd been the town pharmacist since Lucy was in pigtails. He was also a big believer in natural remedies and acupuncture—a strange combination for a pharmacist who dispensed pharmaceutical pills for a living. An array of homeopathic remedies was stacked on a shelf beside the checkout counter.

"Hello, Mr. Magic," Lucy said as she slid the prescription across the counter.

Theodore looked up to give her a toothy grin. "Well, hello there, Lucy."

Lucy noticed a copy of the *Town News* beside the cash register. The picture of Kebab Kitchen on the front page jumped out at her. Her fingers itched to reach across the counter and rip the article to shreds.

Theodore glanced at the prescription slip. "Ah, so your father finally saw the family doctor for a checkup and blood work?"

Lucy rolled her eyes. "Not by choice."

Theodore chuckled. "Did your mother finally force him?"

"Unfortunately, no. He experienced chest pains and was taken to the hospital, but thank goodness it turned out to be only a panic attack."

"A panic attack? I suppose he's been under a lot of stress after what happened. 'Tis a shame."

Lucy glanced at the newspaper again. Just what did the whole town think after reading the damaging article?

Noticing her obvious distress, Theodore took off his reading glasses and looked at her kindly. "Don't fret, Lucy. I don't believe a word of that printed nonsense. I've been eating at your parents' establishment for years, and I consider them good friends."

Gratitude welled in her chest. "Thank you."

He waved a pen at her. "Now look on the bright side. Your father's a lucky man not to have heart disease. I'll be sure to stop by your parents' house on my way home and say hello."

"They'd like that very much."

"Meanwhile, I'll fill this prescription while you wait. But just so you know, there are other holistic remedies that I can recommend to lower cholesterol."

A thought occurred to Lucy. From what her mother had always said, Theodore Magic was highly intelligent and a wonderful source of information. But how was she going to ask what she wanted to know without being too obvious?

Lucy rested her hands on the counter. "May I ask you a question?"

"Of course. I answer them all day."

"Well this question may be a little from left field. I have a girlfriend, a fellow lawyer in Philadelphia, who has rambunctious toddlers. She worries about the best way to baby-proof her home."

His lips pursed thoughtfully. "Always a good idea."

The fabricated story came more easily. "Her husband is an exterminator. He has chemicals in the garage, and she's concerned about her young, mischievous sons getting into things."

He nodded. "Any mother would be."

Lucy took a deep breath. "Her husband uses cyanide in his work."

Theodore's brows arched into triangles. "Cyanide? To kill bugs?"

She needed to improvise and fast. "He has to exterminate all types of vermin. You know"—she waved a hand—"rats and rabid raccoons and squirrels."

"I should have considered that. Cyanide can be an ingredient of rat poison."

"I thought you would know," she said, tilting her head to the side. "So she has a reason to be especially cautious. Anything else I should tell her about it?"

"Yes . . . well . . . cyanide is highly toxic and very little is needed for a fatal dose. It's also a very interesting poison from a pharmacist's perspective."

"How so?"

"Cyanide has a long history. Did you know it is so old that even Egyptian hieroglyphics mention using it to murder someone?"

"Really? We were never taught that in public school," she said, looking at him with avid interest. "Anything else?"

Thankfully, Theodore was easily distracted by her rapt attention, and she got the impression that not many people wanted to listen to his encyclopedic lessons.

"Oh, yes. It's quite fascinating, really. Some forms of cyanide have industrial uses, such as to make paper, textiles, and plastics. Photographers use cyanide in their chemicals to develop pictures. Other forms of cyanide have medicinal uses. For example, Laetrile is an anticancer drug."

"I never knew it had positive uses." *But let's go back to how could it be used to kill someone.*

"My friend told me there are government restrictions on cyanide, so how could someone obtain that much?"

"She's right, but if one wanted to obtain it there are always ways. For instance, did you know that cyanide occurs naturally and that it's even in some of the foods we eat?"

Lucy tilted her head to the side. Now they were getting somewhere. "What types of food?"

"Cyanide is prevalent in certain seeds and pits of popular fruits, such as peach, apple, cherry, apricots, and plums. That's why you are never to grind those seeds and consume them in fruit smoothies. In large doses, it causes internal asphyxia."

Lucy already knew about apple seeds and cherry and peach pits from her internet search. But something else he'd mentioned caught her attention. "Wait. You said apricots?"

"Oh, yes. I remember a recall a while back of packages of roasted apricot kernels—which are the seeds inside the pit—sold in health food stores as a snack. Each package contained more than double the minimum lethal dosage for an adult human. So it's safe to say that if a large enough amount of apricot kernels were consumed, they could cause cyanide poisoning."

Lucy felt as if her world had just tilted on its axis. *Apricots.*

Apricots were prevalent in Mediterranean cuisine. Her father had once mentioned that Lucy's grandfather's family owned acres of apricot orchards back in Armenia before the First World War and the Armenian Genocide.

She recalled her first day back in Ocean Crest. Big Al had made a delivery to the restaurant, and she'd glimpsed inside the box to see fresh apricots, their peachy skins soft, ripe, and juicy, perfect for eating. She remembered something else. One of her mother's new hummus varieties included apricots and pine nuts.

Could the apricot hummus be the source of the poison that killed Heather Banks?

But how? Dozens of customers had eaten from the hummus bar and sampled the apricot hummus. Her mother didn't use the pit or the kernel of the apricot, just the fruit. As far as Lucy knew, the pits were discarded in the trash.

The same trash that the police collected. Would Calvin Clemmons or Prosecutor Walsh even identify the apricot pits and know that they contained cyanide?

Even that was a stretch. The apricot pits would have been tossed in a large Dumpster of trash. Picking them out as particularly suspicious would be like finding a needle in a haystack, or in this case, a pit in a mound of rotten food.

Her gaze snapped back to the pharmacist. "How much?"

Theodore blinked. "Pardon?"

"How much cyanide is fatal?"

"Not much. Only a small amount is needed for a fatal dose."

"Thank you for the lesson. Oh, and what can I tell my friend about baby-proofing?"

"The safest method is to not keep the cyanide in the house or the garage. Other than that, we carry some baby-proofing items in aisle seven." Theodore smiled and handed her a bag. "If your father has any questions about his prescription, please call."

"Thank you." Lucy was in deep thought as she walked to her car.

Who'd had access to the apricots?

Her mother, of course. But she wasn't the killer.

Azad had helped her come up with some of the recipes, including the apricot hummus. Why did everything always come back to him?

Butch had been in the kitchen, but he didn't make the hummus.

Big Al had delivered the apricots. But he had no motive and no connection to the victim.

Nothing made sense. She couldn't say for certain that ground apricot kernels had killed Heather. It was more probable that Guido Morelli or Mac McCabe had poisoned Heather's iced tea. And Paul Evans was still a suspect.

So was it death by hummus, the tea, or something else?

"Wow! That is one hot dress," Katie said.

Lucy looked in the full-length mirror in the bedroom. Katie sat in the wicker chair, a pair of five-inch black heels dangling from her fingers.

"I'm not sure about this," Lucy said.

"Why? You look great."

"It's a bit dressier than what I'd intended." She'd borrowed one of Katie's dresses for Michael Citteroni's surprise party. She had to admit she did look good in the sleek cocktail dress with spaghetti straps. Katie was taller than Lucy and she'd insisted Lucy take the dress to the seamstress for hemming and to let out a seam or two to fit. Katie had insisted she had no plans to wear the dress again and intended to donate it. Lucy wasn't sure, but Katie had convinced her.

"You said yourself it's a black tie affair at a Victorian Cape May mansion. Everyone will be dressed to the hilt."

Lucy took the offered heels and tried them on. "Good grief. They're so high. With my luck, I'll trip walking into the place and break a leg."

"You need the height."

Lucy scowled. "Don't remind me." If there was one thing Lucy envied about Katie back in high school it was her long legs and five-foot-seven-inch height.

"What's wrong? You have that faraway look on your face." Like any best friend worth her salt, Katie could always tell when Lucy was upset or distracted.

"I'm thinking about what Theodore Magic told me this morning about the apricots."

"You don't seriously think your mother accidentally poisoned her hummus, do you?"

"No, of course not. But it would explain a lot. How

Heather died soon after eating from the hummus bar. She ate a lot of hummus."

Katie leaned forward and the wicker chair creaked. "Think back. What types of hummus did she eat?"

Lucy recalled the numerous dollops of hummus on Heather's plate. She remembered how each different type of hummus had been placed around the perimeter of her plate like an artist's palette. She'd thought it weird then. "Heather ate from every bin in the hummus bar."

Katie exhaled. "It doesn't add up, Lucy. You said yourself only the apricot pits contain cyanide. My first bet is on Paul Evans. Second would be Guido or Mac spiking Heather's iced tea. She saw all three of them right before coming to Kebab Kitchen."

A disturbing thought crept forward. "What about Azad? He admitted to helping my mom come up with the apricot and pine nut hummus. He also often comes by to help out in the kitchen, and he was there the day Heather died."

"You still think he's capable of murder?" Katie asked.

Deep down she didn't, but the evidence against him kept creeping up. "He's still a suspect."

"What about Mr. Citteroni?" Katie asked.

Lucy recalled the mobster. "He admitted to being at the bike shop that evening. Sometimes we keep the back door open so workers can carry trash to the Dumpster. Do you think he slipped in and delivered poison?"

Katie shook her head. "Not him, but one of his goons. Maybe the same young, good-looking one we saw in the alley of the massage parlor meeting with Paul Evans. He could have injected her in the toe with a lethal dose of poison in the restaurant parking lot for all we know. I saw a movie where the villain did just that and the medical examiner missed it."

Lucy had never thought of *that* scenario. "You watch way too many detective shows and movies."

"We can't rule out any possibility," Katie insisted.

"Great. Now I'm even more nervous to go to tonight's party. Mr. Citteroni will be there."

"Good. Keep your ears open."

"I doubt he'll confess to hiring Heather's killer."

Katie picked up a black clutch and handed it to Lucy. "You never know. Now hurry up or you'll be late."

CHAPTER 19

The Queen Victoria was located in Cape May on a street lined with three hundred-year-old sycamore trees. The stunning nineteenth-century home looked like an elaborate dollhouse with a breathtaking view of the Atlantic Ocean. The three-story building was painted burnt sienna with pale yellow shutters in striking contrast. Tonight, lights shone brightly in the windows and guests with glasses of wine and sparkling champagne mingled on the wrap-around porch.

Lucy climbed the steps, crossed the porch, and entered the vestibule. Sparkling chandeliers illuminated cream-painted walls, velvet curtains, and elaborately ornamented wood-trimmed furniture. Glass table lamps with marble bases sat on dainty rosewood tables. Figurines of dogs, cats, and farm animals decorated built-in bookshelves. A lush Oriental carpet covered the gleaming wood floor. Wood chairs with curved backs and a settee covered in red velvet were situated around a fireplace, welcoming guests.

Men dressed in tuxedos and women wearing cocktail dresses with glittering diamonds looked dapper and elegant. Lucy smoothed her skirt with nervous fingers. Most of the guests were unfamiliar, but a few were Ocean Crest residents she recognized. Two ladies from the town council, Gertrude Shaw and Francesca Stevens, were standing by the fireplace balancing drinks and scallops wrapped in bacon on cocktail napkins as they talked. Lucy quickly turned away. Gertrude was a notorious gossip, and Lucy had no intention of drawing attention to herself and risking the nosy woman quizzing her on her presence at tonight's party.

A passing server carrying a tray of hors d'oeuvres halted before Lucy. She took a spring roll and a cocktail napkin, then searched the sea of faces. The guest of honor hadn't yet arrived. For a man who rode a motorcycle and enjoyed his freedom, she wondered what Michael would think of such an elaborate setting for a party. No doubt the big shindig was more for the father than his son.

She bit into the spring roll.

"Lucy!" A deep masculine voice bellowed.

Lucy whirled around to see Anthony Citteroni approach. He wore a tuxedo with a checked black-and-white bow tie nestled just below his ample chin. "Michael will be happy that you came."

Lucy nervously swallowed a lump of spring roll. "Thank you for inviting me. This house is lovely."

He snatched a bubbling flute of champagne from a passing server's tray and offered it to her. "Eat. Drink. Enjoy."

She clutched the delicate stem of the crystal. "When will Michael arrive?"

"Soon. His sister, Teresa, is bringing him. He thinks it's a surprise party for one of his cousins." Suddenly Mr. Citteroni's bushy eyebrows drew together like a hairy caterpillar and he glared at her. "You didn't say anything to him to ruin the surprise, did you?"

"No, of course not."

He pointed a thick finger at her. "I told you I always know everything that happens in town."

Her eyes widened and a trickle of apprehension coursed down her spine. "I don't doubt it."

He grinned. "Just joking. No need to look so fearful, Lucy." His smile couldn't entirely disguise his ominous nature, and the hair on her nape stood on end.

"Come. There's someone I want you to meet." He took her elbow and tugged her along to a group of four men drinking what looked like whiskey in the corner of the room. "Luke Santiago is a business associate of mine. He's going to run my Ocean Crest trash pick up and linen supply businesses this summer. Since one of the establishments he'll serve is your parents' restaurant, I thought you should meet him."

They reached the group of four men and Mr.

Citteroni called out in Italian. One of the men immediately turned around.

Lucy's heart skipped a beat.

"Lucy, meet Mr. Santiago." Mr. Citteroni turned to his associate. "Luke, Ms. Berberian's family owns the Mediterranean restaurant next to one of my bicycle shops."

A corner of Luke Santiago's lips curled in what resembled a grin. There was no mistaking his height, the swath of tawny hair that brushed his forehead, or the goatee. Up close, Lucy knew women would find him attractive. He was also the man that had met Paul Evans in the alley outside the massage parlor.

Luke Santiago extended his hand. "It's a pleasure to finally meet you, Ms. Berberian."

Finally? What did he mean by that? As Lucy shook his hand, a mocking look flashed in his icy blue eyes.

A frightening realization washed over her as her mind turned back to that night. Could there have been video surveillance outside the massage parlor that she hadn't seen? Or maybe someone had spotted them spying and had reported it to Mr. Citteroni?

That could only mean one thing. Mr. Citteroni knew she and Katie had been there that night.

Well that worked out splendidly, Lucy mused as she turned away after the brief introduction. She wondered if Anthony Citteroni's true motive for inviting her tonight was to put her on notice that he was aware of her clandestine surveillance. Was the mobster toying with her? Or did he really want her there for Michael?

Thank goodness Mr. Citteroni and Luke Santiago had lost interest in her. Both men had wandered off to greet other guests. Neither had directly confronted or questioned her, but the warning was clear—*keep your nose out of our business.*

Lucy reached for her second glass of champagne from a passing tray. The bubbling alcohol had served to take the edge off, but she knew she'd have to stop drinking in order to drive home.

Despite what had occurred, she wanted to stay until Michael's arrival.

A hushed murmur ran through the crowd and Lucy knew the guest of honor would arrive soon. Minutes later, Michael stepped inside the entranceway with his sister.

"Surprise!" the party revelers shouted in unison. Colorful balloons were released from nets in the ceiling and guests blew party bugles.

Michael kissed his sister's cheek as men stepped forward to shake his hand, and women rushed to embrace and kiss him. He looked handsome in a tuxedo, which accented his dark hair and vivid blue eyes, but she noticed his smile did not quite reach his eyes.

He's not pleased.

Lucy stayed back and watched. Teresa, stunning in a red dress and platform silver heels with rhinestone buckles, appeared to enjoy the attention much more than Michael did. Her coloring was similar to Michael's, with long, dark hair and blue eyes, but there was a sharpness to her features and a shrewdness in her eyes that Michael didn't possess. Lucy was reminded of what Michael had said about his sibling. She was more like their father, whereas Michael seemed to favor his mother and wanted to be his own man.

Uncomfortable to intrude with the crowd of well-wishers—many of whom appeared to be relatives—Lucy waited until the group dispersed.

The guests thinned out and Michael spotted her. He grinned as he approached. "Lucy," he said, his gaze traveling her from head to toe. "You look beautiful." His smile was genuine, not strained.

Her cheeks grew warm under his admiring look. The noise of the party faded until it seemed like just the two of them were standing there. "Happy birthday."

"I'm glad you're here."

"I wouldn't miss it. Did you suspect the party was for you?"

"No. Although I'm not all that surprised. My father loves throwing large parties. He conducts more business at these types of gatherings than he does all year in his office."

She thought of the way Mr. Citteroni had introduced her to Luke Santiago. Yes, he'd conducted business with her, too.

Michael glanced at the near empty glass of

champagne in her hand. "May I get you another drink?"

She shook her head. "This is my second, and I need to drive home."

"I'll drive you. We can come back for your car tomorrow."

She motioned to her cocktail dress. "I don't think this outfit is suitable for a motorcycle."

He threw back his head and laughed. "I drove my sister in my car. She wouldn't be caught dead on a motorcycle."

She smiled. "Then I may take you up on your offer."

Two men approached and began talking to Michael. Lucy knew she couldn't dominate his attention for the entire party, but now that he had arrived, she was more at ease. Mr. Citteroni's presence or that of Luke Santiago didn't frighten her.

She motioned to the dining room to let Michael know where she was headed. Stepping into the room, her eyes widened at the lavish buffet spread on a long mahogany dining table and sideboard. All manner of Italian delicacies were being served from chafing dishes. The aroma of Sicilian seafood soup with couscous, sausage stuffed potato gnocchi, marinated artichoke hearts, and dozens of additional delicious dishes filled the air. Fine china and polished silver flatware wrapped in crisp cream-colored linens tied in satin bows invited guests to dine.

Lucy filled a plate with orecchiette pasta with

cauliflower and sausage, baked ziti, and lentil and faro salad, then wandered to a room that appeared to be a parlor. It was a lovely room with red velvet settees and large windows. A few other guests were finishing their own food and rose to offer Lucy a seat. The food was delicious, especially the perfectly seasoned lentil and faro salad.

She spied a glossy black grand piano in the corner and carried her plate from the settee to study the instrument more closely. Old sepia photographs of women in Victorian gowns with lace fichus and men in cravats and superfine wool jackets and checked waistcoats were arranged on the piano. The photographs, in combination with the décor, made her feel like she'd been transported back in time to a quaint Victorian parlor.

"Well, I wish my father had invited the famous author. It would have made good entertainment." Teresa Citteroni's voice cut through Lucy's thoughts. She was standing by the fireplace with another dark-haired woman Lucy didn't recognize.

Neither woman noticed Lucy as she froze by the piano. Was Teresa taking about Paul Evans?

"He managed to get himself involved with the wrong girlfriend, that's for sure," the second woman said.

Teresa picked up a brass candlestick from the mantle and appeared to study the workmanship. "I went through my father's files and saw just how much Heather Banks had borrowed to pay off her gambling debts. She had an addiction. Paul Evans was foolish enough to vouch for the loans. Now he owes it all."

"How much?"

"A hundred grand."

A hundred thousand! Lucy couldn't imagine anyone gambling that much money.

"Whew. That's a lot of cash," the second woman said, echoing Lucy's thoughts.

Lucy's heart pounded, and she shifted a few steps in an attempt to hear more clearly.

"That's not the best part. He backed her financially before he knew she was cheating," Teresa said.

"Don't hold out. You know I love juicy gossip," the second woman said.

"She was sleeping with one of my father's men, Luke Santiago."

"The tall, blond one with the goatee?"

"Yup," Teresa said.

The other woman sighed. "I've always thought Luke was hot."

"I once saw Heather and Luke together in a car outside one of my father's businesses. They were kissing and groping each other like randy teenagers."

Lucy's heart did a triple beat. Heather was cheating on Paul with Luke Santiago, Mr. Citteroni's employee? He was the man Paul had met in the alley when he'd handed him a fat envelope, which Lucy had suspected was filled with cash. After hearing Teresa, Lucy believed her suspicion was correct. Paul was making a payment on Heather's loans. And he was making it to the same man Heather had cheated with. Paul must have been humiliated and angry.

Both women giggled. "And Paul found out?"

"Luke told me Paul walked in on them at a seedy massage parlor. They were only half-dressed on the table. Heather tried to claim Luke was her masseuse," Teresa said.

"I wish I were a fly on that wall. He must have been furious."

"He was. He said he wanted to kill her. Maybe he went through with it."

The second woman whistled through her teeth. "You think so?"

"Who knows?"

A server stuck her head in the parlor and Lucy jumped. "Ten minutes until your brother blows out the candles, Ms. Citteroni."

Teresa waved a bejeweled hand. "We can't miss my brother's celebration . . . or a piece of cake."

The two women left the room.

Lucy waited until the parlor was empty before digging her cell out of her purse and dialing Katie. "Paul backed Heather's loans with the mobster Citteroni and then found out she was cheating on him. He then threatened to kill her!" She quickly summarized the night's events and exactly what she'd heard from Teresa Citteroni.

"My God," Katie said. "That's twisted. The guy Mr. Citteroni sent to collect payment on the loans was the same person Heather was sleeping with? Paul must have felt completely betrayed. You said he was livid enough to kill. You know what they say about crimes of passion."

Lucy's grip on the phone tightened. "Except Heather's murder was premeditated. Poisoning takes planning. It would have been easy to poison her iced tea that day. I suspect Paul wanted to frame Guido or Mac for the murder."

"Paul was the one who pointed us to Guido and claimed he hated Heather for repeatedly issuing health violations for his pizzeria."

"Paul also claimed Guido threatened Heather on the boardwalk."

"And Guido pointed us to Mac. He hated Heather for blackmailing him in exchange for passing health inspections of his pub."

"What do I do?" Lucy asked.

"Call Calvin Clemmons. Tell him everything."

As soon as Lucy hung up with Katie, she dialed the Ocean Crest police station and asked to speak with Detective Clemmons. Her call went right to voice mail and she left as detailed a message as the two minutes would allow before cutting her off.

Damn. Lucy glanced at her watch. Eleven o'clock. She heard an out of tune rendition of "Happy Birthday" outside the parlor. She headed straight for the dining room, and pushed her way through the crowd just as Michael blew out a blinding number of candles on a large, double sheet cake with butter cream frosting. A box with a printed logo of Cutie's Cupcake Bakery rested on the sideboard. Guests clapped and a waiter stepped forward with a silver cake server and knife and began cutting the frosted cake and placing pieces on china.

Michael looked up, caught Lucy's eyes, and grinned. She couldn't leave without saying good-bye. Someone handed her a piece of cake and a fork. She took a bite and the sweetness hit her tongue with a sugar shot.

Michael managed to extricate himself from a group of guests and approached. "I'm sorry we couldn't talk more, Lucy."

"Don't be ridiculous. You are the guest of honor. I have to share. I'm just sorry that I have to leave early." It had worked out just fine for her. She wouldn't have overheard his sister's conversation if he'd been with her.

"Do you still need a ride home?"

"No, I'm quite sober. But thank you for the offer."

He offered her his arm. "I'll escort you to your car."

She rested her hand on his sleeve. "That would be lovely."

"One more thing. How about a motorcycle ride the day after tomorrow? I want to take you to the Cape May lighthouse."

"Absolutely, but on one condition," she said.

"What's that?"

"You teach me how to drive."

Michael threw back his head and laughed. "I've created a monster."

They left the house and made their way down the graveled drive. Flowering pots of daffodils and tulips lined the path and the heady scent of their perfume lingered in the air.

"For once, I'm grateful for something my father did—inviting you," Michael said.

"I'm glad I came," Lucy said.

It was the truth. She may have been initially intimidated when Mr. Citteroni had introduced her to Luke Santiago, but her eavesdropping opportunity in the parlor had made it all worthwhile. Plus, she was happy she could be present for Michael.

Lucy pulled out her car keys from her purse and glanced at her cell phone. No messages or texts. She frowned. Clemmons hadn't returned her call. Either he was busy booking a drunk driver on a Saturday night or he thought her rambling message was crazy. Well, if Clemmons wouldn't call her back, she'd go directly to the police station and find a cop who would listen.

Streetlights that looked like old gas lamps cast a faint glow through the canopy of sycamore trees. She glanced back at the Victorian mansion.

Hundreds of decorative lights outlining the frame of the house and the windows gave it a magical appearance. Crickets and locusts sang in the pleasant warm May evening.

They reached the small parking lot. Amongst an impressive number of high-end cars left in the lot—Mercedes, BMW, Lexus, and Audi—Lucy spotted her Toyota and pressed the UNLOCK button on her keyless remote.

Michael opened the door for her. Bending down, he pressed a quick kiss on her cheek. "Good night, Lucy."

"Happy birthday, Michael."

For a heart-stopping moment, she wanted to tell him everything she'd learned tonight. That his father knew she'd spied on Paul Evans and Luke Santiago. That his father had loaned Heather an exorbitant amount of cash. That Paul had backed the loans before he discovered Heather had been sleeping with Luke. And that Paul had threatened to kill Heather after finding her in the arms of her lover.

Instead, Lucy smiled and kept her mouth shut, then slid into the car. She hadn't known Michael for that long and even though he may not get along with his father, Mr. Citteroni was still flesh-and-blood. Lucy didn't want to put Michael in an awkward position or make matters worse for him with his family. He had nothing to do with Heather Banks' murder.

Lucy drove down back roads that led toward Ocean Crest and headed straight for the small police station. She turned on her radio, and the sound of smooth jazz calmed her nerves.

Behind her, an engine roared, loud and throaty. The sound pierced the solitude of a soothing saxophone and the hum of her Toyota. The speed limit was forty-five miles per hour. The driver coming up behind her was doing at least sixty-five.

A drunk driver?

She glanced in her rearview mirror. The car's halogens temporarily blinded her as they came dangerously close to her bumper.

"Pass me!" she yelled even though she knew the other driver couldn't hear.

The blaring sound of a police car drowned out the noise of the car behind her as red and blue flashing lights reflected off her rearview mirror.

Finally, she thought. *The Ocean Crest police when you need them.*

Suddenly, the speeding car veered into the left lane and whizzed past her, spitting gravel that sounded like buckshot against the side of her car.

Alarmed, Lucy glanced to the left to see a white BMW as it flew past. Paul Evans was in the driver's seat.

Sweet Jesus. What was going on?

Seconds later, the police car sped by in hot pursuit. Up ahead, the BMW swerved madly as its tires hit a patch of wet road. Lucy held her breath and gripped the steering wheel as the rear of the BMW swerved like a fish caught on a hook as its tires attempted to gain traction. The car careened off the road and flew into a deep ditch. The police car's brakes squealed and pierced the night air as it came to a stop on the shoulder of the road.

Lucy jammed her foot on the brake and pulled up behind the police car. She threw open her door and ran to the ditch and looked down.

Calvin Clemmons ran up the embankment, his radio in his hand.

"Where's Paul?" Lucy asked.

Clemmons' eyes narrowed as he spotted her on the embankment, but he didn't look surprised, merely annoyed and frazzled. "He wasn't wearing a seatbelt and he banged his head pretty good. I called for an ambulance, and it should be here soon."

"What happened? Why were you chasing him?"

His granite eyes locked on her. "I got your message."

CHAPTER 20

The following day, Lucy arrived at Kebab Kitchen to find everyone—her parents, Emma, Sally, and even Butch—waiting for her.

"You did it! You saved us, Lucy," Raffi said.

Angela cradled Gadoo in her arms as she came forward to kiss Lucy's cheek. Lucy had never seen the calico cat inside the restaurant. Her mother was obsessed with cleanliness and had never permitted it, but today was evidently an exception. Angela's cheeks were tinged pink with happiness as she scratched the cat under his chin.

Lucy had called her parents late last night to inform them that Paul Evans had been arrested for Heather Banks' murder. She knew they were under a lot of stress from the restaurant's struggling business, as well as from her father's recent trip to the hospital. She wanted to ease their worries. Plus, she knew how fast news traveled in town. The Internet had nothing on Ocean Crest when it came to the information superhighway.

"Dad, I didn't really do much."

"I knew it was the boyfriend all along," Angela said, though she had never once mentioned her suspicion.

Lucy rolled her eyes.

"Katie told us you overheard something and called the police. When Detective Clemmons went to question Paul, he ran. It was the car chase of the century in Ocean Crest," Emma said.

Lucy wondered if it had been the *only* car chase to ever occur in Ocean Crest. "It didn't end well for Paul."

Sally beamed. "People have already told me they knew it couldn't have been the food here."

"Our problems are over!" Angela said as Gadoo purred in her arms. "Just in time for tourist season. The earlier vacationers are already arriving."

Butch took off his red bandana and smiled. "I had faith in you all along, Lucy Lou."

They were all hovering over her like she was a hero and it was making her anxious. "Thanks, Butch, but I—"

"That busybody prosecutor can go home now," Sally added.

"You haven't had breakfast yet, have you?" Lucy didn't have a chance to respond before her mother pulled out a chair at the nearest table. "Sit. You need to eat."

"I'm fine, Mom," Lucy insisted, uncomfortable with the attention.

"Nonsense. You had a late night. I can tell when

one of my daughters doesn't eat properly. I'll put Gadoo outside, then get you something."

"Let me, Mrs. B. I know just what she likes," Butch said as he made a beeline for the kitchen.

"Emma, please get your sister a cup of coffee," Angela said.

"Glad to." Emma traipsed off, and Angela followed, carrying the cat.

It was just like her mother to use food as reward for a good deed.

Before Lucy could protest further a feta and spinach cheese omelet was placed before her. Picking up a fork, she took a bite. *Yum.* The feta blended harmoniously with the eggs and the spinach added an extra texture. Her mother had often made feta and spinach omelets when Lucy had lived at home. How long had it been since she'd eaten one?

Her mother returned without the cat, followed by Emma. Her sister set a mug of coffee and the *Town News* before her. "It made the morning paper."

Lucy set down her fork. "Is it bad?"

Sally answered. "Nope. Stan Slade printed the truth this time."

"Does it mention me?" Lucy asked.

Emma shook her head. "No. But it mentions the big chase last night through Ocean Crest and it shows a picture of Paul's car being towed from the ditch and the ambulance in the background."

"Let me see," Lucy's unfolded the paper. The headline read FAMOUS SUSPENSE AUTHOR ARRESTED ON SUSPICION OF MURDER. The article mentioned that the police received an anonymous tip from a concerned citizen. When the police went to question Paul, he ran.

She scanned Stan's article and thankfully she wasn't mentioned. If it had named her, there was a good chance Mr. Citteroni or his daughter Teresa would have figured out Lucy was the concerned citizen. She was already on the mobster's radar. He wouldn't be pleased if Paul told the police about Mr. Citteroni's unethical loaning practices, and if Paul was incarcerated, no one would pay off the remainder of Heather's debts.

Others would be pleased that they were no longer under suspicion. Guido Morelli and Mac McCabe came to mind.

And Azad. Deep in her gut, she'd never truly believed him capable of murder, even though the evidence kept pointing his way.

"Hello, Mr. and Mrs. Berberian." a familiar voice said.

Lucy turned. Azad stood by the hostess stand, hands in his jean pockets, and grinned. It was as if she'd conjured him from her thoughts.

"Hi, Lucy. I heard the good news."

Lucy glanced at her mother. "Did you call and tell him?"

"Nope," Azad answered. "I heard it from no less than four people at Lola's Coffee Shop. You should know that the *Town News* gets delivered there before five in the morning."

"The restaurant is saved!" Raffi slapped Azad on the back.

Something flickered far back in Azad's eyes as he grinned.

Lucy stopped at Lola's Coffee Shop on the way home. Katie had grown fond of cappuccino and had asked Lucy to pick up a cup for her. She stepped into the coffee shop and breathed in the heavenly scent of ground coffee beans and warm pastry. As usual, there was a line at the counter, and Lola was busy filling orders

Lola's eyes lit up when the customer in front of Lucy left and she stepped up to the counter. "Everyone's talking about Paul's arrest," Lola said as she slipped a protective sleeve around a paper coffee cup. "The newspaper said he hit his head and is in the hospital."

Lucy shifted her feet. "I read about it in the paper." Once again, she was grateful the newspaper article had never mentioned her name. Lola would have grilled her for details if she knew Lucy had been at the scene of Paul's crash or that she had been the concerned citizen to call Detective Clemmons with incriminating information about Paul's involvement.

"Paul was a regular customer here." Lola leaned across the counter and lowered her voice. "He was so polite. Who would have thought he was a murderer?"

"I guess you never really know someone."

Lola straightened and reached for another paper cup behind the counter. "Hmm. Maybe you're right. It's always the quiet ones in the movies that have the worst secrets."

Lucy suppressed the urge to laugh. Lola sounded like Katie when she talked about her detective shows.

Two cappuccinos in hand, one for her and one for Katie, Lucy said farewell to Lola and headed for the front door. Halfway through the coffee shop, she stopped short in surprise.

Guido Morelli and Mac McCabe were sitting together at a corner table. White mugs and plates of scones sat before them. They were drinking coffee and eating pastries like longtime friends. If someone had told her the two businessmen would be there together, she'd have called them crazy.

She halted at their table.

"Well, hello there, Lucy," Mac said.

"Hi," Guido said.

"Hello, Mr. Morelli and Mr. McCabe. I'm surprised to see you two here together."

Mac set down his mug. "We're celebrating."

"You mean about the arrest of the suspect for Ms. Banks' death?" Lucy asked.

Guido shook his head. "That's a great reason to celebrate around here, but that's not why."

Lucy's brows drew downward in a frown. "Then what else? You both led me to believe that you disliked each other."

"You're right. We did. But we also discovered that we have more important things to focus on rather than a silly business rivalry," Mac said.

"Your children," Lucy said as realization dawned.

Guido nodded. "Maria and Connor are going to the senior prom together."

"That's wonderful." Lucy recalled Mac saying Guido's daughter, Maria, had a crush on his son, Connor, and that she'd asked him to the senior prom. If Connor had accepted, it sounded like the two teenagers had romantic feelings for each other.

"We may not have thought it was a good match at first, but teenagers have a remarkable ability to help a parent come to their senses," Mac said.

Lucy grinned. She could just imagine how her niece, Niari, would turn out in a few years. Emma and Max would have their hands full. Lucy wanted to remain an involved aunt. Spending time with her niece building Lego towers, eating pizza, and watching movies was fun and rewarding. It was another reason to want to stay close to her family and remain in Ocean Crest.

"My wife is helping my beautiful Maria shop for the perfect prom gown," Guido said, a note of pride in his voice.

"And my wife went with Connor to order his tuxedo and to the florist to pick out the corsage," Mac said.

Lucy smiled at their eagerness. "I'm proud of both of you. I'll leave you two to your coffee and pastries." She turned to leave.

"Oh, and thanks Lucy," Mac said.

She turned back to them. "For what?"

Mac rubbed his chin with his forefinger. "We both suspect you had something to do with finding Ms. Banks' killer."

Lucy blinked. "Why would you think that?"

"We've been talking. You visited us at our businesses and asked questions. We also learned that your parents own Kebab Kitchen where Heather died," Guido said.

She shouldn't be surprised. If both men had set aside their differences and started talking, it wasn't a far leap to compare notes and figure out the truth. Talk of the murder had been a regular topic of conversation in town, and Paul's arrest would only add fuel to the fire.

"We also believe that we were on your list of suspects," Mac said.

Lucy squirmed beneath their stares. "Well now . . . I was just asking questions. I'm not a cop."

Both men laughed, and Lucy's nerves eased a bit.

"No hard feelings," Guido said. "We don't blame you. After all, it all worked out in the end."

CHAPTER 21

The front door of Kebab Kitchen opened to welcome a flood of locals and a few early tourists. The tables were full within fifteen minutes, and Lucy's parents were grateful for the show of support from their friends and the community. Her mother was in a particularly happy mood, and alongside Butch, offered scrumptious specials of fried eggplant appetizer, curried chicken, cheese bake called *sou boreg*, and green bean salad. Lucy tasted them all. The curried chicken was divine and the cheese bake was even better.

Lucy spotted Susan Cutie from the bakery and Lola Steward from the coffee shop with their families. Theodore Magic was seated with a group of elderly widows, including Mrs. Kiminski, the old lady who'd first welcomed Lucy as she'd driven into town weeks ago. The white-haired ladies were peppering Theodore with questions about their ailments and he answered each one enthusiastically. The next customer to walk through the doors surprised Lucy the most.

Stan Slade gave her a cocky grin. "Do I still get that exclusive?"

Lucy plucked a menu from the hostess stand. "If you really want it, but there's not much to tell."

"I disagree." He sat at a table and waved away the proffered menu. "I'll start with the hummus bar."

"Research for your next article?"

"No. I want to know what all the fuss is about."

"The plates are at the end. Help yourself," Lucy said.

Azad had put on an apron to help Butch and her mother in the kitchen. Her father handled the register and floated around chatting with customers. Lucy, Emma, and Sally were busy waiting tables.

Everyone was working efficiently and happily, yet Lucy was feeling tense and uptight.

The events of last night should have made her content. Not because Paul Evans had driven off the road and had been taken away by ambulance, but because he'd been arrested for Heather's murder. She should be relieved and just as joyful as the rest of her family. So what was her problem?

With a pang, she realized she still had questions. Paul had seemed so sincere when he'd said he loved Heather and had pulled out the impressive diamond ring from his desk drawer. Was he that good an actor? Was a cheating girlfriend enough to turn him into a killer?

She kept thinking as she greeted customers with

a smile, took orders, delivered food, and tallied checks. Two hours later, when the lunch shift slowed, Lucy wiped her brow. "Can you cover my tables, Em? I want to call Katie."

"Sure," Emma said, waving her off.

Lucy went to her parents' office in the corner of the storage room and called Katie's cell. She answered on the first ring.

"What's the latest on Paul?" Lucy said without preamble.

Katie lowered her voice a notch. "Bill told me he's at the Ocean Crest Medical Center."

"Is he okay?"

"He hit his head on the steering wheel and is being treated for a concussion and bumps and bruises."

Lucy recalled Clemmons saying that Paul wasn't wearing his seat best. "He's lucky it wasn't worse."

"True. He's a flight risk so he's handcuffed to the bed and a police officer is stationed outside his door."

"I feel sorry for him," Lucy murmured.

"Why? He killed Heather. No matter what we thought of her, she didn't deserve to be murdered."

Lucy bit her bottom lip. "That's true, but—"

"But what?"

"I'm wondering how he administered the cyanide. Has he confessed?" Did Paul lace Heather's iced tea? If so, did the police find a cup? Or did Paul toss it out? And how did Paul obtain cyanide in the first place if it was regulated by the government and difficult to obtain?"

"Bill said Clemmons is meeting with Prosecutor Walsh this afternoon to put all the pieces together," Katie explained.

"Hmm."

"Lucy, I never thought I'd say this, but stop thinking about it. Paul is guilty. Our investigation is over."

Logically, Lucy knew Katie was right. But if it was that simple, why did so many questions still plague her?

After the lunch hour, Lucy stayed with Azad in the kitchen while her mother saw to a delivery in the storage room. Emma and Sally left for a couple hours and would come back for the expected dinner rush. Raffi went home grumbling after Angela insisted he go home to rest. His hospital stay was fresh in all their minds.

The reservation book was nearly full for that evening, which made everyone ecstatic, especially her parents.

"Lunch service was great. Things are looking up," Azad said to Lucy.

They were slicing ripe tomatoes for a salad that would accompany a *mezza* appetizer plate tonight. To be fair, Azad was doing the cutting and Lucy the watching. His knife skills were impressive. The sharp serrated blade easily sliced the delicate tomatoes with impressive speed without squishing them into a bloody pulp like Lucy did whenever she'd tried.

Lucy nodded. Every seat had been full, the food

was delicious, and the staff enthusiastic. The place had worked like a well-oiled machine, and she'd found it thrilling. She realized what she'd been struggling with since coming back to Ocean Crest.

She *wanted* to stay.

She wanted to take a crack at running the restaurant. She'd need help, of course. Her parents' expertise and guidance. Emma and Sally's support. Butch would have to remain full-time, and eventually she'd have to hire another chef to replace her mother.

One name sprang to mind.

She gave Azad a sidelong glance. Would he want to work as the head chef instead of the owner?

The more she thought about taking over, the more it made sense. She'd make some changes. She'd computerize the place for certain. And update and refresh the décor. But the essence of the place, a casual family Mediterranean restaurant offering mouth-watering dishes, would remain the same.

If her parents were willing to give Azad a loan, then surely they would give her one. Or maybe they would agree to have her manage the place, and they could work part-time and ease into retirement. Azad might be upset at losing the opportunity, but if he was still interested in her afterwards, well . . . then . . . she just might let him woo her.

But how could she consider a serious relationship with one man when Michael Citteroni and his motorcycle rides were too much fun to give up?

She pushed her thoughts aside. It was too much to contemplate. "Hey, Azad. I've been thinking."

"Oh?" He kept slicing, his blade like quicksilver. A lock of dark hair fell across his forehead and gave him a roguish look.

"I may want to stay," she said.

He looked up, his knife halting in midair. "Stay?"

She shrugged a shoulder and hoped for an air of nonchalance. "You know. Stay in Ocean Crest."

A corner of his lips curled in a smile as he looked at her. "That's great. Did you find a law job in town?"

"No. I was thinking of taking over the place."

His brow crinkled. "What place?"

"Kebab Kitchen."

He stopped cutting, and his dark eyes became flat and unreadable as stone. "You mean taking over for your parents?"

"I know you hoped to buy it yourself, but yes."

He set the knife on the cutting board. "Why? You never wanted it before."

Her mind was a crazy mix of hope and fear. "I know . . . but things have changed for me."

"In a little less than two weeks' time?" he pressed.

Things weren't going well. He was clearly upset.

Anxiety spurted through her. "Look, I haven't even spoken about it to my parents. It's just something that's been in the back of my mind. I felt it for real today."

"One good lunch service and you decide you want to manage the place," he said, his voice cold. He was getting hostile.

Her anxiety increased. "There's no need to get angry."

"I'm not angry. I'm just trying to understand you. After our breakup, you ran, and you've kept running for years. You hardly ever came back. When you did come back for longer than a quick visit, you decide to take over the family business?"

Lucy opened her mouth, then closed it, unsure of what to say.

The restaurant's phone rang, piercing the awkward silence and making her jump. She wiped her hands on a towel. "Excuse me. It's probably for a reservation. They've been calling all day." Relieved to have an excuse to escape, she rushed into the dining room to answer the landline by the hostess stand. "Hello. This is Kebab Kitchen."

"Lucy Berberian?" said a low raspy voice.

Static crackled through the line. "Yes."

A cough. "I need to see you."

Lucy frowned and pressed the receiver closer to hear. "Who is this?"

"It's Paul."

"Paul Evans?"

Another few coughs. "Yes."

"Why are you calling me?" Lucy asked, her voice sharp.

"I need to see you."

Her body stiffened in surprise. "No. I don't think that's a good idea."

"We need to talk."

"I'm listening now."

"No. In person. They could be listening. Please."

Who could be listening? And why was he so desperate to meet with her? Katie had told her that Paul was restrained and under guard at the hospital. She didn't think she could meet with him even if she wanted to.

"First, I heard you're handcuffed to your bedrail with a police guard outside your hospital door. Second, you should be talking with your lawyer," she said.

"You're a lawyer."

Lucy gritted her teeth. "I don't represent *you*."

A woman's voice sounded in the background. "Time for blood work, Mr. Evans."

"I'm in room 323. Please come," he pleaded.

"Lucy!" Azad shouted from the kitchen and she jumped, automatically covering the receiver with her hand. "How many appetizer trays did your mother want?" His voice was hoarse with frustration.

Lucy suspected he wanted to finish and leave after their discussion. "I'll be right there," she shouted.

She lifted her hand and uncovered the receiver, but Paul had already hung up.

CHAPTER 22

"You're not seriously thinking about going to see Paul in the hospital, are you?" Katie looked at Lucy as if she'd lost her mind.

Lucy paced back and forth in Katie's living room. "I am. You should have heard him. He sounded so desperate."

Katie folded her arms across her chest. "Of course, he did. He was arrested for Heather's murder. He'd say anything to get someone to believe him."

"But why call me?"

Katie threw up her hands. "I don't know. Maybe because he knows we were investigating on our own."

"Hmm. Maybe—"

"You really have doubts about his guilt." It was a statement more than a question. Katie always knew what she was thinking.

"I can't help it," Lucy said. "I remember the first time we went to Paul's house and he pulled out that diamond ring. He really seemed sincere and broken up over Heather's death. And then there's the question of how he got his hands on cyanide to begin with."

"All right. I'll help."

"What?"

"You're my best friend, and I trust your gut," Katie said. "If you need to talk to Paul to put your mind at ease, I'm in. What's your plan?"

Lucy blinked. "My plan?"

"You need to get past the front desk and obtain a visitor's pass, and then you need to slip by the armed police officer standing guard outside Paul's door."

"Yikes. You're right. I do need your help."

Katie rubbed her chin. "You're in luck. I spoke with Bill this morning and he told me the cop on duty at the hospital today is Don Stevens."

"Why does that make me lucky?"

"He was the only Ocean Crest police officer who didn't show up at Kebab Kitchen the day Heather died."

Lucy's pulse pounded. "He won't recognize me."

"That's right."

"But I still have to get past him to see Paul."

Katie reached for a pen and pad on an end table, and Lucy immediately thought of a military sergeant drawing up battle plans.

Katie tapped her pen on the pad, then eyed Lucy's waitressing uniform. "I have an idea, but it requires a change of clothes."

Lucy nodded. "Then let's get to work."

* * *

Lucy pushed open the door to the Ocean Crest Medical Center and stepped inside the lobby. She was immediately reminded of when she'd visited only a day ago when her father had been admitted for what had turned out to be a panic attack masquerading as a heart attack.

Whether or not she should be there today was another question entirely. According to Katie, the police considered the case closed, and Heather's killer was wrist-shackled somewhere in the building.

Yet there she was, trying to figure out how to sneak into a guarded hospital room. At least Katie supported her. Lucy realized for the umpteenth time how valuable she considered Katie's friendship. It was one more reason to stay in Ocean Crest.

Lucy smoothed the skirt of her navy business suit. After Katie had explained her plan, Lucy had rummaged through her suitcases until she found the right clothing. She prayed the ploy would work. Katie had stayed behind to visit Bill at the station with a box of doughnuts from Cutie's Bakery. If she saw a policeman leaving for the hospital, she would text Lucy, who would hightail it out of the hospital.

Lucy halted by the snack machine in the lobby. Feigning interest in the selection behind the glass, she eyed the receptionist. Thankfully, she recognized the middle-aged woman with dyed red hair and a prominent gap between her two front teeth. Paul had told her he was in room 323, but she couldn't just waltz up to the receptionist and ask for a visitor's pass for a guarded room.

Lucy approached the front desk. "Good morning. I'm here to visit my father, Raffi Berberian, in room 306B." Lucy smiled and held her breath.

"Ah, yes. I remember you. I hope your father is feeling better. Here you go." The woman handed Lucy a visitor's pass. Thank goodness, she didn't bother to look up her father's name to realize he'd been discharged yesterday.

"Thanks," Lucy took the badge and hurried to the elevators, feeling like a security guard would seize her by the arm and yell, "Stop!" at any second.

The elevator doors opened and Lucy pressed the button for the third floor, only letting out a breath once she was alone. The elevator dinged and the doors opened. Glancing out, she scanned the floor and spotted the policeman.

A stocky cop with a mustache stood guard outside a door. Lucy's mind spun back to the night of Heather's murder and the group of policemen, EMTs, and the coroner who had descended upon the restaurant. Katie was right. The policeman stationed outside room 323 wasn't one of them.

Thank her lucky stars.

Scanning the hospital floor, she was relieved to find it busy. A group of people stood outside one room, speaking in hushed whispers. By their somber looks it was obvious someone they cared about was not doing well. Lucy's heart went out to them.

Two doctors in white coats and hospital scrubs talked to a nurse at the desk. A woman pushed a multi-tiered food cart, quickly stopping at each room to deliver a meal. A patient in a hospital gown and socks walked past Lucy, reaching back to ensure his gown stayed closed.

Taking a deep breath and straightening her navy jacket, she headed for Paul's room, her high heels clicking on the tile floor. It was the first time she'd worn business attire since her arrival home, and the skirt, pantyhose, and heels felt more uncomfortable than she'd ever remembered.

The police officer glared at her as she approached. "This room is off limits."

Lucy glanced at his nametag which read OFFICER STEVENS. Her eyes snapped to his, and her voice was cold and precise. "My client is in there. I need to see him."

Stevens straightened. "I'm sorry, but I have my orders. No one is allowed inside but authorized medical personnel."

"I'm not anyone. I'm Mr. Evans' attorney and he's entitled to legal representation."

The cop wavered a bit, then shook his head. "Sorry."

"Do you want me to call County Prosecutor Walsh?" Lucy knew it was an empty threat, but hoped he didn't know. The prosecutor couldn't care less whether Paul Evans had an attorney or not.

A flash of uncertainty crossed Officer Stevens' face, and Lucy leaped. "I only need a few minutes," she pressed.

"All right. But make it quick, Counselor." He stepped aside, and Lucy opened the door.

When he moved to follow, she scowled up at him. "I must meet with my client alone. Attorney-client confidentiality."

Stevens frowned, but backed away. "He's drugged pretty good. I don't think he'll be much use to you anyway."

"Thank you for your concern." Lucy shut the door and turned to the room.

Paul was unmoving in the bed, the sound of his deep breathing and the hum of the monitors the only sounds in the room. He looked ashen in the artificial light.

She glanced at his IV. One of the bags of fluid was labeled OxyContin. Not for the first time, she wondered about the extent of his injuries from the accident. "Paul," she whispered.

Nothing.

"Paul," she said louder, then gently squeezed his shoulder.

His eyes opened a crack, glassy and unfocused.

"It's me, Lucy. Wake up. You wanted to see me, remember?"

He blinked twice. "You came." His voice was weak and gravely.

"Yes, I did. But we don't have much time. What did you want to say?" A confession? An admission of how he poisoned Heather? An explanation of how he got his hands on the cyanide?

"I didn't do it." His voice was strong, then more forceful. "I didn't kill Heather."

Lucy shot him a doubtful look. "Heather was cheating on you with Luke Santiago. You found out after you backed her loan to Luke's boss, Mr. Citteroni."

"No . . . I loved her."

"You said you wanted to kill her," Lucy insisted.

Paul rubbed his temples. "I didn't mean it. We were working out our problems. I wanted to marry her. You saw the ring!"

She had, and it had caused her second thoughts . . . but she had to remain logical. "Tell the police."

"I did. They don't believe me."

"It didn't help that you ran," Lucy pointed out.

"I was scared. I panicked. I know how bad it looks. The huge loan. Heather's affair. My threat. The police don't believe me."

"Then tell your lawyer," she said.

"It's not the same. You know this case and everyone involved. You're investigating it."

"I *was* investigating it." Was he going to accuse Guido or Mac again? Paul was clearly desperate to point to anyone.

"You came. You must know something doesn't add up," Paul said.

He had her there. She did have questions. Not about his motives, because there were plenty, but about how he'd done it. Had he stumbled across a black-market supplier of cyanide when he'd researched one of his suspense novels? And how exactly did he administer the poison?

"I came because I felt bad for you." There was a grain of truth to that.

Paul needed a good criminal defense lawyer. A zealous advocate who would argue on his client's behalf.

Not Lucy.

A beep sounding from one of the machines made Lucy jump. One of the bags of fluid was almost empty.

"I have to go." She decided to make a hasty exit before a nurse arrived.

"Wait!" Paul reached out to clasp her wrist, his grip surprisingly firm for a drugged patient. "Promise me you'll think about what I said. That you'll consider looking into things a little more."

Lucy's lips parted to answer, then froze. Her eyes were glued to where Paul gripped her wrist. A glimmer of light from the parted window blinds reflected off his hospital identification bracelet.

Paul Basher.

Not Paul Evans.

Her mind struggled to comprehend as her eyes flew to his face. A sudden thought struck her and she couldn't believe she hadn't considered it earlier. Paul must write under the pseudonym Paul Evans, but his legal name was Paul Basher.

"Hello."

A nurse in scrubs stood in the doorway with an IV bag of fluid in her hands. "Time to swap out your meds." She stopped short as she noticed Lucy. "Oh, I didn't realize he was allowed visitors."

Lucy forced herself to smile. "I'm his attorney, but I was on my way out." She hurried from the room.

Officer Stevens shot her a glare as he stood guard outside. She didn't wave on her way to the elevator.

CHAPTER 23

By the time Lucy made her way back to Kebab Kitchen, her mind was in overdrive.

Paul Basher.

The day she'd met Paul, he'd said he was originally from Ocean Crest and had recently returned. The surname Basher was vaguely familiar, but in her agitated state she couldn't quite place it. She rubbed her temples. The stress was getting to her.

Think, Lucy! After years of owning the restaurant, her mother knew everyone in town. Perhaps she'd heard of his family.

Lucy pulled into the restaurant's back parking lot. Her mother's car was gone. Azad's blue pickup truck was missing, as well. Both must have left for a break before the dinner hour.

She'd call her mom. Using her key to open the back door, Lucy made her way through the storage room and into the kitchen. She pulled up a stool to the prep table where she'd prepared baklava at the break of dawn, and took her cell phone out of her purse.

A delivery box on the table caught her eye. A slip of paper sat next to it. Big Al must have made a delivery and left his invoice as usual. She reached for the invoice and froze as she read the printed red letters at the top of the paper—ALI BASHER, SPECIALTY MEDITERRANEAN FOODS.

Of course! She'd forgotten Big Al's name was Ali Basher. For as long as she could remember, everyone called him Big Al.

Was it a coincidence? Or were Ali Basher and Paul Basher related? Father and son?

If it were true, how on earth could she not have known that Big Al had a son who happened to be a famous best-selling author? She'd never heard of him having a family. And if he did have a son who was a bestselling novelist, wouldn't he have proudly mentioned it to her parents?

Plus they looked nothing alike. Big Al was short, fat, bald, and waddled when he walked. Paul was average height, thin, and had a full head of brown hair.

She reached for her cell and called her parents' home. They didn't answer. She tried her mom's cell. Still no answer. She called Katie who thankfully picked up on the first ring.

"Did you talk to Paul?" Katie asked.

"I did. Paul's real name is Paul Basher, not Evans," Lucy said.

"What?"

"When we first met Paul at Mac's Irish Pub, he told us he was born in Ocean Crest, moved away with his mother when he was young, then recently came back," Lucy said.

"So?"

"Well, I just remembered that our food supplier's last name is Basher. Big Al is Ali Basher."

"Do you think they're related?" Katie asked.

"I need to ask my mom."

"What else did Paul say?" Katie asked.

"He insists he didn't kill Heather, and I still have doubts myself."

"Where are you?"

"I'm by myself at the restaurant."

"Is it safe?"

Lucy blinked. "I locked the door behind me. Why?"

"Stay where you are," Katie ordered. "I'm calling Bill."

As Lucy hung up the phone, she heard the sound of a key in the back door. Relief coursed through her. Her mother must be back. Maybe she'd get answers now. The storage room door slammed closed.

"Hello!" Lucy called out.

"It's Big Al. I forgot a second box for you, Mrs. Berberian." He entered the kitchen, carrying a medium-sized box, his feet shuffling across the tiled floor. He halted when he spotted her. "Well, hello there Lucy."

Lucy pushed back her stool and stood. "The door was locked. How did you get inside?"

He placed the box on the prep table. "It's not a problem. Your parents gave me a key years ago so that I could make my deliveries." His large smile melted in his buttery face.

If Paul was his son, she felt horrible for Ali Basher. His son had been arrested for murder and was lingering in a hospital room, handcuffed to the bedrail, with a policeman standing guard outside. Al must be devastated.

"Isn't it late for a delivery? I'm sure your family is waiting for you." She was fishing, but she wanted answers.

Big Al shook his head. "Sadly, no. My wife died many years ago."

So, he had married. "I'm sorry. What about your children?" she prodded.

Something flickered far back in his eyes. "A son. He's grown. I didn't know about him until recently."

"What do you mean?"

He shifted his feet, and his brow furrowed. "I never married his mother. We were very young, just shy of eighteen, and she didn't tell me about him. I only learned of his existence when he came searching for me months ago."

Lucy took a step forward and lowered her voice. "Is his name Paul?"

Big Al blinked once, then his brown eyes sharpened.

Lucy's heart gave a jolt and the truth struck her like a blow to the gut. "It was you, wasn't it? You poisoned Heather Banks. Why?"

He swallowed. "Heather Banks was a bad person. I had finally connected with my son, my only child. He'd been raised to believe I was dead. He'd only learned the truth when his stepfather became ill and told Paul everything in confidence. Even though I'm proud of Paul for what he has accomplished with his books, I agreed to keep our relationship private at his request because his mother is still alive."

"I don't understand. What does that have to do with Heather?"

Perspiration beaded on his brow, and he wiped his broad forehead with a meaty palm. "Paul met Heather soon after returning to Ocean Crest. At first, I thought she was good for him, then one day as I was making a delivery, I saw her in a car, kissing another man. She cheated on Paul and caused him nothing but pain. I had just discovered I had a son. I couldn't let her ruin his career or his future."

"Did you tell Paul? Explain how you felt?"

"I tried," he said his expression pained. "He refused to listen. I thought with her dead, my son would be free of her, but instead he was arrested for her murder."

"You didn't have to kill her." Lucy couldn't fathom murdering someone just because they'd cheated.

Al's eyes flashed and he looked fiercely protective. "I didn't have a choice. When I confronted Paul and pleaded for him to stop seeing her, he told me he had a ring for her. A ring! He planned to ask her to marry him. I had to do something."

"It was the apricots, wasn't it?" Lucy held her breath.

"I've sold them for years. I know the crushed kernels are poison."

The blood pounded in Lucy's ears. "You were here that day. You made a delivery and were talking in the kitchen with Azad when Heather came to eat."

"I followed her for a week. I saw my son visit her during one of her inspections that day. Then I followed her here and knew what I had to do."

"You used a delivery as an excuse to show up at the restaurant while Heather was here."

He nodded once. "I sprinkled crushed apricot kernels on the hummus bar."

"You could have poisoned someone else!" Lucy said.

"No," he said in a dull and troubled voice. "She was the only customer in the place."

Another thought came to Lucy. "What about the day Azad and I were locked in the walk-in refrigerator? Was that you?"

"You were in the kitchen with Azad. Your mother was in the office. All I wanted was to return unnoticed and get my apricots. But then you and Azad came into the back of the kitchen and I would have been seen, so I jammed the broom against the door and locked both of you inside the refrigerator."

"We could have been in there for hours."

Big Al shook his head. "No. I knew your mother would discover you before then. I just wanted my apricots."

"What now?" Lucy asked.

He licked his lips and swallowed. "You don't have to tell the police."

"You killed Heather!"

He flinched. "You're right. My son must not go to jail for something he didn't do."

Lucy was relieved. He was going to do the right thing and turn himself in to the police with a full confession.

"My son is in the hospital. If another murder occurs, they will know they have the wrong man."

Another murder? He couldn't mean—

He did.

Lucy stared in disbelief as Big Al snatched the knife Azad had used earlier to slice tomatoes.

He wielded it at her. "I'm sorry, Lucy. I never meant for you to get involved. You just kept asking questions. You wouldn't give up."

Panic and anger simmered inside her. "Put that down. Killing me makes no sense."

"It will if I put the cyanide powder on you. They will think you poisoned Heather."

"You're not a killer." *Stupid, Lucy! He already was.*

"I have to fix this."

"By killing again!?"

His face crumpled, but his hold on the knife remained firm. "You know too much."

Lucy's eyes darted to the prep table for a weapon, but the surface was clear of other knives or utensils. The delivery box was between them. She inched toward it, holding up her hands as if surrendering. She needed to buy time, appeal to him emotionally. "Think of my parents. They're your friends. How do you think they'd feel if you stabbed me?"

The knife wavered. "I have no choice. You know the truth."

"I've changed my mind. I promise not to tell anyone. Just put the knife down," she pleaded.

He shook his head. "It's too late."

She lunged for the box and pushed it with all her might at him. It slid across the table and hit him in the stomach. He cried out as Lucy sprinted from the kitchen into the storage room. Big Al bellowed and she heard the shuffle of his footsteps as he charged after her.

She was faster and more agile. All she had to do was run out the back door and sprint to the neighboring bike shop and scream for help. Michael or his father might even be there. She pushed a rolling cart into Big Al's path as she ran through the kitchen and into the storage room. She reached the back door and turned the handle.

Locked.

She struggled with the deadbolt. In her panic, her fingers fumbled and she tore a nail. Just as she managed to unlock the dead bolt and throw open the door, she ran straight into Azad. "Look out!" she cried.

Big Al charged into the storage room with the knife in hand. Azad reacted automatically, picking up a glass jar of tahini from a nearby shelf and throwing it at the supplier. It struck him between his eyes, then shattered on the ceramic tile. Big Al stumbled back, clutched his head, then dropped to the ground like a felled tree as the knife clattered to the floor.

"My God. Are you all right?" Azad asked her, concern etched between his brows.

Lucy's heart was racing. "It was him all along. Big Al poisoned the hummus bar with cyanide and killed Heather. He's Paul's father. He thought he was protecting his son."

Azad reached for his cell phone in his pocket. "I'll call the police."

Just then sirens sounded outside. Lucy placed a hand on Azad's sleeve. "Katie already called Bill."

They glanced at Big Al lying unconscious on the storage room floor. He'd been stopped by a jar of tahini that would have been used to make hummus.

Despite her racing adrenaline, Lucy couldn't help but think how fitting it was. She took deep breaths.

"Big Al will get his wish. Paul will be exonerated, but I doubt his son will forgive him. Despite everything, I think Paul truly loved Heather."

"Love is blind."

Her gaze snapped to his face. "Why did you come back?"

"I thought about what you said about wanting to take over the restaurant. You have just as much right to want this place as any prospective buyer. Even more. The place belongs to your family."

"Oh, I . . . well . . . thanks."

His gaze traveled over her face and searched her eyes. "I also came to ask if you'd like to go for a second cup of coffee."

Lucy's pulse leapt, and she felt a ripple of excitement. She smiled and looked up at him. "Coffee sounds great. By the way, how did you plan to get inside? The back door was locked."

He held up his keychain. "I've had a key ever since I've worked here."

Her parents were too trusting in handing out keys . . . but, this time, she was grateful they had.

CHAPTER 24

"To family and friends!" Raffi Berberian cheered as he opened a bottle of expensive cognac from his own private stash. It was the following day, and they were seated around a large table in Kebab Kitchen's dining room. Lucy's entire family, along with Katie and Bill, Sally, Butch, and Azad were all present. Even Gadoo lounged on the window sill, his jewel green eyes watching them curiously.

"To Lucy for solving the case," Emma said.

"To Lucy for deciding to stay," Mom said.

"To Lucy for taking over the business," Azad said.

Lucy had been shocked and pleasantly surprised that Azad was okay with her decision. "There's a job opening for head chef," she said.

"I'm thinking about it," he drawled.

If that was the best he could offer, she'd have to be patient.

Her parents had been thrilled with her decision. They'd also been relieved. Kebab Kitchen would stay in the family. Of course, her mother had taken the opportunity to remind Lucy if she ended up with Azad it was just as she'd wanted all those years ago. Somehow her mother's meddling was more humorous than annoying, and Lucy had simply rolled her eyes.

Meanwhile, she had other things to think about. She'd need to find her own place for starters. Katie and Bill had graciously told her she could stay in their guest room as long as she wished. Her parents had asked her to live with them—but that was *not* something she was considering. Even Emma and Max had offered her their basement. Lucy had options, but she knew that she eventually wanted her own place.

She scanned the dining room, its tables with pristine tablecloths and the maple booths. She'd never envisioned staying when she'd arrived. But somewhere in the back of her mind, she'd known she wasn't happy with her legal career. She hadn't given a single thought to updating her résumé the entire time she'd been home.

A glass of cognac was handed to her. She tossed it down and coughed as the strong alcohol burned her throat and every inch of her esophagus all the way down to her stomach.

"It's smooth as silk," her dad protested.

"You can try my sparkling apple juice, Mokour Lucy," Niari said as she giggled and held up her own glass.

Lucy grinned at her niece. "I just might."

The front door opened and Anthony and Michael Citteroni walked inside. Mr. Citteroni was holding a bottle of champagne. "We wanted to congratulate our neighbors. May we join you for a drink?"

"Anthony, how gracious of you," her mother said as she approached Mr. Citteroni and kissed his cheek.

"Good to see you." Lucy's dad shook the mobster's hand.

Michael stopped in front of Lucy and winked. "Good to see you, too, Lucy."

A pop sounded and flutes of bubbling champagne were handed out. "To neighbors and friends." Mr. Citteroni raised his glass.

Michael tapped Lucy's flute. "To new business ventures."

She swallowed. From the corner of her eye she saw Azad stiffen. Was he jealous?

A tiny thrill coursed through her. She never could have imagined how things would end up after she'd quit her job in the city and come home. Big changes meant big hurdles, but she was looking forward to each one.

Her mother kissed her cheek. "I know we've told you already, but we are so happy you have come home for good."

Lucy's heart squeezed as she looked at her family and friends. There was no place in the world she'd rather be. She held her glass up in the air and smiled. "To home, to family, and to good friends."

Author's Note

This book is a mystery straight from my heart. For twenty-eight years, my Armenian-American family owned a restaurant in a small town in South Jersey. My mother was a talented cook and the grapevine in our backyard was more valued that any rosebush. I'd often come home from school to the delicious aromas of simmering grape leaves, stuffed peppers and tomatoes, and shish kebab. Lunch at school would be hummus and pita instead of peanut butter and jelly at a time when hummus wasn't as popular as it is now. It wasn't always fun as a teenager to have an eccentric, ethnic family, but I've grown to value my roots and my own colorful cast of family members. In contrast, my husband is like Katie's family—they can almost trace their roots back to the Mayflower. We have two young daughters who have the best of both worlds, and yes, they both know how to make hummus and like it.

I loved writing this book, and I'm happy to share my own favorite family recipes with you. Enjoy the food!

RECIPES

Angela's Famous Traditional Hummus

This is my own secret recipe. It can be served as a dip with wedges of pita bread or vegetables, and goes well with broiled or grilled meat. It can also be used as a healthy alternative to mayonnaise on sandwiches.

1 can (15 ounces) chick peas
3½ teaspoons tahini (sesame seed puree)
3 cloves minced garlic (1½ teaspoons)
1 teaspoon salt
5 tablespoons extra virgin olive oil
2 tablespoons lemon juice

Drain can of chick peas and reserve ¼ cup fluid. Mix tahini thoroughly before using to incorporate oil that separates during storage. Using a food processor or blender, combine and blend all ingredients until smooth. If hummus is too thick, add a few tablespoons of reserved fluid from chick peas and blend again. Pour into serving platter. Enjoy!

Azad's Tabbouleh Salad

This parsley and bulgur salad is a favorite and a healthy alternative to any mayonnaise based potato or macaroni salad.

½ cup small bulgur (cracked wheat)
4 cups freshly chopped flat leaf parsley
1 cup chopped scallions or onions
2 cups chopped tomatoes
⅓ cup freshly chopped mint leaves or
     2 tablespoons dried crushed mint
salt and pepper to taste
½ cup extra virgin olive oil
½ cup fresh lemon juice

Soak bulgur in a small bowl for a half hour, then drain and squeeze out all excess water. In a large bowl combine all ingredients and mix thoroughly. Refrigerate and serve cold.

Lucy's White Almond Cookies

¾ cup unsalted clarified butter
½ cup vegetable shortening
1¼ cups sugar
2¼ cups flour
almonds

Preheat oven to 275 degrees. Combine butter, shortening, and sugar and mix. Add flour and mix well. Take two full teaspoons of dough and roll into a rope, then make a circle and pinch the seam together. Lightly press an almond into the seam. Repeat for remaining dough.

Arrange on cookie sheets and bake for 20 minutes until lightly golden on the bottom. Cookies should remain white on top. Transfer cookies from baking sheet to cooling racks to cool. Makes about three dozen cookies.

ACKNOWLEDGMENTS

Writers create stories in solitude, but publishing a book is a team effort. I'm thankful for all the wonderful people who have helped me along the way. I'd like to thank my parents, Anahid and Gabriel, for their love and for all their hard work as owners of a restaurant. I will forever be indebted to them for teaching me to never stop reaching for my dreams, and I miss them every day.

I'm eternally grateful to my family—John, Laura, and Gabrielle—for their support, encouragement, and never-ending love. Thank you for your patience when Mom is in the throes of plotting, writing, editing . . . and editing.

Thank you to my wonderful agent, Stephany Evans, who encouraged me to write this book when I pitched her the idea.

Thank you also to my great editor, Martin Biro, for taking a chance on me and helping to polish the book and make it shine. I'm grateful! Also, my heartfelt thanks to the entire Kensington team for their work on my behalf.

Last, thank you to my readers. Without you, there would be no books!